MERROWKIN

JENNIFER ALLIS PROVOST

CONTENTS

Dedication V

1. The Cliffs 1

2. The Height And The Wind 11

3. An Unexpected Holiday 18

4. Sullivan's Surf Shop 25

5. Cold Chicken And Hot Kale 31

6. Sad Potatoes 41

7. Come Sail Away 47

8. The Natural Order Of Things 59

9. A Key, Or An Old Rotted Piece Of Junk 64

10. The Sword 77

11. Oyster Thieves 85

12. Lemons And Thyme 90

13. Close, Yet Hidden 99

14. Murphy's Maniacs 105

15. A Party? 122

16. Archeologists Of Questionable Intent 135

17. Keep Moving 154

18. Ready To Listen   165

19. The Truth About Calliope   172

20. A Proper Gang   178

21. The Shannon Pot   185

22. The Wormhole   192

23. A Right Traitor   198

24. Gold Bars And Shepherd's Pie   206

25. Caves   219

26. Jewel Of The Sea   225

27. Below   238

28. Badass Warrior Queen   243

29. The Most Law Abiding Gang In Ireland   252

30. The Holy Island   266

31. Merrows And Stones   275

32. Reliable   289

33. Happy Endings All Around...   296

34. But It's Not Yet The End   305

35. Death's Door: Chapter One   310

36. Glossary Of (mostly) Irish Terms   318

Acknowledgements   320

Also By Jennifer Allis Provost   321

About The Author   323

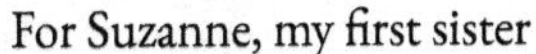

For Suzanne, my first sister

THE CLIFFS

I burst into the kitchen and tripped over the threshold, but managed to catch the edge of the table before I hit the floor. I wasn't usually so clumsy, but this wasn't an ordinary Monday. For the first time, I was going on the school field trip to the Cliffs of Moher. Also of note, I was defying my father for the first time in my life.

The kettle whistled as I carefully forged my father's name on the permission slip. It wasn't perfect, but it was passable. My hands shook as I poured the water, but I made my tea without scalding myself. That done, I got the bread that I'd set out to rise the night before into the oven, and took stock of the larder. We had fish, fish, and more fish. Yum. That, coupled with the bread, meant Kevin and I would eat today, and perhaps again tomorrow, but the day after that was looking a bit uncertain. It was Kevin's turn to do the shopping, and his version of a balanced meal was a bag of crisps with a glass of milk. And for the love of all that is holy, couldn't he bring home a vegetable for once, or maybe some fruit? It would be terrible to expire due to scurvy, what with us living in the twenty-first century and all.

I also noticed two bottles of whiskey standing at attention on top of the refrigerator, one more than usual. Interesting.

I jotted a few items on a list and taped it to Kevin's bedroom door. Hopefully, he would notice it when he woke. Shopping list sorted, I sought out lunch money. Being that Da had already left for his fishing boat I went to the tall hutch in the dining room and opened the drawer on the left.

There were two envelopes in the drawer, and in those envelopes was where Da left our allowances. On one of them was written *Meri girl*, and on the other *Kevin lad*, both in Da's messy scrawl. I have never opened Kevin's envelope, and I trust that he's never opened mine. Even siblings need privacy now and then. *Especially* siblings.

I pocketed the euros, and by the time I'd got myself showered, the bread had baked up nicely. I set it aside to cool while I dressed, then I took a big slice and left for my classes at Saint Senan and Saint

Conainne's Academy. That name was a mouthful, so we students called it The Saints.

School was... Well, it was there. I've never been one of those studious sorts, the ones who lived and died depending on their marks. I was a good enough student, and my grades reflected that, but the classes were just so boring. Once I was taught a bit of science or mathematics and understood how the concept worked, I lost all interest in the subject. And don't get me started on the atrocious reading material my literature teachers assigned with grim enthusiasm. I don't care if James Joyce was a national treasure, *Finnegan's Wake* is nigh on unintelligible.

Beyond the boring classes, the worst part about school was that everyone knew me as the mermaid's daughter, and that was no one's fault but my own. When my mother had left us all those years ago, I was inconsolable. I'd only been three years old, and I could not understand where Mama was or why no one would tell me when she was coming home. Da, in his kindest, most foolish moment, told me that my mother was in reality a mermaid, and had returned to her people under the sea.

At that, my tears had given way to a proud smile. My Mama was an important mermaid, of course she couldn't be mucking around up here on land. There was work—important work—to do down below, and she'd return to us soon enough.

I don't know if Da had expected me to believe him, or if he'd told me that story the way other parents warn their children to be wary of fairy circles and black cats crossing their path. But believe him I did, and when I started school, I told all my classmates about my beautiful mermaid mother. In hindsight, that had not been a very good idea. Somehow, I endured the resultant name-calling and teasing into my fifth year, though I'd considered leaving school many times. I didn't want to live as an uneducated minor, so a student I stayed.

Relentless teasing aside, the only subject that had ever interested me at school was music. I loved singing, and whenever I sang, the world fell away as I lost myself in the ebb and flow of the notes. Even though I was one of the strongest voices in the choir, I kept to the chorus. Standing in the front of the pack with the entire auditorium staring at me was quite a bit more attention than I could handle. What with all the backhanded comments regularly tossed my way—*Meri's got a voice like her mum, have a care or her siren's song will make us follow her to our doom*—I didn't need the added scrutiny.

Let me tell you, if I could have controlled that lot with a song, I would never have them follow me like a modern day Pied Piper. Sending them off in the opposite direction, now that would be a fine trick.

When I arrived at school, I was greeted by the mad chaos that was a hundred or so students being herded onto buses for our day trip to the Cliffs. The weather was grey and cold, but that hadn't dampened anyone's enthusiasm. It was a day out of school, after all. I saw which bus Aodhan was queued up near, turned on my heel and went to the farthest one from him.

It's not that I didn't like Aodhan. I did, very much so, and I'd spent countless hours wondering if his hair felt as soft and silky as it looked. But I was only seventeen, and the last thing I needed was to be someone's girlfriend. I needed to figure out for myself who Meri Murphy was before I could go around sharing her with others.

After I handed off my forged permission slip, I boarded the bus and scored a window seat. As I stared out the window, I wondered if Da was aware of this trip, and if that was why he'd stockpiled the extra bottle of whiskey at home. No matter why he'd got the booze, I refused to stay behind—again—while the rest of my class got to visit one of the greatest sights in Ireland. This time, I wouldn't be left behind, and I'd see for myself the place where my parents had met all those years ago.

I could use a drop of whiskey myself.

A wadded-up ball of paper hit my head and bounced onto my lap. Behind me, I could hear Kelsey McGrath and Sarah Haynes snickering. They'd been the architects of my troubles for as long as I could remember, though to my knowledge I'd never done anything to either of them. I smoothed the paper out against the back of the seat in front of me to learn what today's torment entailed. It was a rather nice sketch of a mermaid, bare breasts and all.

My face went hot and my hands trembled. Even after years of being teased, a simple sketch could still reduce me to a weepy, snotty mess. I bit the inside of my mouth and got myself under control, then I tilted my head back and yelled, "It's a lovely likeness. Thank you for your consideration."

There was a great deal of laughter toward the back of the bus. The school's headmaster, Seamus MacCreehy, got up from his seat to investigate. "What's all the yelling about?" he demanded.

"Nothing, sir," I said in a rush. MacCreehy was an absolute terror, on account of his loud rumble of a voice and his tall, broad frame, which was better suited to a rugby player than a professional educator.

His eyes narrowed. "You're certain it's nothing?"

"I am." I hadn't made the mistake of attempting to seek justice against those bullies since I was ten. "Someone drew a picture of a mermaid and tossed it up to me. It's really quite good."

I handed over the wrinkled paper. His brow creased when he saw the sketch. "Times past we called them merrows."

"What was that, sir?"

"Mermaids. We once called them merrows, and their children the merrowkin." Mr MacCreehy blinked and refocused on me. I could see his inner battle waging; should he reprimand whomever had sketched the mermaid, or just let it go? Eventually, he jerked his head toward the back of the bus and asked, "Has that lot been bothering you, Meredith?"

Ugh. I hated my given name. "Not at all," I said with a smile. "Just a bit of fun."

He grunted, then he stuffed the paper in his back pocket and returned to his seat. Just as I was congratulating myself on that small victory, Aodhan Sullivan slid into the seat beside me.

"Hey, Meri," he said. "What's the what?"

Aodhan was as much of an outlier at school as I was, though for different reasons. His father was not only black, but American to boot. The elder Sullivan had been some kind of surfing celebrity in California, and after winning all the trophies and setting several world records, he'd relocated to western Ireland and opened a surf shop. The school lasses all followed Aodhan like lovesick puppies, describing him as worldly and cultured compared to the rest of the boys. Never mind that Aodhan had been born right here in County Clare, and was therefore about as exotic as a goat.

If I cared about such things as boys I'd say he was a handsome one, tall and lean with dark hair and wide brown eyes. But I don't care about those things, so to me he's just regular old Aodhan.

"Is this seat taken?" he asked, when I only stared at him in silence.

"I saw you getting on a different bus," I blurted out.

"I was, then I saw you get on this one and I switched. What was that about?" he asked, jerking his chin toward Mr MacCreehy.

"Same old," I replied. "Someone thought it would be smart to bonk me in the head with a picture of a mermaid."

"Sullivan," MacCreehy yelled. "Quit bothering Meredith and find a different seat."

"Can't, sir. The rest have all been claimed." Aodhan gestured behind him, indicating the full bus. MacCreehy opened his mouth, but the driver shut the door and announced that we were pulling away from the school, and could everyone please sit down and buckle up? After shooting a final warning glare at Aodhan, MacCreehy returned to his seat.

"Wasn't that a bit of excitement," Aodhan said, then he tipped his head toward the back of the bus. "Why do you let them act that way? Really, Meri, you need to stand up for yourself."

"If I do, they'll just find some other way to harass me."

"But, Meri—"

"I don't want to talk about it." I turned my face toward the window, because damn it all I was not going to cry on a bus to a school field trip after getting bonked in the head with a drawing of a mermaid. I do have some dignity left.

I felt a soft warmth on my fingers. I looked down; Aodhan had placed his hand on mine. Any other time I would have shooed him away, but right then I needed a friend. I curled my little finger around his, but didn't acknowledge him in any other way. He smiled, and we rode in silence to the Cliffs.

Less than an hour later, our caravan of buses pulled into the car park at the Cliffs of Moher. Once they were properly arranged, we disembarked, crossed the road to the Visitor Centre, and got ourselves sorted out. The centre itself was built right into the hillside, and it sat quite near to the cliff's edge. The whole effect made me feel like we'd reached the end of the world. Surely we'd reached the end of Ireland proper.

Since there were four busloads of students, we were organised accordingly into four tour groups. That meant that I was in the group with those who found it amusing to pick on my unfortunate family situation. It also meant that I was in the group with Aodhan. His presence made the rest a bit more bearable.

"Have you ever been here before?" Aodhan asked.

"I think once, when I was small." I didn't add that any trips I'd made to the sea would have taken place back when Mama was still with us. Ever since she'd left, Da hated the very notion of Kevin and I possibly following her into the waves, even though he's out on his boat every day, trawling for fish and guzzling whiskey. It's a wonder he hasn't drowned.

Luckily, Da was still with us, but despite the way he chooses to spend his days, he has forbidden both Kevin and I from ever approaching the sea. A challenging thing to do when you live on an island, yes, but being that I hate the idea of swimming, it's not too difficult for me to avoid the beach.

"Meri!"

"What?" I turned away from the water and stared at Aodhan.

"Have you heard a word I said?" he demanded.

"I was looking at the waves. What were you saying?"

"Are you excited to see the Cliffs?"

"I guess I am excited," I said.

Aodhan's grin returned. "Me, too."

I turned back toward the sea. "My parents met here."

Aodhan's brows rose. "They met at the Visitor Centre?"

"No, at a beach down below. Da was out on his boat and Mama was stranded. He rescued her."

"Huh. I guess that's where the mermaid bit came from."

I swallowed the lump in my throat. "I guess so. Let's queue up with the rest."

It was a windy day, but I guessed it always was there on account of the Cliffs' amazing height. If I remembered correctly, we were about two hundred metres above sea level, and it was a sheer drop straight down to the water. While the school administrators and park officials were deciding which group of students should take the nature walk first, I turned toward the ocean.

Even though I couldn't see the waves crashing against the shore, I could hear them mercilessly beating the rocks. An island sat atop the waves, so small it was like a pebble lying on a vast blue rug. At first, I assumed it was one of the Aran Isles, but then a bit of gold flashed on the ocean's surface.

I closed my eyes and shook my head. It had to have been a trick of the light, or perhaps it was due to me being unaccustomed to the great height. Any gold would have to be the reflection of the sun on the water, though since the day was overcast, I didn't know how that could be. I opened my eyes and looked again; yes, there was the gold, surrounding the island and scattered across the top. If I craned my neck just so I could make out a roof—no, make that a cluster of roofs—and what looked like a church's spire...

Shouts from behind roused me. I looked down, and saw nothing but the sea crashing against the rocks. Just like mama had done, I was going home.

The Height and the Wind

Aodhan threw his arms around me, and I fell back against him. The two of us hit the cold earth as an undignified heap of limbs. "What the devil is the matter with you?" I demanded.

"Me? What in God's name were you doing?" he countered.

"I was looking at the golden—"

I turned back to the sea, but we weren't in front of the Visitors Centre. We were right on the edge of the cliff, a metre back and a few hundred up from certain death. I glanced at the waves. The golden island was gone.

"H-How did I get here?" I whispered.

"You ran," Aodhan replied. "You looked toward the ocean, and you ran. You moved so fast it was like there was fire at your back." He held me a bit tighter. "I didn't know if I'd catch you before, you know."

"I wasn't going to jump," I snapped.

Aodhan put his mouth close to my ear. "Did you see something?"

"No," I said, but I tasted the lie, acrid on my tongue. Aodhan's brow pinched, but before I could defend myself, the grown-ups were there. They pulled Aodhan and me apart, demanded to know if I felt ill, if I was sick or on any medication. They crowded around me as they walked me back toward the visitors' centre, but I caught a glimpse of Aodhan's stricken face. He'd heard my lie, too.

"I was not going to jump," I said. Again.

In fact, I'd denied wanting to jump several times, beginning with when the park rangers and Mr MacCreehy dragged me away from Aodhan. What was worse than them not believing me was when they marched me right past every student from The Saints, all of them staring and whispering about me. Kelsey and Sarah had laughed and pointed and called me the lamest student in history.

"Then what on earth were you playing at?" Mr MacCreehy asked. "The other students said you ran for the edge as if you'd decided to end it all."

"Another few minutes here, and I just might," I muttered. We—Mr MacCreehy, two park rangers, a medic, and myself—were in the Visitor Centre's lovely and well-stocked first aid room; I knew that last bit because all the brochures advertised it as such. Mind you, the only medical treatment I needed was a salve for my wounded pride, but there was none of that. Instead, they asked me if I was drunk or on drugs, even if I felt suicidal. No one had yet asked me if I'd thought I was a mermaid, but only just.

The medic shined her little penlight into my eyes, then she examined my hands. Apparently, the dirt underneath my fingernails spoke volumes. "You seem to be all right, physically at least," she said. She reminded me of a school nurse from a daytime drama with her light blue scrubs and hair scraped back in a tight bun. Pinned to her lab coat was an enamel pin featuring a puffin, in honour of the local wildlife.

"Your name's Meri?" she asked. When I nodded, she continued, "I'm Cara. Are you thirsty?"

"A bit," I replied.

She reached into a metal cabinet and handed me a bottle of water. "Sip that. I'll try to get these men out of your hair."

I dutifully drank my room temperature water while Cara drew the rest to the far side of the room. They bent their heads together and whispered furiously for a few minutes, then one of the rangers tilted his head and regarded me the way one would size up livestock at the fair.

"That's the Murphy girl, then?" he asked.

I held myself still, not acknowledging I'd heard him while straining my ears to catch anything further. I didn't need to wait long.

"Aye, she is Calliope Murphy's daughter," Mr MacCreehy said.

"I remember when Calliope's husband—Brian, was it?—would come here looking for her," the ranger continued. "He never made any trouble, just showed around a few pictures of his wife, and asked if anyone had seen her." The ranger glanced at Mr MacCreehy. "She never came back, then? The wife?"

"Not as far as I know," Mr MacCreehy replied.

The ranger shook his head. "Sad, isn't it, that he couldn't accept he'd been the one left behind."

Cara saw me watching them, and said, "All right, why don't the lot of you clear out and give us girls a bit of breathing room." Mr Mac-

Creehy and the rangers left, and I was alone with Cara. She bustled about on the other side of the room for a bit before she approached me.

"I know you heard what they were saying," she began. "Now, I don't pretend to know anything about you, but I am certain about one thing. Gossip is just about the most useless thing out there."

"In this case, it's not gossip. These are all facts," I said to my bottle of water. "I was a toddler when my mother left us. That was fourteen years ago, and she's never come back."

"Do you know what happened?"

"Not really," I replied. "I hardly even remember her. What I do know is that my father's a drunk, and tells everyone who'll listen my mother was a mermaid that left him to return to the sea." I blew out a breath. "I really wish he'd stop telling that story."

"Maybe he believes it to be true."

"I guess." I looked toward the door MacCreehy and the rest had left through. "They think my mother jumped off the edge, don't they?"

"Honestly, I've no idea what they think of her." She regarded me for a moment before she continued. "The truth is that there has been an increase in jumpers over the last few months. No one knows why, but these increases do seem to happen in cycles. The last upsurge was about seven years ago."

"This would be a rather effective place to end it all." I realised what I'd said and clapped my hand over my mouth. "I did not mean that how it sounded."

Cara patted my knee. "I understand." She withdrew a business card from her pocket and offered it to me. "If you ever need an un-judgmental ear to talk to, I'm here for you."

I took the card, but I didn't look at it. "Why? I mean, you don't even know me."

She shrugged. "Maybe someone was there for me once. Maybe I need to do some penance of my own." Cara winked at me, and added, "Maybe I'm really a mermaid, and I can sneak you into our next gathering."

We laughed, and I decided she wasn't so bad after all. "What do I do now? I imagine I'm in a bit of trouble."

"Yes and no," she said. "I've convinced them that you just had a bit of confusion due to the height—many visitors experience the same—and that you'll be fine after a few days' rest. They've called someone to bring you home."

"Who would they call to come get me?" Da was on a boat, and the rest of our family lived clear across the island.

She shrugged again. "I've no notion. Perhaps someone from your school?"

As it turned out, the school couldn't spare a body to take me home, not that I was surprised. What did surprise me was when my brother pulled into the centre's car park in Da's old beater.

I watched as Kevin got out of the car. When he saw me, he leaned against the driver's door and waited. We looked a great deal alike, with our matching dark brown hair and blue eyes, and while we were both on the lean side, Kevin was a few centimetres taller than me, though our father towered over both of us. When we were younger, people often thought us twins, even though he's three years older than me. The main difference between us is that Kevin had garnered sympathy about our missing mother, and had never once been teased. Sadly, I did not inherit that bit of luck.

Having been released by both Cara and the school, I approached the car. "Hi."

"Are you all right?" he asked.

"I am." Kevin jerked his head toward the car, and I got in. "Thank you for picking me up."

"Da will have a stroke when he hears of this," Kevin said as he drove away.

"Then let's not tell him." I shrunk down in the seat and started out the window. "Like the medic said, I was just disorientated. It happens a lot here, what with the height and the wind and all."

"It's not that you got sick, or whatever happened out there," Kevin said. "It's that you were here. Christ, Meri, you of all people know how he feels about the Cliffs."

"It's just a school trip," I said. "It's not like I was out on a boat casting a net and calling Mama's name." I watched the passing countryside for a moment. "Do you know her name?"

"You know it was Calliope."

"No, that's what Da says he called her. Never once has he said that's her real name. He's probably forgotten her real name."

"Meri!"

"It's possible and you know it." Da's drinking had worn holes in his memory, and while he remembered some things with blinding clarity other details of his life—like the name of our old dog, Shep, and most of his time with Mama—seemed to be gone for good. How much whiskey does it take for a man to forget his wife's name? Ask my Da, he can tell you.

I studied Kevin's profile; this was the most we'd talked about our mother in years, and he'd been older that I was when she left. Not much older, but I reckoned that a six-year-old could recall much more than a three-year-old.

"Don't you ever wonder where she is? Where she went?" When he only pursed his lips, I added, "Don't you miss her?"

"Aye. That I do." He stopped at a turn, and said, "Just as I'd miss you if you went off and did something foolish. Promise me, Meri. No more Cliffs. No more running toward the sea."

I glanced back toward the ocean, and the waves that still called my name. Had they once called my mother's name? Had Calliope Murphy gone over the edge as I almost did, or did the rangers catch her in time? Was she pronounced mad and sent to an asylum?

I didn't want to go over the cliffs or go mad, but even as I rested my forehead against the cool window glass, I felt the sea beckoning me to stay. But I couldn't tell Kevin about that, now could I?

"I promise."

An Unexpected Holiday

Thanks to my antics at the Cliffs, and a letter written to the school on my behalf by Cara the medic, I was excused from classes for the rest of the week. Being that the entire mess had happened on a Monday, I found myself looking forward to an unexpected holiday.

Kevin had agreed to never, ever tell Da what had happened, and I had to hope that whatever bits of information the gossip mills churned out would miss Da's ears entirely. I had no idea how he would react to learning that I went to the one location I'd ever been forbidden from, other than badly. Neither Kevin nor I thought our physically strong yet emotionally fragile father could handle the knowledge.

Tuesday morning turned out to be just as cloudy and gloomy as the day before, but I've never been one to let the weather affect my mood. I tended toward foul regardless of the number of clouds in the sky. I rose early as ever, got the bread going, and took my shower. After I dressed, I checked my envelope in the hutch. The money had been replenished yet again. As I claimed the euros, I wondered how much savings I'd really need to make a go of it elsewhere, since after yesterday I was seriously debating never showing my face at The Saints ever again.

Of course, I could just stay home and not attend classes, for all that Da would notice. It's what Kevin had done, in a way; he'd taken his transition year, found a job in the village, and never went back to school. To this day, I wondered if Da realised what had become of his son's education.

Close to noon, there was a knock at the side door. I peeked around the window shade, and saw none other than Aodhan standing there, clad in his school uniform with his bag slung across his shoulder.

"Can I help you?" I asked after I opened the door.

"When you weren't in school, I got worried," he said. "I came to see if you were all right."

"As you can see, I am." When he frowned, I added, "I'm off school for the rest of the week. It's a gift from the medic at the Cliffs, so to speak."

"If you're fine, why are you home for a week?"

"The medic thought I, ah, needed some rest." I left off the part about me blubbering to Cara about how I'd be mercilessly teased about what had happened, and she'd taken pity on me and thus crafted my out-of-school note. I didn't think a week was near enough time for the rest of the school to forget what had happened, but it was better than nothing.

Aodhan nodded. "Rest is good." He didn't budge, and neither did I. "Can I come in?" he asked, eventually. "I want to run something by you, and it would go better over tea than out here on the steps."

"What makes you think I'll be making you any tea?" I stepped aside, and Aodhan entered my dingy kitchen. If he noticed the cobwebs or the peeling wallpaper, he kept his opinions to himself.

"I'll make the tea myself," he said, as he set a duffle bag on the table. "I'll cook you a five course meal if it will get you to sit down and listen to me."

I scowled at Aodhan, then I filled the electric kettle and set two mugs on the table with rather more force than was necessary. Aodhan ignored my deplorable hostess skills, then he took a few battered books from his bag and set them on the table.

"What are those?" I asked.

"I've a few ideas about what happened yesterday," he said. "Have you anything to eat? I skipped lunch to come here."

I set out what was left of the bread I'd made that morning, along with a lump of butter and some jam. As I grabbed some plates, the kettle whistled. While I saw to the tea, Aodhan sampled the bread.

"This is excellent," he said. "Did you get it from the baker by the green?"

"I made it." I sat across from him. "Now, will you please tell me why you're here?"

"I will, but first I need you to tell me the real reason why you ran toward the edge." When I did nothing but butter a slice of bread, he added, "It's all right. It's just you and me here, no MacCreehy or medic or anyone else passing judgement."

"The medic was nice," I said. "She gave me her card."

Aodhan set his hand on top of mine. "Meri."

"I thought I saw something on the water," I said in a rush. "It looked like gold, and at first I thought it was just a reflection from the sun. Then I realised it couldn't be the sun, since it was cloudy. I moved to the side, leaned around the others for a closer look, and I saw rooftops and what might have been a church. No, it was more of a castle spire, not like how the castles are here but how they look in Germany, like real life fairy tale castles..." My throat went dry. I blew on my too-hot tea, took a sip. "And the next thing I knew, you were dragging me away from the edge."

"I've never been so scared in my life as when I thought you were going over." He rubbed his thumb between my first and second knuckle. "I'm a fast runner. Best on the team. I almost didn't catch you."

"I... I just wanted a closer look."

"I believe you, Meri." Aodhan withdrew his hand and slid the stack of books he'd brought between us.

"Where did you get these?" I asked. "The school library?"

"Some are from the library. The rest I ordered on the internet."

I regarded the pile of books. "You've been ordering a lot of books."

"I have. Anyway, I think what you saw coming up from the waves was Kilstiffen."

I cocked an eyebrow at him. "What, now?"

"You know, the lost city at the bottom of the sea," he continued. "According to the stories, the roofs and the castle towers in Kilstiffen are all clad in gold. That's what made me think of it, when you said you said you saw gold on the water. Here's a drawing of it." He opened one of the books and flipped to a rather crude sketch of a castle situated on top of some waves.

"That's Kilstiffen?" I asked.

"It's no photograph, but you get the idea," he replied. The page opposite the drawing told a story about the island:

In times long past, the Tuatha dé Danann warred with the Milesians over who held rights to the noble land of Ireland. After much bloodshed, a truce was called, with each party to receive half of the island as recompense. The Milesians took Ireland above, while the Tuatha dé Danann claimed Ireland below. Betwixt the two was the city of Kilstiffen.

Kilstiffen was no ordinary city. Within it was a portal that kept those who walked above safe from what lurked below, as much as mortal flesh could ever be safe from gods and monsters. But the two lands could not be wholly separate, and every seven years Kilstiffen rose atop the waves, its gleaming gold spires announcing to all that the way below was open, albeit for a short time, if only they'd care to make the journey.

Things came up during those times as well, which accounted for the odd beasties sighted on Ireland's western edge over the past centuries. The land has never wanted for monsters, nor heroes to slay them.

Tasked with guarding Kilstiffen were the merrowkin, for they could move easily between the mortal folk of above, and the immortals that resided below. All was as it should be until an arrogant and foolhardy merrow thought to raise the city once and for all. Knowing that this would be disastrous to those both above and below, the king's daughter did the unthinkable and stole the key to the city. Without it, Kilstiffen cannot rise, and the way below is blocked.

Many have searched for the key, but the king's daughter hid it well. Some say that the Tuatha dé Danann are dead and Kilstiffen will never rise again; others say that the old gods are biding their time until they reclaim Ireland above. And as for the key, it remains missing to this day.

"Anyway, the city has these magic gates, but the key's been lost," Aodhan continued. "Some say it's hidden beneath a grave marker, or at the bottom of a lough."

"So this city was destroyed, yes?"

"Oh, no, it's still there. It's supposed to be guarded by some kind of sea people."

"Sea people. People who live in the sea?" I pinched the bridge of my nose. "Like mermaids?"

"Uh, yeah. I guess."

I couldn't believe my ears. All this time I'd thought that Aodhan was my one real friend, but here he was, spouting garbage about mermaids like the rest of them. "Why are you here?"

"I told you, I came by to check on you."

"No, I mean why are you here, telling me about a city under the water," I clarified.

"Don't you see, Mer?" Aodhan asked. "Your ma, she might be from Kilstiffen!"

"You're telling me you think my mother came from a drowned city at the bottom of the sea?"

"It all makes sense," he said. "Your Da claiming she was a mermaid, them meeting each other on a beach near the Cliffs, and then her returning to the sea. I reckon while she was up here, she was searching for the key. Perhaps she even found it, and when she left it was to bring the key back to the king."

I closed my eyes. I could almost hear my heart breaking, quiet yet so, so painful. "The only thing that makes sense here is that you are using my mother against me."

"No, Meri, that's not it at all!"

"Isn't it?" I slammed down my mug, then I stalked over to the sink and gave him my back. Over my shoulder, I said, "I expect this kind of rubbish from Kelsey and Sarah. I even expect it from my teachers and the folks in town. I never expected it from you, Aodhan."

My voice cracked when I said his name. I hadn't meant to sound so pathetic, so I faced the window and stared at the clouds. Aodhan had been the one person—the only person save Da and Kevin—that never treated me like a crazy man's daughter. He'd been the only schoolmate I'd ever had who hadn't played nice just to get me to lower my defences so they could ask about my drunk father and missing mother.

I was wrong. He was just like the rest of them.

A moment later, I felt warmth at my back; Aodhan was standing right behind me.

"Meri. Mer." He put his hands on my elbows, and it was all I could do to not lean into him and bawl against his shoulder. "I didn't mean to upset you, or make fun of you. Or your ma. I'm serious about all this."

"Go."

"Meri, I only want to help."

"I can't hear this right now." He began to speak, but I held up my hand. "Just go. Please."

"Would you like me to leave the books, so you can have a look at them?"

"No."

I heard him pack up, then he let himself out of the kitchen. The door shut with a soft click, and only then did I let myself cry.

SULLIVAN'S SURF SHOP

After Aodhan left, I stayed in my room for the rest of that day and into the next morning. I normally considered myself above wallowing in self-pity, but this was an exception. Aodhan knew how I'd been tormented about my mother. He'd witnessed most of it first-hand, and on more than one occasion, he'd been the only one trying to stop the bullies from harassing me. I'd long since ceased hoping for the taunts to end. Not Aodhan, though; he was determined to make my tormentors pay for each and every hurt they'd caused. If only he had discouraged them, but they were a tenacious lot.

And yes, Aodhan was also aware of how much the teasing bothered me. Outwardly, I ignored the comments about my mother; how she'd probably run off with another man, or how she'd left because she couldn't bear having such a pathetic daughter, or that she couldn't deal with her husband's drinking any longer. By all accounts, Da hadn't started drinking until a year after she'd gone. My entire family was hurting, not just me.

The bullies at school didn't care when or why my father drank, only that he did. The first time Aodhan had found me crying in the schoolyard, we'd been ten, and he held my hand and told me the most awful jokes until I laughed. I cried less often now, but he remained the only one who knew the extent of my pain. Until that grey afternoon in my kitchen, he'd also been the only one who hadn't joined in the taunts, as well.

When I woke on Wednesday, I was too depressed to make my usual morning bread, and by the time the afternoon rolled around, I was starving. Neither Kevin nor I made regular trips to the market, and I'd been taking for granted how much of my daily food intake was supplied by the school's canteen services. Not to mention, I was sick to death of cooking for myself.

I pulled on some clean jeans and a jumper, and headed to the centre of town. My original plan had been to stop by the market for a few days' worth of supplies, then I passed by the fish and chip shop. The aroma made my mouth water and my belly rumble. I hadn't splurged on fish and chips takeaway for months, and I decided to treat myself. I'd just queued up when I heard them.

"There she is, the suicidal one."

I glanced over my shoulder, and saw Kelsey and Sarah sitting near the windows. I faced forward, and hoped they hadn't noticed me noticing them. How were they always right behind me? Do they follow me around?

I took a deep breath and stared at the clock behind the counter. I just needed to endure their presence for five more minutes, then I'd have my food and leave. I could do anything for five minutes.

"I can't believe we got in trouble over that cow."

"Too bad her boyfriend saved her."

That last part was what straightened my back. I'd never had a boyfriend, and if my relationship status changes, that lot will not be on the need to know list. "Shouldn't you be in class?" I asked without looking at them.

"We got suspended," replied Kelsey. "Both of us. It seems someone told MacCreehy that a certain drawing made you want to take a flying leap."

"They made us talk to psychologists," Sarah added. "Worst twenty minutes of my life."

"I'm sorry for your unfortunate circumstances, but I never mentioned your names," I said. "Any parallels drawn between your actions and mine are the result of MacCreehy's overactive imagination."

"I saw how he pocketed my drawing," Kelsey said. "Think we can get him on a porno charge?"

"So you did draw it," I said, not that I'd thought otherwise. Kelsey's sour face told me she'd rather I hadn't made that connection. She glared at Sarah, who had whipped out her phone and was texting furiously.

"Maybe that's where your mother's been all this time," Kelsey said, sneering. "Doing pornos."

I clenched my fist. They weren't worth a drop of emotion on my part. They weren't.

Not one single drop.

"Gonna search topless mermaid pictures," Sarah said.

Not. One. Drop.

Kelsey giggled. "Wait, is that her?"

"Next," called the chipper. When I didn't move, he jerked his chin toward me, and said, "Next." It seemed it was my turn to order.

"You know what? My appetite's just been ruined," I said, then I shoved my way out of the shop and away from Kelsey and Sarah and the rest. I walked through town like a robot, blinded by both my tears and the bright sun. I made my way toward a park near the centre of town, intending to sit by myself for a time. Despite what I'd said to the chipper, I was ravenous, and I fully intended to get something to eat once I'd calmed down. Instead, when I got to the park, I kept going.

And going.

I didn't know where my feet were taking me. My anger at Kelsey and Sarah was all I felt, and I wanted was to get as far away from them as possible. No, that wasn't exactly true. I wanted to punish them for how they'd hurt me, punish them until tears flowed down their cheeks for once. As much as they deserved my wrath, it would be wrong to turn the tables on them. As Da always said, when they go low, we go high. If I get any higher, I'll leave the atmosphere.

The next thing I knew, I was at a beach, shivering cold and kneeling on the wet sand.

How did I get here? My clothes and hair were soaked with seawater, which made me wonder if I'd knelt down in the surf. Stiffly, I got to my feet, and only then did I notice the sun. It was close to setting, which meant I'd lost hours since I'd torn out of the chip shop. What's more, I was far from home, and it would be dark soon.

"What is happening to me?" I whispered. I'd blacked out twice in three days, and both times I'd been pulled toward the sea. Either I was doing my best to leap into it or just marching along the beach and straight toward the waves. It was enough to make me wonder if my subconscious was trying to drown me.

My gut clenched; when Da said that Mama returned to the sea, is this what he'd meant? Did she wander into the waves and drown herself, and he hadn't the heart to tell me?

Sobs threatening to strangle me, I covered my face with my hands. The saltwater residue on my hands got in my eyes and the sand caked around my fingers scratched my cheeks. Tears leaked from my eyes, and the salt's sting brought me out of my despair. Da had never acted like a widower, and neither he nor Kevin had ever referred to Mama as being deceased.

Good, then. As far as any of us knew, Mama was still alive. While that was a solid piece of good news, I still needed to sort out why I kept struggling to jump into the waves.

Lucky for me—my first and so far only luck that day—I knew someone who spent his afternoons on the same beach I'd ended up on. Aodhan, the very same person who'd saved me from jumping to my death, and the only one who'd thought to check on me afterward. I didn't know if he'd be glad to see me; I was near certain he wouldn't be, especially after how I'd treated him only the day prior. However, me turning up at home full of sand and seawater would only upset Da and Kevin, and I had nowhere else to go.

It was after sunset when I reached Aodhan's family business, Sullivan's Surf Shop. The walk had taken longer than I'd anticipated. I was shivering so hard my arms and sides were stiff and sore, and my feet ached in my wet runners. I tried the door, grateful the shop was still open, and stepped inside.

I'd never been inside the surf shop before. For a moment I just stood in the main room staring at the items for sale, dazzled by the brightly coloured surf boards and printed tee shirts. Most think of surfing as a sport that only happens in tropical locations, like Hawaii or Fiji. Little do they know that the Atlantic side of Ireland offers up some of the best waves on the planet.

Aodhan knew. Just like he knew me, and like he'd somehow known what was going on beneath the waves. Aodhan understood me.

"Can I help you?"

Having been startled by the voice, I looked toward the sales desk. A dark-haired man was frowning at me. When all I did was stare at him, he asked, "Do you need some help?"

"I'm, ah, looking for Aodhan," I replied. "Is he here?"

The man nodded and called Aodhan's name over his shoulder, his other hand on the phone. Suspecting he was about to call the garda, I moved toward the exit.

"Meri?"

I turned around, and saw Aodhan rushing toward me. "I'm sorry to appear unannounced," I began, but he pulled me into his arms. It was awkward and unexpected and I stood there stiff as a tree trunk.

"What happened to you?" he asked, his hands pausing against my back when he felt my wet shirt. "You're soaked to the bone, cold as death." He held me at arm's length, and asked, "Why did you come here?"

"If you still want to talk, I'm ready to listen."

He nodded. "Of course. First, let's see about getting you dry and warm."

Cold Chicken And Hot Kale

I ronically, me getting dry involved me first getting a good deal wetter. Instead of the sea, this time it was in the form of a shower.

It was a wonderful shower, and even though it was the shop's bathroom, it was decked out like a rich person's private spa. The massive showerhead rained litres of steaming water onto me, and the tiled ledge was filled with scented soaps and shampoos that Aodhan insisted belonged to his sisters. Being that I'd been dealing with bare bones toiletries for years, it was a welcome if somewhat overly floral change.

But I couldn't stay in there forever and ignore the present, now could I? When I exited the shower I found a short-sleeved knit shirt and a pair of black tracksuit bottoms neatly folded on the counter, and my own clothes were nowhere to be found. I remembered that Aodhan had said he'd have my clothes washed and dried, and was momentarily mortified; had he seen me showering? I shook my head, and decided that it didn't matter one way or the other, since we had much bigger problems to sort out. That, and the shower curtain was opaque plastic. While Aodhan was amazing in many ways, I was certain he did not have x-ray vision.

I dried off and got myself dressed, rolling up the tracksuit legs so many times it looked like I had tyres around my ankles, then I exited the bathroom into what looked like a loft-style family room. It was furnished with a couch, table and chairs, and a little kitchen area sat in the corner. Aodhan was sitting at the table, staring at his phone. "I didn't realise you lived here at the surf shop," I said.

"I don't, not really," he replied. "But we do have some nice amenities." He gestured toward the seat opposite him, and I sat. My gaze travelled back to the kitchenette. Now that I was thawed out, I remembered how starved I was.

"I know I should be apologising right now, or thanking you, but I haven't eaten since yesterday," I said. "Would there happen to be any food in this very nice establishment?"

Aodhan chuckled—which was irritating, since I was dead serious—then he rose and rummaged about in the small fridge. A few moments later he set out a loaf of bread and a few plastic containers on the table. My stomach overruled my manners, and I started popping lids while he grabbed plates and forks.

"I can heat that up for you," he said when he saw me tearing into some cold chicken.

"This is perfect," I said around a mouthful of food. He laughed again, out loud that time, and scooped some mashed potatoes and soggy green vegetables onto a plate and set it to warm in the microwave. While the appliance worked away, he filled a glass at the tap and set it before me.

"Thank you," I said after I'd had some water.

"Would you like some tea?"

"You don't have to go through all this trouble."

"It's no trouble." The microwave beeped, so he retrieved the plate and set it next to my glass, then he filled a second plate for himself.

"Do you always have supper here?" I asked as he set his plate in the microwave to warm.

"Supper?" he asked with a grin. "This is but a snack." I gaped at the amount of food he'd set out. If this was a snack, he must eat whole pigs for dinner.

The microwave beeped again, and we sat together eating our left-over chicken and potatoes. The green mess turned out to be kale, and it tasted a good deal better than it looked.

Aodhan didn't ask me anything while we were eating, he just tucked into his plate and finished his own food. I don't know if I'd ever been more grateful for anything in that moment than Aodhan's friendship, and his stalwart, mule-headed presence that somehow made him remain by my side even when I treated him like rubbish. I didn't know which one of us was crazier.

"Thank you," I said when we were both finished eating. "The food was wonderful. I can, um, wash up if you'd like."

"We can do it together."

We brought our dishes and such to the sink, and Aodhan scraped the plates into the bin while I rinsed and then set them in the dishwasher. When that was done, he filled the kettle and set it on the hob. If I had to endure another moment of this forced domesticity, I would definitely go mad.

"What happened with my clothes?" I asked.

"We have an industrial washer out back. I tossed your kit in with the rest of it." He glanced at me, then turned away as red dusted his cheeks. "Sorry I didn't have any knickers to loan you."

Did he have to go and remind me that I was sitting about, eating plates of cold chicken and hot kale whilst not wearing proper undergarments? Suddenly, I remembered why he irritated me as much as he did.

"I'd have been rather more surprised if you'd had a pair lying about." Face on fire, I coughed and looked away. "Really, Aodhan, I don't know how I can ever thank you for all of this."

The kettle whistled. "Telling me how you ended up here would be a good start," he said. We fixed our tea, then he guided me to the couch. I took a deep breath, then I told him everything that had happened at the chip shop, ending with how I'd somehow turned up on the shore hours later, waterlogged and with no memory of having got there.

"So it bugged you when Sarah called me your boyfriend," he said. "Interesting." I moved to swat him, but he held up his mug as a sort of shield.

"It was yet another lie, that was what bothered me," I said. "That's what they've been doing for years, bending the truth to make my life into something worse than it already is."

He frowned. "Would me being your boyfriend really be that bad?"

"That's not what I meant." I hadn't meant to hurt Aodhan, but I excelled at sticking my foot in my mouth. "You know that. Don't you?"

"I do." He flashed a quick grin. "Besides that, not everything they said to you was a lie. The school did have all the students meet with counsellors. They asked us if we'd ever felt like harming ourselves or others, stuff like that."

"You never told me that."

"I would have if you hadn't kicked me out of your kitchen yesterday," he retorted. I scowled at my tea. "And you haven't yet said if you'll forgive me, for showing up out of the blue like that and forcing my ideas on you. I am truly sorry about that, Meri."

"Are you apologising to me, for me having to ask you to leave?"

"I suppose I am."

"Then I suppose I forgive you."

Aodhan curled his fingers around mine and squeezed. "Thank you."

"You know the best way to thank me?"

His thumb glided across my knuckles. "Tell me."

"Explain to me how you got the idea of my mother being from a lost city at the bottom of the ocean," I said as I withdrew my hand from his. "That notion's nearly as daft as her being a mermaid."

He ran a hand through his hair. "I'm on the water almost every day, either surfing, manning one of the tourist boats, what have you. I've seen things."

"What sort of things?"

Aodhan shook his head. "Things that shouldn't be there... Things that just shouldn't exist. The first time I saw a roof beneath the waves, I thought my eyes were playing tricks on me; the second time, I figured an earthquake had destroyed a village way back when, and it was an archaeological site or something."

Aodhan had seen something. If we'd both seen something on different days, that meant I wasn't crazy. Or it we were both crazy. That was still an option. "What made you decide it wasn't?"

"I did a bit of research. You're not the only aces student in Sister Mary Katherine's classes, you know." We grinned at each other for a moment, then he went on. "My research told me that the place where I saw those structures hasn't been above water in recorded history."

"What about unrecorded history?"

"That's what I thought at first, but deep sea dives have proven that nothing manmade is down there. Which begs the question, what the devil have I been seeing? So I moved on from archaeology to some of the local legends, and learned about Kilstiffen." He set down his mug, then he leaned back against the cushions and said, "There's more."

"Christ, Aodhan, what more could there be?" I squealed. "Have you seen people down there?"

"Well, I haven't seen any mermaids or merrows, if that's what you mean." He winked, and added, "It seems that only the Murphy clan is allowed that bit of mystery."

That time, I did swat him, albeit gently. "I'll forgive you that, on account of yesterday. What more, then?"

"Out on the water, you hear things."

"What kind of things?"

"Voices, for one," he replied. "The sound is somewhere between a song and a wail, but it's always there. It's like it's following you, keeping you from harm."

"And that's what made you think of my mother?" I asked, and he nodded.

"Everyone who remembers her mentions her voice."

"Her singing is my only real memory of her." Since we were having a moment, I asked, "Was I really that bad at the Cliffs?"

"It was worse than you can imagine," he said. "I really didn't know if I'd catch you in time, and then you would have been gone forever..." He cleared his throat, and asked, "Did you know that there are many jumpers at the Cliffs?"

"Aodhan, you know I wasn't trying to kill myself!"

"But you were trying to jump," he said, and I didn't disagree. "I could see it in your eyes, feel it in the way you struggled to get free from me. And how did you end up on the beach earlier?"

"I really don't know," I said. "Kelsey and Sarah made me angry, so I left the shop and started walking. I don't know if I walked for hours, or if I'd been kneeling in the water for half a day." I looked at Aodhan. "Why didn't anyone stop me, ask me what was happening?"

"I don't know," he replied. "Maybe when you were walking, people just let you go about your business? And did you see anyone else at the beach?"

"No, it was empty when I came to myself. Empty, and freezing cold." I suppressed a shudder, and wrapped my arms around myself. "It was like the water was calling me."

"Calling you how?"

"Not with a voice," I said, since I hadn't actually heard anything, either with my ears or inside my head. "It was pulling me, like it had thrown a rope around me and was yanking me along." I thought about my time on the beach, grasping for any shred of memory: sand yielding beneath my knees and shins, dappled rays of sunlight streaming from above, the feeling of my hair and clothes floating, the bone-chillingly cold water pressed against my skin.

"I-I think I was underwater," I said.

"For how long?"

"Long enough for the water to be over my head." I held my head in my hands. "How is that even possible? Wouldn't I have drowned?" I shook my head. "That must not be a real memory. M-Maybe I hallucinated it."

"Maybe. Or maybe whatever was calling you wanted you to feel that way. What if some of those who had jumped from the Cliffs felt that same pull?" Aodhan asked.

"Aodhan, you can't think all of them felt like me," I said.

"Not all, *some*," he clarified. "How many times have you read a news story about someone who ended it, and all their friends and family are shocked? Claiming he or she wasn't suicidal or depressed, that it really must have been a terrible accident, or maybe even an unsolved murder?" Aodhan put down his mug, then took my hands in his.

"Meri, I have felt the sea's call many times, and you've felt it twice in three days. There is something out there, isn't there?"

"I think there must be," I replied. "You've really felt it?"

"I have. Many times."

My relief over not being crazy was overshadowed by my recent near-death experiences. "Does that mean we're doomed to drown as well? Aodhan, I don't want to die."

"I don't think the voice wants to harm us. I think it needs help, just as it tries to help us." Aodhan squeezed my hands tighter. "Ever since I first heard it, I've wanted to learn more about it. It's why I started buying books about the sea and what might be lurking beneath it... But now it's calling you, too." He paused, searching my face. "Will you help me find out what it wants, what it needs?"

I stared at our hands. "Do you think it might lead us to my mother?"

"I don't know," he admitted. "I think it might get us closer to her, yeah."

"What if it doesn't?" I asked. "What if we try to follow it, but we can't?"

"We're Meri and Aodhan. Together, we can do anything."

The next thing Aodhan and I did was sleep. Not together, mind you.

Spending the day telling people off and stomping around town had been exhausting. The subsequent hot shower and hearty meal had both contributed to my exhaustion, and it wasn't long before we were awkwardly discussing sleeping arrangements.

"I can go home," I said around a yawn.

"Your father and Kevin won't have something to say about you getting home so late?" Aodhan asked. "Wearing my clothes?"

"My clothes aren't done yet?" I asked. Before he could respond, I said, "I'm sure they're fine. I can wear damp clothes."

"If you think I'm going to let you walk home in the cold dark night wearing wet clothes, you're daft." With that, Aodhan opened a press and withdrew a heap of blankets and pillows. He tossed the lot of it onto the couch, then he grabbed a sleeping bag and an air mattress.

"Do you sleep here often?" I asked.

"Often enough to keep the proper supplies on hand." He plugged in the air pump, and the mattress came to life like a writhing ocean beast. I hoped that wasn't indicative of whatever was calling me from the bottom of the sea. "The air bed is more comfortable. You take that, and I'll take the sofa."

"That won't work," I said. Now that the mattress was inflated, it had to be a queen size, whereas the couch was shorter and narrower. Aodhan was at least a head taller than me. "You'll fit better on the mattress."

"I'll be fine." Aodhan tossed a few blankets and a pillow at me, then set about making his own bed.

"Why aren't you going home?" I asked.

"I stay here all the time. The shop's closer to school than home is, so it works out well." He pulled out his phone and sent a text. A moment later, it beeped, and Aodhan set it on the table.

"There, my ma knows where I am," he said. "Do you need to text your brother?"

For a moment I panicked, thinking my phone had got lost in the sea, but I remembered plugging it in to charge before I'd left for the market. I considered how Kevin usually came home after I went to bed, and woke up after I left for school. I also considered how Aodhan had assumed Da would be too drunk to wonder where his only daughter was sleeping, and damn it all if I didn't agree with him.

"It should be all right for just the one night," I said. "Are you going to set an alarm?"

"Why? I thought you were off this week."

"What about you?"

Aodhan shrugged. "Maybe I'll take the rest of the week off too, and keep you company. After all, we've a mystery to solve."

I smiled at his ready support. "That we do."

Aodhan shut off the lights, and I snuggled underneath the blankets. He was right about the air mattress being comfortable, and it wasn't long before I felt myself drifting off to sleep. I only hoped I wouldn't dream about water.

SAD POTATOES

When I woke the following morning, I blinked and stared at the textured off-white ceiling tiles. I'd painted my bedroom ceiling sky blue months ago, and what's more, I had a flat plaster ceiling. For a moment, I panicked, having no idea where I was. It came back to me little by little: the chip shop, my lost afternoon, the sea. Aodhan.

I blew out a breath and rolled over. I didn't know what time it was, but it was still dark in the apartment; thanks to the dull light, I could just make out the kitchenette across the room. While I was wondering why the teakettle was on the counter and not the hob something brushed my neck and I jumped, assuming a spider or who knows what had crawled across me. But it was only Aodhan. His arm was dangling off the edge of the too-small couch he was lying on, and his fingers had got caught up in my hair.

I watched him for a moment, then I slipped out from under the blankets and into the frigid air, and made quick use of the facilities. By the time I returned, any leftover body heat was gone from my makeshift bed, and I burrowed deep looking for any warmth I could find.

"How'd you sleep?"

I looked up and saw Aodhan smiling at me from under a mess of dark curls. "Well, until I got up a moment ago. Haven't you got a heater in this place?"

"It's on a timer, kicks on at ten. The shop opens at eleven, and there's no point in heating an empty building. Be right back."

Aodhan made his own journey to the bathroom. When he returned, he was hopping up and down and rubbing his arms.

"I need to call a meeting about that heater. This isn't just unheated, it's positively bitter in here." He sat on the couch, eying me in my heap of blankets. "You're warm under there?"

"I am."

"Good," he said, then he dived off the couch and onto my mattress.

"What are you doing?" I shrieked. He burrowed underneath my blanket and pulled me against him, then he put his cold feet on me. "And why aren't you wearing socks?"

"Come on, warm me up," he said. "I warmed you up last night!"

"Not like this." I gave him another halfhearted shove before I settled against him. It was nice, being held for once. I was the only one holding it together at home, and I was glad to let Aodhan take charge for a moment.

"There. I'm not so bad, am I?"

"Your feet are. Have you got ice cubes for toes, or something?"

"Or something." He tucked my head underneath his chin, and we lay together for a time. I couldn't remember having ever been held by anyone, though I'm sure my parents had done plenty of that when I was a wee babe. After Mama had left us, Da hadn't been interested in outward displays of affection. Truly, the loss of her had broken him.

Aodhan smoothed my hair back from my face. "Tell me, what's on our agenda for today?"

"I don't know. What do you think we should do? Look into these legends you dredged up?"

"An excellent idea." Aodhan's mouth was right against my forehead, and I felt his words vibrating throughout my body as surely as I heard them. "Which one should we read first?"

"Perhaps we should get up and pick one out?"

"I found some of them online. We could stay here, and read them on my phone."

"Aren't you hungry? I'll make breakfast."

"Is that what you want to do?"

"Yes." Actually, I never wanted to move from that nest of blankets and the warmth of Aodhan's arms, but I worried if I didn't get up now something irrevocable might happen. "Yes. That is what I think we should do."

Aodhan exhaled heavily, then he untangled himself from me. I jumped up from the air mattress and headed toward the kitchenette. I turned to say something to Aodhan, but he was already folding up the blankets and stowing them in the cabinet. I watched him for a moment, then I filled the kettle and took stock of the refrigerator. I found mostly pre-made food, along with a few dozen eggs, a package of rashers, milk, and some very sad potatoes. The shelf over the countertop held more boxed and packaged snacks, along with a loaf of store-bought bread.

"You have quite a lot of food on hand for someone who only stays here occasionally," I said as I rummaged about for some pans. "And why have you got the potatoes in the fridge?"

Aodhan shrugged. "To keep them from going bad? And as I told you, I do get hungry."

I prodded a potato with my fingertip. The indentation remained like a crater. "These must have turned days ago."

Aodhan scooped up the potatoes and tossed them in the bin, then he resumed folding blankets. Even without the rotted spuds, there was enough food in that tiny kitchen to feed both of us for a week, and that was counting Aodhan's superhuman appetite. That, coupled with the air mattress and blankets he kept at the ready, was interesting. More than interesting, even. I left it for now, since there were several things about my home life I'd rather not discuss, and set a skillet on the stovetop.

Aodhan, having put away all of the bedding and the deflated mattress, investigated the ingredients I'd lined up on the counter. "Making me a full breakfast?"

"It's the least I can do," I replied. "Besides, who knows what the day will bring. If I'm going to lose my mind and wander the countryside for half a day again, I'd like to do it on a full stomach."

"That won't happen," Aodhan said. "Meri, I won't let you walk into the sea."

His intensity was more than I could handle at the moment, so I turned on the heat and arranged some rashers in the skillet. While they sizzled, I popped some bread into the toaster, then I finally turned to Aodhan.

"Would you like a fried egg, too?"

"I can handle the eggs," he said as he set a second pan on the burner. He'd already opened the beans and put them on the cooker. "We'll have quite the feast this morning."

The kettle whistled, so I busied myself with our tea. Once that was done, I turned the rashers, then I found some plates and went to set the table. As I was laying out the forks, Aodhan caught my wrist.

"I didn't mean to make you uncomfortable earlier."

"You didn't," I said. After all, it was myself I didn't trust, not Aodhan.

"You cook when you're upset." He looked pointedly at the table, and then at the food cooking away on the stove. "Even in play school, whenever things didn't go your way, you'd grab the pretend food and make the class a feast."

"All right. You did make me uncomfortable, but I know you didn't mean to." I went back to setting the table. "You're a nice enough lad, and I like you, Aodhan. Truly, I do. But I'm not here for any of that. You must understand, I've got to fix one situation before I can tackle another."

"You're going to fix me next, then?" he asked. "All because you like me?"

I swatted his arm, but gently. "You're incorrigible, you know that?"

He grinned. "Of course I do. It's why you like me so much."

That broke the wall of tension that was looming between us, and soon enough we sat down to a hot breakfast. I tucked into my plate straightaway, much to Aodhan's amusement.

"When you gobbled down your dinner last night I assumed it was due to a long day," he said around his own mouthfuls of food. "But you've a right appetite, haven't you?"

"Is that bad?"

"Not at all, Mer. Not that you can keep up with me," he added.

"I've always had a good appetite," I said. "When Kevin and I were small, we never knew when the next batch of food would show up in our larder. Whenever it did, we always ate so much that afterward we could hardly move."

Aodhan frowned. "Was your family bad off?"

"Well, yes, but not how you're thinking," I replied. "We've always had plenty of money, thanks to Da's business, but he would often forget to visit the market. The pub is what was on his daily to-do list, not the grocer." Aodhan opened his mouth, probably to say something I'd heard so many times before, either sympathy about my drunk father or an encouraging word about how better days were coming. I didn't want to hear any of that, so I kept talking.

"Anyway, once Kevin was old enough to get the messages on his own, he and I started doing our own shopping. We've been right as rain ever since."

Aodhan nodded, then he poked at his food. "After my ma and my stepfather married, things were off for a time. I know how it can be, wondering when the grownups will take notice of us wee ones again."

"I didn't know you had a stepfather." I'd always thought of Aodhan as the American's son, even though his father had died some time ago, and Aodhan almost never mentioned his family.

"Ma married him a few years back. He hasn't really taken to country life. Prefers to keep to his business in Cork."

"Isn't that an awfully long commute for him?"

"Yeah. He keeps an apartment down there so he doesn't have to make the drive every day." Aodhan gestured to encompass the shop with his fork. "This shop is my real father's legacy. It's why it's so important to me, why I'm always here. Got to keep his memory alive however I can, you know?"

"I surely do." We ate in silence for a moment. "Thank you, for sharing that with me."

Aodhan nodded, but he didn't smile. "You are quite welcome. I've a feeling we'll be doing a lot of sharing in the days ahead while we figure out what's going on underneath the sea."

I stabbed at my eggs. "I fear you're correct."

Come Sail Away

"Well, Meri my girl, where should we start today?"

I slid my gaze toward Aodhan. We'd finished our breakfast and handled the washing up, then Aodhan had retrieved my clothes so I could change out of his things. He had washed and dried them as promised, and the casual observer would never guess I'd spent the prior afternoon kneeling on a beach in the surf. "I'm your girl now, am I?"

"That you are," he replied. "Just as I'm your man, and we're solving a mystery together."

Usually, I liked Aodhan's boundless enthusiasm, but it was awfully early in the day. Instead of saying something I might regret, I focused on tying my shoelaces. My runners had dried out, but when I wiggled my toes, I felt the sandy grit left behind from yesterday's unplanned adventure.

"Since you think all of this hinges on Kilstiffen, should we start with that?" I asked. "You said it's at the bottom of the sea?"

"So the legends say."

"Can we have a look at what's left of it?"

"Not likely. There's a reef out there that some think is a sunken forest, prehistoric and all, but it's not easy to get to." Aodhan reached above the fridge and grabbed two water bottles. "I have an idea, but I don't know how you'll feel about it."

"The best way to learn is to ask me."

Aodhan looked at me, rather seriously for a goof like him. "Has your father ever told you exactly where he first met your mother?"

I pursed my lips and turned away. "Officially, they met at the pub on Fisher Street; not the tourist one, but the one with the *céilí* on Thursdays and Saturdays. He saw her across a crowded room, it was love at first sight, and they danced the night away. That's what he tells people, these days." I cleared my throat. "But when he's deep in his cups, he talks about finding her stranded on a beach below the Cliffs of Moher."

"Stranded?" Aodhan repeated. "How could a mermaid be stranded on a beach? Unless..."

"She is not a mermaid," I snapped.

"But why did everyone think she was?" Aodhan countered.

"Right after she left, Da told me a story about her going back to the sea," I replied. "I was so young... I believed it was true, until I started telling people and they all laughed at me. Turns out I'm the only one who fell for that tale."

"No, Mer, everyone fell for it," Aodhan said. "You haven't told that story in years, and you don't have to. Everyone in town is still telling it, going on about how they know the fisherman and his mermaid bride. There must be a reason."

"They also say my mother ran off with another man. The whole town is crazy."

"That, I do not dispute." Aodhan rifled around in a drawer. After a moment, he withdrew a map and unrolled it on the table. It was a nautical map of the west coast of Ireland. "There are a few beaches along the bay that only appear at low tide. You can't really climb down to them, what with the cliffs being nearly vertical in most spots. You would need to approach them from the sea. Perhaps she was on one of these?"

"Perhaps," I said. "I mean, she could have been out for a swim, and got stuck, then Da rescued her. That could account for the merrow aspect of it all."

Aodhan gave me a look, but refrained from saying that no one went out for a swim in those waters unless they had a death wish. "That's it, then. We'll start by going out to investigate the beaches."

"Um, how?"

"I happen to have access to a right fine boat."

It wasn't long before we were aboard Aodhan's—or rather, the surf shop's—watercraft that took sightseers on tours around the bay. The shop's vessel was both newer and in better nick that my father's boat, but I supposed that was a necessity in order to convince tourists to hand over their hard-earned cash; that, and Da hadn't got himself anything new in over a decade. It's a wonder his clothes haven't all disintegrated.

I tried offering my assistance while Aodhan got the boat ready to launch, but it was soon apparent that I had no idea what I was doing.

"How are you so clueless when it comes to boats?" Aodhan asked after we'd set off. "What with you being the daughter of a fisherman and all."

I laughed through my nose. "You're assuming that Da takes me out with him. Neither Kevin nor I have been on his boat since before Mama left us. I hardly ever look at the sea, much less go near it."

Aodhan pondered that for a moment. "Based on how you behaved at the Cliffs, and yesterday at the beach, perhaps your dad is on to something."

I frowned, then I turned my face into the wind. "I don't feel the sea's pull now, even though I'm right on top of it."

"Even if you did, I won't let the waves take you."

The gravity with which he said that made me pause. "Who did you lose?"

"My father," he replied. "And I didn't lose him so much as he just left for work one day and never came home." He turned away, gazing at something beyond the waves.

"Can I ask what happened?" I remembered when Aodhan's father had died, but I'd never known any details.

"It was seven years ago. When he didn't come home for dinner, my ma thought nothing of it, since he would always find things to do around the shop and not close up until later than expected. Do you know that when the guards came by and told us Dad wouldn't be coming home again, I thought he'd got lost? I tried to go out after him, bring him a map so he could find his way back."

"Aodhan." I moved to stand next to him, but I stared straight ahead and didn't look at his face. I understood that sometimes people needed a moment. "Had he just lost his way?"

"No. It was a sudden storm. Took him and his boat down." Aodhan faced me, gave me a tight smile. "I know what you're thinking, Meri, that I'm helping you with your ma so I can make peace with what happened to my dad. It's not like that."

"I wasn't thinking that at all!"

"Good. I know Dad's not coming home."

I patted his forearm. It was the first time I'd ever initiated contact between us, and I was momentarily mortified. Then Aodhan laid his hand atop mine and squeezed. He and I, we understood each other.

A moment later, he retreated into the cabin and surveyed the many knobs and controls. When he emerged onto the deck, Aodhan gestured toward the waves as if he'd done something grand.

"We are now above Kilstiffen reef," he declared.

"How can you tell?" I asked. We'd reached an expanse of water that looked just like all the other vast expanses of water we'd sailed through.

"Coordinates."

"Of course. Coordinates." I leaned over the side and peered into the dark water. "Is the reef very far down?"

"Oh, yes," he replied. "I believe it's about fifteen hundred metres down. Can't even see it at low tide."

I straightened and looked past Aodhan to the drawer labelled "diving equipment". "Can you dive? Maybe we can get down to it."

"I can dive a bit, but that reef isn't for amateurs. From what I hear tell, diving there is like diving in the open ocean."

"Oh." Since I had no idea what diving was like in any part of the ocean, open or closed, I changed the subject. "What's the point in coming out here if we can't see the reef from the surface or get down to it?"

"I was thinking that we could start here, and then cruise by the low tide beaches," he explained. "All good detectives begin by retracing past steps. Puts them in the perpetrator's mindset." He frowned, and added, "Not that your parents are the perpetrators of anything."

In spite of the fact that we were out in the middle of the bay for no real reason, I smiled. "All right. What direction are these beaches in? Are they far?"

"Not far at all," he replied. "I know of a few. I figured we'd start with those closest to the reef, and work our way toward where we were on the Cliffs. We'll take our time and see what the water decides to show us."

Aodhan busied himself steering us across the water, and I looked toward the shore. I'd never say this out loud—certainly not after what had happened at the Cliffs a few days ago—but being out on the sea made me feel centred. Complete. I wondered if the sea was what I'd been missing all my life.

I sang a few lines from an old rock song. It was about sailing, and finding a new path... and aliens. American music was strange.

"You like Styx?" Aodhan asked.

"Kevin does," I replied. "I'm not really into rock music, but the song seemed appropriate."

"My dad loved that band," Aodhan continued. "He played them all the time, them and a bunch of other bands from when he was a kid. Drove my ma batty."

I imagined a young Aodhan playing air guitar with his father. "Will we see the beaches soon?"

"Aye. Soon."

Aodhan was right, and soon enough we could see a narrow strip of beach below the cliffs. The waves lapped at the sand, reminding the land that it would soon be drowned again.

Drowned, just like the city Aodhan thought my mother came from. I shivered, and moved away from the shadows cast by the boat's cabin and into the sunlight.

"There are caves on some of these beaches," Aodhan said. "Some fill right up at high tide."

"Could someone hide in there?" I asked.

Aodhan shrugged. "I suppose so, as long as they had space for air. Or maybe a breathing apparatus, like scuba gear."

I tapped my forefinger against my chin. "I wonder if anyone's ever lived in those caves."

"Anything's possible, Mer."

We sailed up and down the coast and saw quite a few more beaches. Since I didn't know which beach Da had found Mama on—or if that had ever really happened—we didn't accomplish much more than looking at them. But it was nice to be out on the water, away from the Kelseys and Sarahs of the world, and the rest of the nonsense of life. I was beginning to understand why so many gravitated toward the sea.

I heard a strange beating sound coming from above. I turned toward the sound and saw a red and white helicopter speeding toward the shore.

"Search and rescue," Aodhan said. "I see them all the time out here."

"Where are they going?" I wondered aloud.

"Let's find out."

Aodhan steered the boat to follow the helicopter. Within a few minutes, we were approaching the rocky shore below the Cliffs of Moher, near where we'd been on Monday. Near where I'd almost run off the edge and into the sea. Several individuals in bright yellow jackets were moving about on the beach, and there was a boat anchored just offshore. A red tarp covered what could only have been a body.

I gazed upward at two hundred metres of hard, unforgiving stone. Even if the jumper had changed their mind, or just slipped and accidentally gone over, there weren't any ledges or handholds jutting out that might have saved him. Once he'd taken that fateful step, it was over.

"It's a jumper," I said. "That could have been me."

"But it wasn't you." Aodhan turned the boat around. "Let's leave them to do their work."

Even though someone had felt the same compulsion I had, and succumbed, I felt no urge to be one with the open water. The voice I'd felt as much as heard, twice now, was silent. I don't know if that was because I was already on the water or for a more complex reason, but I was glad to have my wits about me.

"I suppose this was a wasted trip," I said. "We didn't learn anything."

"We did, and we didn't." He moved the knobs on the control panel. "We saw where it all began—well, where we think it began. And this trip gave us time to clear our heads. Never underestimate the power of taking a step back. My dad always said that's the best way to see the big picture."

"When do you ever take a step back?" I asked. "All you do is run and surf."

"Surfing is when I do my best thinking. I go out past the breakers, sit on my board, and watch the shore. It's all so tiny from out there. Really puts things into perspective."

I looked toward the shore. Out here on the water, we were far removed from the hassles of everyday life. Even Kelsey and Sarah were like footnotes in a dusty old essay.

After we returned to the surf shop and docked the boat, Aodhan declared that he would walk me home.

"You don't want to investigate further?" I asked.

"I do, but first we need to figure out what we need to look into next," he replied. "And I also need to figure out how I'm going to get out of class tomorrow."

I ducked my head, having forgotten all about school. "You don't need to become a delinquent because of me. I can amuse myself these few days."

"It's no bother. Besides, you need me."

"I do?"

"Who else keeps you from jumping off cliffs, and warms you up and feeds you after a day spent in the cold sea?"

Yet again, I smiled at him. "You have me there."

Aodhan extended his arm. "Let's be off, then."

I opened my mouth to protest a few things, namely that I'd walked here by myself and I could certainly get myself back home without incident. But Aodhan had been so kind to me, not to mention my literal life saver twice now, and the last thing I wanted to do was upset him by declining. There was also the fact that I enjoyed being with him, and that I didn't want our time together to end just yet. Not that I was going to tell him that.

We laughed and talked all the way back to my house. He went so far as to escort me down my long, winding footpath and right up to the front porch. When we were standing in front of my door, Aodhan got serious.

"Meri," he said as he took my hands. "I've meant everything I've said to you. I will help you find answers."

I swallowed the lump in my throat, but before I could speak the door flew open. Standing on the threshold was Da, furious as a raging bull.

"Where have you been all day?" he demanded. "And where were you last night?"

"I've been with Aodhan," I blurted out, then realised that probably wasn't the best fact to lead with. Da leaned closer to me, his face red and a vein throbbing in his forehead.

"You were on the sea. I smell it on you," he accused. "First you go to the Cliffs—a place that I, your father, have forbidden from you—and now you take off with nary a word and go out on the bloody sea!"

"How do you know about the Cliffs?" I asked.

"That MacCreehy from the school came by the docks and gave the lot of 'em an earful." Da crossed his arms over his chest. "Why, Meri girl? Why did you go to the Cliffs?"

"I didn't want to upset you," I wailed. "I just wanted to see where you and Mama met. Why won't you tell me what really happened?"

Da lowered his head toward me, and I could see dried tears on his cheeks. "I've told you so many times. What you need to do is hear me." He straightened, then looked at Aodhan. "You're Lucas's boy?"

"Yes, sir," Aodhan replied, as startled as I was that Da knew who he was.

"And I assume you know all about what happened with my Calliope?" Da continued.

"Yes, sir, I do."

"Don't take Meri to the sea again," Da said. "Promise me you won't let what happened to my Calliope happen to Meri."

"I won't," Aodhan said. "I promise you, Mr Murphy. I will keep Meri safe."

Da nodded. "See that you do." He looked between us, and shook his head. "Run home now, Aodhan, and thank God that you still have a mother. Get inside, Meri girl."

I looked at Aodhan, wanting to speak to him but not wishing to further anger Da. Aodhan nodded, which I hoped meant he understood. Then I went inside and Da closed the door, shutting out both Aodhan and the sea.

"I'm sorry, Da," I began, but he waved it away.

"Truly, the fault is mine." Da sat at the table and held his head in his hands. "I must not have fully explained to you the horrors of the sea. Just as it was with Calliope, the fault is all mine."

I sat across from him and touched his hand. "No, Da. I was just curious, and my curiosity got the better of me. Would you like to know where Aodhan took me earlier today?"

Da glanced up. "Do I want to hear it?"

I shrugged. "You can only learn by listening."

Da nodded. "All right, then. Tell me where Lucas Sullivan's boy took my only daughter."

I cleared my throat, and ignored the sudden warmth on my face. "We went to look at the beaches below the Cliffs, the ones that only come out at low tide. Isn't that where you met Mama?"

"Aye," he replied. "She was a right beauty, standing there on the sand like a queen surveying her court. I loved her in that moment, you know."

I squeezed his hand. "I believe you."

"She won't go back there," Da said. "When she returns, it will be to a different spot."

"Do you really think she'll come back to us?"

"I believe it with all my heart," Da said. "When she finds a way, she will come back to us."

Da had said as much many times, and I'd always dismissed it as a drunk man's ramblings. After the past few days, I wondered if my mother had felt the same urge as I had to go to the water. If I followed the sea's call, would I find her at last?

THE NATURAL ORDER OF THINGS

Da and I sat together for a time, making awkward small talk about my marks and the weather. Eventually, he cracked open a fresh bottle of whiskey, then he poured out two measures and set one of the glasses before me.

"What's that for?" I asked, eyeing the amber liquid dubiously.

"You're old enough now," Da said. "Thinking about the state of your mother often requires a stiff drink."

"I, ah, think I'll make some dough instead."

"Suit yourself."

I got up from the table as Da downed his glass of whiskey, and then mine. It seemed that my Da being drunk was the natural order of things. Some of my earliest memories were of my father stumbling in after a night at the pub, then crashing about the kitchen as he searched for more whiskey in the press or under the sink. Sometimes he found a drop or two, and took the bottle with him to bed. Usually he found the kitchen devoid of all but the basics and I'd find him in the morning, passed out at the table.

No matter how much Da drank, he never missed a day of work, which was a feat in and of itself. He was a fisherman, and every day before dawn he was on his boat, casting his nets and doing whatever else fishermen did to earn a living. The town folk think he must truly be blessed by the sea gods, for drunks on boats usually tipped overboard.

Thanks to Da's chosen occupation, we always had food in the house. Actually, Da was an excellent fisherman, and if he hadn't drank to excess, we would have been quite comfortable. By all accounts, we had been quite comfortable, back when Kevin and I were young, and Mama was still with us. Then Mama went back to wherever she came from, and Da dived into a bottle and never resurfaced.

No, not never. Every time I see him sober, I hope for better days to come.

"She was so beautiful," Da said out of the blue. I knew without asking he was referring to Mama. She was never far from his thoughts. "And her voice... 'Tis why I called her Calliope."

"Wasn't that her name?" I asked as I kneaded the batch of dough. Aodhan was correct in that I cooked when I was upset. I was as good at baking as Da was at fishing, and kneading dough is an excellent stress reliever.

"She made me forget her true name," Da replied. He never attributed his faulty memory to his whiskey-soaked brain, instead insisting that my mother had somehow forced him to misremember details of their life together. Rather weak as excuses go, but I assumed it was yet another side effect of Da's drinking.

"It isn't written down anywhere?" I asked.

"No, she made sure it wasn't," he replied. "Said it was special, said it would bind me to her and hers." He took a long draught straight from the bottle, then wiped his mouth on the back of his hand. "Christ, as if marrying me weren't binding enough."

"Perhaps she thought a name was worth more than a bit of paper," I offered.

"Aye, Meri girl, that sounds like something your mother would say." Da crossed his arms on the table, and laid his head down upon them. "Meri, my Meri girl, so like her you are. But you'll never leave me. You'll never go to the sea."

He was snoring a moment later. I got the dough into the rising bowl and covered it with a tea towel, then I wiped my hands and draped a blanket across Da's shoulders. Depending on what Da was drinking, his nostalgia was tinged with either bitterness or fondness for the woman who bore me, usually the latter. But no matter Da's mood, no matter how he sobbed or what epithets he flung about, one thing was certain: he still loved my mother, and he missed her terribly.

Kevin and I wrestled Da up from the kitchen table and got him onto his bed. He'd be up again before dawn, as he always was, but at least he could have a few hours rest. After we left him sprawled out on the bed, I lingered in his room for a moment. On his bedside table was one of the two existing photographs of my mother. It had been taken on their wedding day, and both she and my father were grinning ear to ear, so obviously happy and in love. Da was sober, as evidenced by his clear, steady gaze, and Mama... Well, she was just as beautiful as Da had always said she was.

She had shoulder length, just wavy enough blonde hair, as if she'd spent the day at the beach and hadn't yet rinsed out the salt. The picture was too small to discern her eye colour, but I knew for a fact they were as blue as the sea. I saw them in my reflection whenever I looked in a mirror. Those eyes, and her singing voice, were her legacy in me.

As for Da, he was tall and strong in the photograph, with a head of dark hair and a reddish beard he'd passed on to Kevin. We were more than twenty years on from my parents' wedding day and my father was still strong, hauling fishing nets for decades had seen to that, but his dark hair was streaked with grey, and the lines on his face weren't from laughing.

Da grunted, but a quick glance assured me he remained asleep. I set down the picture frame and pulled a blanket across him, then I left his room and eased the door shut. I turned to walk down the hall, and was confronted with the other surviving photograph of my mother from where it hung among the other images of my family.

It had been a beach day, and Da wasn't in the picture because he'd been wielding the camera. Kevin was digging a hole in the sand, plastic bucket at the ready. I, being that I'd just been born, was a wee bundle at Mama's breast. Even though I had no real memory connected to that image, I liked to think it had been a good day. I liked to think we had been happy.

I looked toward Da's closed bedroom door and sighed. More than anything, I wished we could be happy again.

I retreated to my room, and saw my cell phone lying on top of my dresser. I wished I hadn't forgotten it when I'd left for lunch the day before, since a well-timed text to Kevin could have prevented Da from having a meltdown. I plugged in the charger, and waited for the device to come back to life. As soon as the screen lit up, I texted Aodhan.

Meri: Sorry about Da. He was just worried.

Aodhan: I get it. I would worry too, if my beautiful daughter was out all night with a boy.

My face went hot. Did he really think I was beautiful, or was he just trying to rile me up? Naturally, I assumed the latter.

Meri: And a strange boy at that. One who thinks the sea talks to him.

Aodhan: I am an odd one.

I grinned; sending him flirty texts was fun. And much easier than flirting face to face.

Meri: Well? Where should we go next?

Aodhan: Dinner?

Meri: I meant on this epic quest.

Aodhan: ;)

Aodhan: I did a bit of research, might know where to find the key.

Meri: Key?

Aodhan: Key to Kilstiffen. The missing one.

Meri: WHAT

Meri: I thought the key was missing?

Aodhan: It might be on land.

Meri: Why didn't you bring this up earlier? I could have helped research.

Aodhan: Sorry. Forgot, what with going out on the boat.

Aodhan: Need to check a few more things. Talk soon?

Meri: Yes, very soon.

I set the phone down, then I lay back and looked at my ceiling. My mind was racing with so many things; the day on the sea, Aodhan, the key. How could Aodhan know where the key was? And if he knew where it was, then the key was real. Kilstiffen was real.

The story about Mama might be real.

A Key, Or An Old Rotted Piece Of Junk

I was dreaming of bees.

My body was surrounded by a swarm that didn't sting. I'd never been frightened of bees, and I wasn't scared of this friendly group. The bees were warm and comforting, and they tickled my nose and arms with their beating wings and tiny, fuzzy bodies. Their buzzing was so intense I could feel it in my bones...

I blinked myself awake, and saw my phone vibrating on my bedside table. I supposed that was better than a swarm of bees congregating in my room. A quick glance at the screen told me that Aodhan was calling.

I accepted the call. "Yes?"

"You're awake, then." I swear I could hear the grin in his voice. "Up for an adventure?"

"Does it involve the mystical key to Kilstiffen?" I asked. Aodhan ignored my sarcasm.

"Of course it does. Have you ever been to Milltown Malbay? It's near Spanish Point."

I was familiar with the town, being that the one and only formal dress I've ever worn had been purchased from a shop there. "Yes, I've been there."

"It seems that the missing key to Kilstiffen might have been hidden under a grave marker near the town."

"A grave marker?" I squeaked. "The landscape is littered with our dead ancestors! Can you be more specific?"

"This marker is on Slieve Callan."

"Well, that certainly narrows it down. We've only an entire mountain to look over."

"It'll be easy to pick out. It's unique."

"Unique how?"

"It's inscribed with ogham."

I closed my eyes and leaned my head back against my bedroom wall. Ogham was an ancient alphabet, and for all that some said those lines and slashes represented letters, to me they looked like nothing more than random scratches. "So we're looking for an ancient stone, not a relatively new one marked in a language we're able to read?"

"So it would seem."

"Where did you even learn about this supposed grave?"

"It's mentioned in several books." He rattled off a list of titles.

"If you think I'm writing all of that down to check your work, you're daft."

"Does that mean you're in?"

"Will there be any seawater or waves involved?"

"Of course not," Aodhan replied. "I promised your father I wouldn't take you back to the sea. Do you doubt that I'm a man of my word?"

"What I doubt is your grasp on reality." Even as I said the words, I went to my closet and picked out a pair of jeans, and boots suitable for a hike. A long, steep hike, for if I recalled correctly, Slieve Callan was one of the higher points in County Clare. "How are we even going to get there? It's a bit far to leg it."

"I have access to proper vehicle, and GPS on my phone," he replied. "Don't worry, Meri, we won't get lost."

I sighed; I was sure to end up regretting this, but I couldn't pass up a possible lead on my quest. "All right. When will you be picking me up?"

After I sent a quick text to Kevin in which I informed him I was going a few towns over for the day, and left Da a long note on the kitchen table stating much the same, I walked down to where my driveway met the main road and waited for Aodhan to collect me. Soon enough, a bright blue car came screeching 'round the bend and halted directly in front of me.

Aodhan leaned over and opened the passenger door. "Morning, Meri."

"Nice car," I said as I hopped into the passenger seat. It was one of those environmentally friendly compact cars, which meant that tall, lanky Aodhan was folded up like a contortionist behind the steering wheel. "How did you get yourself in here?"

"Oh, quiet, you," he said good-naturedly. "My stepfather got me this for my last birthday. Based on the fact it's smaller than I am, it's living proof he's never actually looked at me."

"That was nice of him, to get you a car," I said. "Wait! At the shop you went on about not wanting me to walk home in the dark, yet you could have driven me!"

"Your point?"

"Why didn't you offer to drive me home?"

"Honestly?"

"Yes, honesty is preferable."

"I wanted you to stay."

"Oh." I hadn't expected that, and decided to end that line of inquiry at once. "How long has your stepfather been around?"

"About as long as I can remember, really," Aodhan replied. "He was my father's business partner. Not at the surf shop, that was Dad's labour of love, but in finance and such. My ma says that Dad only held the finance job to support the shop, but the shop's done right well ever since."

"Who runs the shop now?" I asked. When he gave me some side eye, I added, "I know you spend a lot of time there, but you can't possibly have been running a business by yourself all these years."

"You're right about that. In the beginning, Dad's old store manager took care of everything. After a year or so, my uncles—Dad's brothers, not Ma's—stepped in to help out. Of course, Dad had willed the shop to me alone. On my eighteenth birthday, everything became mine in fact."

"You mean you own the surf shop? The entire thing?"

"That I do."

"Then why are you still taking classes? You're a business owner, Aodhan!"

He laughed through his nose. "I reckon I am. I also reckon I would be a poor businessman if I didn't have at least a basic education to fall back on."

I studied his profile as he drove. "Look at you, being all wise beyond your years. Your father did right to leave you the shop."

He glanced at me. "Think so?"

"Know so."

It wasn't too much longer before we were in Milltown Malbay. Aodhan found a car park right off the R474, and after a short walk to the mountain proper, we started up the trail toward the peak of Slieve Callan.

"So we're looking for a grave marker," I said as we trudged up the trail. The hike was steep but not too difficult, even though the trail was a bit soggy. I was glad I'd worn my boots. "I don't suppose it's someplace convenient, such as in a graveyard?"

"What fun would that be?" Aodhan countered. "There's supposed to be one of those ancient burial mounds called a cairn, and the stone is set upon it."

"Wouldn't the cairn itself be the grave marker?" I asked.

Aodhan shrugged. "We'll know once we find it."

We had a few early moments of excitement, being that we happened upon a cairn almost right away. Being that this was Ireland, it was the wrong cairn. We'd found a monument called Knockalassa, also referred to as Diarmud and Grainne's Bed.

"I hope these boulders being called a bed is part of a legend," I said as we looked it over. Even though it was the wrong cairn, it was interesting nonetheless. It had two massive side walls and was topped with a third slab, all of it ancient, weathered stone. "This doesn't look the least bit comfortable."

"Agreed," Aodhan said, then he checked something on his phone. "Our cairn's situated on a slope north of the lough."

"That should make it easier to find."

It took us some time but eventually we did find the lough, though for my money it was more of a pond. We then spent a small eternity scouring the hillside, searching for a legendary gravestone that may or may not exist, not that we were certain of the key's existence, either. We were betting an awful lot on faith. I'd all but given up when Aodhan called me over.

"Meri," Aodhan yelled after we'd searched for more than an hour. "I think I've got it!"

I followed his voice, and found him kneeling next to a stone peeking out of the dirt. He was comparing the stone in front of him to a picture on his phone. "That's it?" I asked.

"It's the exact stone," he replied. "We've found it!"

"I thought it was on a cairn."

Aodhan frowned; the stone in question was pale grey, and it was covered in scratches that I guessed could have been ogham. It was set flush into the ground, and based on how the grasses crowded around the edges at least some of the stone was hidden beneath the soil. "Maybe the rest of the cairn is covered in sod?"

"Maybe." While Aodhan took a few pictures of the stone, I looked up the site's history on my phone. This had all seemed a bit too easy for me. Well, easy save for the mad search among the dust and rocks. I soon found an article that confirmed my suspicions.

"They say this grave is a fake," I announced. "Some local scholar carved the ogham stone himself and left it here a few hundred years ago."

"It's supposed to mark the grave of Conan Maol, of the Fianna."

I gave him a look. "So you've taken me to a tourist trap."

Aodhan met my gaze with a grin. "We're searching for a key to a legendary drowned city. Don't you reckon this being a tourist trap is the least of our concerns?"

I couldn't help it, I laughed. "I suppose you have a point there." I looked at the stone. Less than a metre of it was exposed, but there was no telling how big this stone actually was. If there really was a full cairn beneath it, we could be dealing with an actual ancient monolith. "May I ask another somewhat mundane question?"

"As you like."

"If this key is underneath this stone, how the devil are we supposed to lift it? If it's of a size like Knockalassa it might weigh a literal tonne."

Aodhan shoved his phone into his back pocket and ran a hand through his hair. "Christ, Meri, you've got a point there. We would need a crane just to budge it."

"That we would. Not to mention that I think you need clearance to disturb one of these sites," I said. "From an antiquities order, or some such. We can't do much more than take pictures."

"Right again," Aodhan said. I'd never been so right in all my life. "Let's have another look 'round the lough, make sure we didn't miss anything."

We snapped a few farewell pictures of the stone, then we circled the lough again. I was not surprised when we didn't find a map of Kilstiffen lying upon the shore. When we came around to the far side, I saw a heap of stones in the distance. Since stones didn't pile themselves up of their own accord, I moved in for a closer look.

"What's that?" I wondered as I started toward it. It turned out to be a trickle of a spring surrounded by moss-covered stones. In other words, it was a holy well, which were rather common in this part of the country. At the top of the stones was a flat slab on which those who'd come before us had left offerings, though who they'd been leaving them to was a mystery. I didn't see a saint's likeness or name anywhere about the stones. Perhaps they'd been leaving offerings to the god of the spring, whoever that was.

"Aodhan, come see this," I called. He yelled back that he was on his way. Once arrived, he crouched down and examined what I'd found.

"You've found a holy well," Aodhan said. "Tiny one, isn't it?"

"Yes, and no clue who it's dedicated to." I walked around to the rear of the well, but there weren't any crosses or other religious iconography present on that side, either. "Think it's old?"

"It's certainly not new construction." He leaned closer and poked at the offerings. "Have a look at this."

I crouched down beside him. Among the polished stones and other trinkets was a key. It was one of those old time skeleton keys that were as much for show as locking doors, and it was huge. The bar of the key was longer than my hand, with the ornate top loop being almost as wide as my palm. I suppose it might have been shiny once, but it was so weatherbeaten that now it was covered in green corrosion.

"We found the key," I said. "I can't believe it, but we really found it."

"My research said that the key is supposed to be under a cairn, and made of gold," Aodhan said. "That's an old rotted bit of junk."

"The article also said that the cairn might be a fake. They must have used a different hiding spot for the key."

"This well isn't exactly hidden. And who are 'they'?"

"According to your own theory, 'they' are the ones who need to keep the door to Kilstiffen locked." I picked up the key and moved to pocket it.

"You can't take that," he said. "That's someone's offering!"

"Or maybe it's something we were meant to find." When he kept frowning at me, I continued, "Look, we came here for a key. We found one. Can't be a stickler for details on something like this."

"We also can't just pick up random junk and hope it fits."

I blew out a breath and returned the key to its ledge. "It drives me crazy when you're logical."

"I know it does. That's why I'm logical so often." Aodhan snapped a picture of the well, then he turned to me. "What now? I bet you're hungry after all this."

"I could eat."

"Off to the chipper, then?"

"Brilliant."

We walked a few paces down the hillside, then I ran back to the well and grabbed the key. Based on the condition of the key, it had been out here for years and no one would miss it. When I returned to Aodhan's side, I handed it to him.

"Why do I have to carry it?" he asked.

"You have bigger pockets."

"You really think this key means something?"

"I'm not sure," I replied. "But I have a feeling, and lately my feelings are all I've had to go on."

"If you're right, this is big."

My hands were trembling, so I shoved them into my pockets. "I know."

We tumbled down the mountain and back to the car. A short drive later found us back in the centre of town where Aodhan re-parked the car, then we wandered among the shops until we found a place to eat. I ordered a bowl of mulligatawny soup and some brown bread, while Aodhan tucked into a sandwich stuffed with turkey, ham, tomatoes, sautéed onions, and cheese. The whole thing was topped off with a fried egg.

"You are a beast," I said as he unhinged his jaw and took a bite. He'd also got himself a side of chips, a slab of bread, and an apple. For dessert, he'd said with a grin.

"Am I?" he asked after he'd swallowed. "I am feeling a bit beastly after that hike. Go on, have some of my chips."

I made a face, then I took possession of a chip and dragged it through some curry sauce. "I'm sorry we didn't find a key alongside the ogham stone, like you'd planned."

Aodhan offered a sheepish grin. "Me, too. I really thought we'd find the stone, grab the key, and be on with it. At least you got that one from the well."

I almost spit out my soup. "What, did you think the key was the be all, end all? What of finding Kilstiffen, if it even exists?"

He took another lion-sized bit of his sandwich, and chewed thoughtfully for a time. After he swallowed, he said, "I thought about that on our way down the hill. It seems that I was putting the cart before the horse, eh?"

That, I could agree with. "Did your agile mind also come up with a solution?"

There was the grin that could never let me stay mad at him for long. "I like that. Aodhan of the agile mind." He leaned closer to me, and waggled his eyebrows. "Most only notice my body."

I kicked his chair under the table. "Solution, please?"

He flinched. "Jeez, Meri, I was just teasing you."

"I know. I'm just not used to that kind of talk."

"I get that."

"What did you come up with?"

"Well, it did occur to me—albeit a bit late—that finding a key is the least of our worries. If we're to find your ma, we need to know two things." He held up a finger. "One, where she came from."

I swallowed hard, and took a sip of water. "And the second?"

"Why she let your dad find her."

"What do you mean? She didn't let him find her. She was stranded on a beach and he rescued her."

Aodhan set down his sandwich. "Yes, he did rescue her. But what did he rescue her from?"

I flopped back in my chair. "I... I don't know." I turned toward the window and frowned. "I have no idea how she got to that beach, if she was shipwrecked or swam there on her own... I don't even know if Da knows."

"A third thing: what did he do once he got her?"

That straightened my back. "Aodhan Sullivan, if you think I am going to speculate on what went on between my parents—"

"Not like that," he said over me. "I mean, did he take her to hospital? To the garda? Was there a missing persons report, something like that?"

"Oh." I felt my face warm. "I-I don't know about any of that, either."

Aodhan smirked. "Dirty-minded girl."

I threw my napkin at him. "Do you think those records might still exist?"

"It's a possibility," he replied. "Think about it. If a fisherman found a woman stranded at sea, he wouldn't just take her to the local church and marry her straight away. He'd try and get her some help, like at a hospital or from the Coast Guard. Perhaps he'd even take her to the local pub for a pint, but the journey wouldn't have been straight to the chapel."

"True. Even Da doesn't claim to have married my mother the day he met her. He's said many times that he courted her for a time. I think they married six months after they met."

"You see? That's what I mean. We need to drill down to the original story, not all the rubbish that's been tossed about since."

I ducked my head and tore at my bread. "Thank you."

"For what, now?"

My throat thickened, and even though Aodhan had just given me the gift of believing in me, I couldn't say as much. "You know."

We ate in silence for a time. Despite what I'd said on Slieve Callan I felt a bit guilty for nicking the rotted old key. I hoped me removing it from the well didn't negate whatever good will the offeror had intended. And if whomever had left it really was hiding the key to Kilstiffen, did that mean that Mama was trapped in the city? Maybe she'd gone back for a visit all those years ago, but she couldn't get out.

"There's something else I'd like that agile mind of yours to consider," I said.

"What, love?"

"After my mother left, where did she go?"

Aodhan squeezed my hand. "We'll work on that, too."

We finished our lunch soon afterward, and made our way back to the car. As we walked, Aodhan swiped away at his phone.

"Meri, I may have discovered a promising new lead. A sword suspected of being many centuries old was recently found in the Shannon."

Ancient relics were not a rarity in Clare. "And?"

"And this sword is unlike any other recovered in the area. It's not an Irish sword, nor is it Viking."

"Well, what is it, then?"

"Even the experts are stumped. The article calls it an Atlantean sword."

"But Atlantis isn't real," I said, then I stopped walking. "Why do they think it's Atlantean?"

"The article says it looks like something that would come from Atlantis. What in the world could that mean?"

"If they're calling it Atlantean, it must look like something from under the sea," I said. "Where is the sword now?"

"It's at the County Clare Museum of History and Artefacts."

"Want to go have a look at it?"

Aodhan looked up from his phone and grinned. "You know I'm going to say yes."

THE SWORD

The museum that held the so-called Atlantean sword wasn't far from Milltown Malbay, which made me wonder if this side trip had been part of Aodhan's plan all along. He did seem to have an awfully easy time of stumbling across clues, and I could just see him plotting to keep the latter portion of our expedition under wraps until we were already nearby. That Aodhan Sullivan is a sneaky one.

We wandered inside the museum like ordinary tourists, picked up our brochures at the front desk and dutifully made our way around the exhibit rooms. The displays were set up in chronological order, starting with the obligatory shrine to the Great Famine. Aodhan and I took in the dioramas and emaciated mannequins with a respectful moment of silence. That done, the exhibits took us backward through history until we were standing in front of a rather pathetic representation of a burial cairn.

"Is that... Styrofoam?" I asked. Whomever had constructed the cairn had used blocks of Styrofoam and papier mâché, a sound choice for a child's after school crafting project, but a bit lacking for a formal museum installation. Evidently, that same individual had thought to spray paint the entire mess in various shades of grey and mud. The whole effect was rather atrocious.

"Nothing like the real sites I brought you to earlier, eh?" Aodhan bumped his shoulder against mine. "Want to find the people responsible for this lovely display and ask them about a certain relic?"

I gave the cairn a final glance. It would be an ideal hiding spot for magic keys or other treasure, since no one would ever want to see that halfhearted construction again. "Absolutely."

Aodhan sidled away from the railing that cordoned off the cairn's display, and I followed him as he meandered through the exhibits toward the front desk.

"Excuse me," he said to the clerk behind the counter.

"Next tour begins at half past the hour," she said, without looking up from her phone.

"Actually, I read an article about a sword you have here that was recently found in the River Shannon. Is it on display?"

"Swords and armour are in the eastern wing."

"But this is a new sword," Aodhan pressed. "A new old sword, that is."

The clerk sighed and set down her phone. I glanced at her screen; she'd been losing a game of solitaire. "You mean our Atlantean artefact?"

"That's the one," Aodhan replied.

"It is here, but it's still in processing."

"How does one process a sword?" I asked.

"Before anything goes on display, it needs a thorough cleaning, for starters," she replied. "Once that's done, it gets dated, and cross-checked with various other sources in order to learn its provenance. We can't very well put an unknown bit of metal on display, now can we?"

"No, that wouldn't be proper at all," I said. "Any word on when this sword was created?"

"Funny you should ask." She leaned over the counter, as if she were about to divulge the museum's deepest and darkest secrets. "We can't date it."

"Really? Why not?" I asked.

"It's tough dating metal as it is, but usually we can use the deterioration of an artefact to pinpoint its age with some accuracy... but this particular sword looks as if it was forged in the last few decades. Perhaps the last few years, even."

"Maybe it was," I said, but the clerk shook her head.

"The craftsmanship indicates otherwise," she said solemnly. *Oh, craftsmanship.*

"Can't you date the layer it was found in?" Aodhan asked. When the clerk gaped at him, he added, "I watch a lot of *Time Team.*"

"That's another problem," she replied. "According to the report, the sword was just lying atop the riverbed, as if it had been dropped there last week."

"Interesting," I said. "But it is here?"

"Oh, yes. It's in the archaeology room downstairs."

A couple approached the opposite end of the counter. The clerk made her apologies to Aodhan and me, then she greeted her new customers. Aodhan tapped his finger on the counter; underneath the Plexiglass surface was a map of the museum, and he'd located the archaeology room. It was on the floor below the main exhibits.

We waved goodbye to the clerk, then we walked toward the dark corridors at the rear of the building and located a staircase. It was narrow and dusty and clearly not meant for public use. After a shared glance, we entered the stairwell and descended to the lower level.

We emerged into a rather nondescript corridor of unadorned beige walls and matching linoleum floors. There was large metal filing cabinet pushed up against one of the walls, and a set of double doors directly in front of the stairwell. The doors were open, and Aodhan poked his head inside for a look 'round.

"Oh, hello," he said. "Is this the archaeology room?"

"It is," came the reply. "Can we help you?"

I peeked around Aodhan's shoulder. The room looked like something out of an academic essay. It had the same beige walls and linoleum floor as the corridor, along with overhead fluorescent lights, and walls lined with metal shelves upon which sat all manner of items and boxes. In the centre of the room was a long wooden table. Two people wearing white lab coats were standing over the table, their heaps of papers and pencils betraying that they were taking careful notes about the item they were examining. I stepped closer, and saw that the item was something long and metallic, not unlike a sword.

"We were on the tour and got a bit turned about," Aodhan said, then he pointed at the table. "Is that the sword just fished out from the Shannon? The one they're calling Atlantean?"

The man looked rather irritated by our presence, but the female scientist was all smiles. "You've heard of our find, then?"

"We have," Aodhan affirmed. When the archeologists just stared at us, Aodhan continued, "Our fathers are fishermen. They know all about things that happen on—and below—the river."

"Good to know you're not from a competing museum, looking to steal our find," she said.

"Does that really happen?" I asked. "Like in the movies?"

"Maybe," she replied with a sly smile. "What are your names?"

"I'm Aodhan, and this is Meri," Aodhan said in his best car salesman's voice.

"I'm Dr Fitzsimmons, and this cranky fellow is our senior archaeologist, Dr MacElroy," she said. "Since you're here, would you two like to have a closer look at the sword?"

We nodded, then she moved aside, and we saw the sword laid out on the table. It was about a metre long, including the hilt, with a shining silver blade that reflected blue in the harsh overhead light. The cross guard was a set of flames moulded in gold metal, the grip was iridescent green, and etched into it was a pattern that looked like fish scales.

I'd seen that design a hundred times before. My mother had worn jewellery with that exact same fish scale pattern. Which was why I blurted out, "That's Mama's."

The archaeologists stilled. "What did you say?" Dr Fitzsimmons asked.

"What?" Cold sweat collected between my shoulders, on my palms. "I didn't say anything!"

Dr Fitzsimmon's eyes narrowed. "Then what did I hear?"

"She said that the sword's marvellous," Aodhan said. "Didn't you, Mer?"

"It really is beautiful," I said in a rush. Never had I been so grateful for Aodhan's quick thinking. I also never thought I'd find something in a museum's research room that so clearly reminded me of my mother.

"Is it real?" Aodhan asked.

"What do you mean?" Dr MacElroy asked.

"It's so perfect," Aodhan replied. "Surely it couldn't have been in the water very long. It looks like you nicked it from a movie set."

"Perhaps it really is nothing more than a movie prop," I suggested. "Or a souvenir from a gift shop."

Dr MacElroy shook his head. "It's too well made, too perfect. And we've already contacted the local prop houses. None of them owned up to making a weapon like this one."

"The style is unlike anything else ever recorded," Dr Fitzsimmons continued. "At first glance, it appears to be a ceremonial sword, what with the heavy ornamentation, but look here." We leaned in, and she indicated the edge of the blade. "See this? The blade has battle scars. This sword has been used, either in an actual battle or for some serious training sessions. It's been re-sharpened several times."

"Why did the reports say it came from Atlantis?" I asked. "I mean, that place isn't even real."

"I believe the confusion comes from the hilt." Dr MacElroy tilted the sword so the engravings on the hilt caught the light. "See that pattern? It's much like fish scales."

"Or a merrow's tail," Dr Fitzsimmons added.

"A merrow?" I repeated.

"It's another word for mermaid," she clarified. "Surely you know what those are?"

I gulped, and nodded.

"Huh." Aodhan rolled back on his heels. "That's amazing. Have you two got cards or something? So we can follow your discoveries and such?"

Dr Fitzsimmons blinked at the abrupt subject change, but she went to her desk and retrieved a few paper rectangles. "Here you are. Are you two in the museum's archaeology club?"

"We'll be joining it straight away." Aodhan flashed Dr Fitzsimmons his grin, and I was pleased to learn it affected adult women just as much as it affected girls my age. "We'll get out of your hair now. It was great meeting you, and seeing the sword. Good luck with it, and all."

We said our goodbyes, then Aodhan and I left the research room the way we came in. Once we were outside the museum, he asked, "What did you really say about the sword?"

I didn't ask him for clarification. "I can't explain it, but that is my mother's sword."

He stopped walking and faced me. "Why on earth would you think that?"

"The handle," I replied. "Did you see how it was a green, scaly pattern? And how the pattern was etched into the green, with gold underneath? I remember her having things with that pattern. She wore these wide bracelets with that same design, one on each wrist."

"Wide bracelets," Aodhan repeated. "Like a set of gauntlets? Like a warrior might wear?"

"Gauntlets are gloves."

"Fine, vambraces."

"What on earth is a vambrace?"

"Armour that protects your forearms."

I started to ask how he knew about armour, but left it. Knowing Aodhan he kept a full suit of armour in the back of the surf shop for research purposes. "What makes you think my mother was a warrior?"

"The sword, for one."

I linked my fingers behind my head and thought about Mama's bracelets. "The bracelets were wide, but they didn't cover her entire forearms. They were more like cuffs."

"You're sure? The sword, all of it?"

"I'm sure." We reached the car. Aodhan held the door for me, then he went 'round to his side.

"Now we have a new thing to learn."

"What's that?"

"How did she lose the sword?"

I swallowed the lump in my throat. "Do you think it was taken from her?"

Aodhan started the engine, then he reached over and squeezed my hand. "Don't fret, Meri. We'll find out what happened."

I sank down in my seat. Now that I'd got closer to an answer about my mother's past, I didn't know if I wanted to hear it.

OYSTER THIEVES

By the time Aodhan dropped me off at home on Friday night, both Da and Kevin had already gone out for the evening. I momentarily debated texting Aodhan, but I was exhausted and achy from our trek around Slieve Callan and the museum. Having a quiet evening all to myself sounded like heaven. Besides, I didn't want Aodhan thinking I couldn't amuse myself without him.

I woke early on Saturday morning, when my father and brother were still sleeping. I considered hanging out in my room, but my rumbling stomach insisted that I head into the kitchen and start a batch of rolls. I didn't usually bake on Saturdays, but it wasn't like I had anything better to do. When I opened the fridge, for a moment I thought I was in the wrong house.

Staring out at me were packages of sausages and rashers, a whole chicken, assorted vegetables, and there was fresh milk and cheese. I closed the fridge and took stock of the rest of the kitchen, and found a carton of eggs, a bunch of bananas, and other sundries like soap and sponges. There was even a sack of potatoes in the corner by the door.

It was as if the market fairy had visited us whilst we slept and left us all of her best treats.

I didn't waste any time in assembling the requisite pots and pans and starting on breakfast. I considered making an all-out feast as I'd done at the surf shop, but without Aodhan present, I feared most of the food would go to waste. The sausages had just begun to sizzle when I heard footsteps behind me.

"Is there enough for me?" Da asked.

"Of course." I put two more links in the pan, and started cracking eggs into a bowl. After I'd beaten them nice and frothy, I asked, "Would you like some beans? Or maybe some tomatoes?"

"Whatever you've got going will be fine with me." He filled the kettle and set it to boil, and I poured the eggs into the hot skillet. Da opened the fridge and withdrew a carton I'd somehow overlooked.

"Orange juice," I squealed. "When did you get all of this?"

"I came ashore early yesterday, and went to the market before, ah, anywhere else," he replied. "I was going to roast the bird last night, but I held off since you and your brother weren't home."

"Sorry," I said, ducking my head.

"Quite all right." Da poured two glasses of juice and set them on the table. "Were you out with Aodhan again?"

"We weren't near the sea," I blurted out.

"Did I say you were?" he countered, in that patient way of his. "I trust that when you make a promise, you'll hold to it."

"Sorry. Again." I poked at the eggs for a moment. "We hiked up Slieve Callan. Did you know there's a lough up there?"

Da snorted. "Yes, I did know that. More of an overgrown puddle, as I recall."

"That's the one. After our hike, we went to a museum."

"You two had a good day, then?"

"Yes, it was very good." I grabbed two plates and served up the sausages and eggs, all the while remembering the sword at the museum.

It had to have been Mama's. The hilt was the exact pattern from her bracelets, and she'd worn those so often the three-year-old version of me remembered them to the smallest detail. I suppose I could have chalked those patterns up to coincidence, but in my experience there were no coincidences, only people ignoring the obvious. I refused to ignore the clues stacking up around me, not when they might lead me to my mother.

Da poured the tea and set the mugs on the table. It was the perfect moment to ask him a few questions about Mama, such as where she'd got those bracelets she'd worn so often, if he recalled her being involved in any sword-related activities, things like that. Instead of asking any of those questions, my courage wilted in my belly. What if he told me things I wasn't ready to hear? What if he didn't know the answers to any of it? After all, it was Da who'd first told me Mama was a mermaid. Maybe he didn't know why she'd left. Maybe she'd really just wanted to leave us all behind.

I took a deep breath and willed myself some composure. That done, I set our plates on the table.

"Here we are," I said. "I can't remember the last time we had breakfast together."

"Perhaps we'll make a habit of it, each and every Saturday," he suggested.

There went my composure; nothing got to me like Da being sober and present in our lives. I cleared my throat, and said, "I'd like that."

"Excellent," Da said after he sampled the eggs. "Maybe you'll be a chef one day."

"I'll never cook as well as you do," I said. "How did you know who Aodhan was?" While Aodhan and I had gone to school together for years, he'd never once been by my house before this week.

"He looks just like his father," Da began. "I've known his parents for some time. Actually, our families have known each other for generations."

"But Aodhan's father was American."

"Yes, and his mother grew up right here in town," Da said. "Bridgette—that's his ma's name—and I went to school together."

"I didn't know that," I said.

"Well, it's the truth. In fact, my da and Bridgette's father—your Aodhan's grandfather—once poached oysters together."

"You poached oysters?" I asked. "And he's not my Aodhan."

Da gave me a look, then continued, "I did not poach anything. There were a few beds that were government owned, and—what with the government being what it was—were sorely neglected. A few enterprising individuals noticed this, and harvested the oysters for themselves."

"I suppose there's nothing wrong with that," I said. "They must have eaten a lot of oyster stew."

"Oh, they didn't eat them. They sold them."

I set down my fork. "Da, that's illegal! Didn't they get caught?"

Da shrugged. "They paid a few fines, went to the courthouse once or twice. Eventually, the government divested itself of the beds and turned them into a local co-op, and that ended that business venture. It's quite a different thing to steal from your neighbour than from the government," he added.

"I imagine so." We ate in silence for a few moments. "Why did you bring home all of this food? I can't remember the last time you went to the market."

"Ah, well." Da downed his juice in one gulp and grimaced. I wondered if he was wishing for something stronger in his cup. "When you came home with Aodhan the other day, I got to thinking about why you were out with him in the first place. And the answer came to me; you felt safe with him. At first I was angry, being that your home is what should be making you feel safe… But then I remembered the state of things here, and that's all my fault. This house isn't much of a home, and it hasn't been since your mother left. I mean to change that, Meri girl."

"Da, this will always be my home," I said. "We're an off bunch, you and me and Kevin, but we're in this together. We'll always be family."

Da smiled. "You truly are the best of your mum and me, together in one tiny package. Now tell me all about this hike up the mountainside, and about the museum you visited."

"The museum was rather boring," I began, looking down at my plate. I resolved to not bring up the sword until I knew more about its history; I'd been dealing with half-truths and fairy tales for so long nothing less than verified facts would do. "As for Slieve Callan, that was quite an adventure."

LEMONS AND THYME

After breakfast was done, Da went to his boat, Kevin went to work, and I stayed home bored out of my mind. My body hummed with energy from the past few days' adventures, and I could hardly sit still. I spent an hour straightening up the house, but that wasn't enough of a workout for my restless limbs. What I really wanted to do was ransack the place looking for clues about my mother, but I wasn't sure when Da and Kevin were coming home. If they caught me searching and asked what I was after, I did not want to explain why I was examining every drawer and cubby. Being that I didn't even know what I was looking for, there was no way I could explain it to someone else.

I went outside to clear my head, and spied the old cottage at the bottom of the garden.

Back when our house had been a working farm, the hired help was allowed to stay in the cottage, if necessary. From what Da says, we'd never had year-round staff, only the occasional extra body or two for the harvest or sheep shearing. Sometimes I wished we still kept livestock. The rest of the time I understood I'd be the one raking out stalls and hauling feed, and realised things were better off as they are now. Still, having a lamb or two frolicking about every spring would be great fun.

The cottage hadn't seen a hired worker in decades, and was now only used for storage. Kevin and I had spent many days in the cottage when we were younger, slaying imaginary dragons, and I recalled seeing dozens of wooden crates in the front room stacked up to the rafters. Many of those crates held women's clothing, mostly Da's sister's things from before she went to university decades ago. But what if some of those old bits and bobs had once belonged to my mother?

I trudged across the fields and garden rows until I was standing in front of the weathered old door. The latch and hinges were rusty, but the door opened with no problems. I left it open, using the sunlight to illuminate the interior; the cottage did not have electricity, or indoor plumbing. Thanks to the sunny day, I didn't need modern lighting to see that everything was covered in a thick layer of dust. Before I could properly search for clues, this place needed a good scrubbing.

An old straw broom leaned against the hearth, next to a bucket of rags. I dumped out the rags and hauled the bucket to the stream that marked the eastern edge of our land and filled it. Three refills and the associated scrubbing later, and I'd got enough filth off the windows to let even more light into the cottage. Since I could now see into the very dark, very dusty corners, I grabbed the broom and swept out the front room as best I could. Once that was done, I was a sweaty, filthy mess. I resolved to take a shower, and come back later to sort through some of the crates. I'd just replaced the broom and bucket when I saw a bit of shining metal on a tabletop. It was a triangle-shaped patch of chain mail, but instead of the usual silver, it was plated in bright yellow gold.

"Well, where did this come from?" I turned the mail over in my hands. As far as I knew, chain mail was the stuff of knights and warriors, and was of no use on a farm.

I stuffed the bit of mail into my pocket, went inside, and had my shower. After I'd dried off and dressed, I went into the kitchen, and found Da surrounded by heaps of vegetables and pans.

"What's going on here?" I asked. "I thought you were needed at the harbour."

"Sunday roast is what's going on for all that we're a day early," Da replied. "I reckoned that since you made breakfast, it was on me to prepare dinner. After all, we don't want to end up eating anything that brother of yours cobbles together," he added, with a wink.

"No, we do not." Kevin could make coffee, and sandwiches, though even the sandwiches were a bit dodgy. I peeked around Da's shoulder, and saw him wrestling with the chicken. "Do you need help with that?" I asked.

"I am perfectly capable of trussing up a bird on my own, thank you very much," he replied. "If your hands need work, you can take care of the lemons for me."

I washed and quartered the lemons, and then I sliced up a few onions for good measure. While Da layered potatoes and onions in the bottom of the roasting pan, I popped out to the garden and grabbed a handful of thyme.

"Changing my recipe?" Da asked as I rinsed off the herbs.

"This *is* your recipe," I said. "You always stuff chickens with lemon and thyme."

"I'm surprised you remember that."

I was surprised too; Da hadn't made a Sunday dinner in years. In fact, he hardly cooked at all anymore, which was a shame. He made the best roast chicken in Ireland. I spied two empty wineglasses on the windowsill.

"What are those for?" I asked, jerking my chin toward the glasses.

"Ah, well." Da picked up one of the glasses and twirled the stem. "The first meal I ever cooked for your ma was a roast chicken. She helped me, as much as a woman who'd never been inside the kitchen could help, and after she nearly destroyed the bird, I asked her to pour two glasses of wine."

"Was the wine for a sauce?"

Da smiled. "It was for us, to pass the time while the bird cooked."

"So you tricked her." Da's brow pinched, so I continued, "You got her drunk, then you fed her the best food she'd ever tasted. No wonder she married you."

Da paused, and I was afraid I'd gone too far. I'd never teased him about Mama before, but here he was, sober and happy and cooking, and I'd dared to take that leap. After a moment's terror on my part, he set down the wineglass beside its mate. "There was a bit more involved than chicken, but my intent was for her to stay and she did. Perhaps you should make dinner for Aodhan?"

I opened my mouth to say I'd already cooked him breakfast, then I caught the gleam in Da's eye. I smiled ruefully instead, and said, "That was sneaky."

He shrugged. "I'm a fisherman. I sneak up on fish for a living."

We laughed, then my phone buzzed in my back pocket. Aodhan had sent me a picture of himself standing on the beach, wearing a wetsuit. He was holding his surfboard, and his wet curls were spiralling out from his head every which way.

Meri: You look like Medusa.

Aodhan: Bam! You're stone.

Aodhan: Just finished my last lesson of the day. What are you doing?

Meri: Been poking about the house. Found some gold.

Aodhan: Please tell me it's a key.

Meri: Not quite.

I slipped into the dining room, withdrew the chain mail, and sent Aodhan a picture of it.

Aodhan: That's so cool! Where did you find it?

Meri: In the cottage at the bottom of my garden. Want to come over and have a closer look at it?

I bit my lip, and added,

Meri: Da's making dinner. Roast chicken.

Aodhan: Thought you'd never ask. Be over in a bit.

I burst into the kitchen, and asked, "Can Aodhan come over for dinner?"

Da eyed me over his shoulder. "I don't see why not. We've plenty of food." He turned back to his chopping, and added, "Remember, Meri girl, the way to a man's heart is through his stomach. Or through the fourth and fifth rib, your choice."

"Ugh," I said. "I hope I don't end up regretting this."

Two hours later, there was a knock at the kitchen door. I opened it and Aodhan was standing there, his arms laden with shopping bags.

"I would have been here sooner, but I stopped at Tesco for dessert," he said, as he thrust the bags at me. Inside were several packets of American-style cookies. "I, ah, don't bake like you do."

"I'm sure these will be delicious." I took the bags of cookies from him, and Aodhan entered the kitchen just as Da was taking the chicken out of the oven.

"Hello, Mr Murphy," Aodhan said. "Thank you for having me over. The food smells amazing."

"Hopefully it will taste amazing, as well." Da set the roasting pan on the hob and pointed at the press. "Around here, the guest sets the table."

"On it, sir."

Dinner with Da and Aodhan went better than I'd hoped. They discussed safe topics like boats and the weather, which was a relief. The last thing I needed was for them to talk about Mama, or worse, me. At one point, Kevin returned home from work, grabbed a chicken leg, and retreated to his room. I don't think he even realised Aodhan was there. As for me, I couldn't stop thinking about the cottage, and what else could be hiding in those crates.

After we'd eaten, Aodhan and I handled the washing up. It took longer than it had at the surf shop, since we didn't have a dishwasher. Still, it was nice to slow down and do something mundane, even for only a short while.

When the dishes had all been washed and dried, I arranged the cookies Aodhan had brought on a platter and the three of us returned to the table. Kevin remained in his room, nursing his lone chicken leg. Da took one look at the cookies, and poured himself some whiskey.

"I've a bit of maintenance to attend to on my boat," he said, after he'd downed the whiskey. "While I'm gone, don't you two do anything I'll need to lecture you about later on."

"Da," I huffed, but he only laughed as he ambled out the door, bottle in hand.

"Well, having him sober for most of the day was wonderful," I said. "Want to see where I found the mail?"

"You know I do."

Aodhan grabbed a stack of cookies, and we set out across the old field toward the cottage. Aodhan couldn't stop staring at the old hedgerows, tumbling stone fences, and our many outbuildings in various states of disrepair.

"I never realised you live on a farm," he said.

"I don't know if you could call it a farm now," I said. "Not a working one, anyway. This land has been in my family for generations, but no one's farmed it for years. My granddad kept a few sheep, but even they've gone."

Aodhan pointed at a dilapidated structure opposite the cottage. "Is that a greenhouse?"

"It is." I gazed longingly at the whitewashed framework. "Someday, I'd love to restore it."

"I'll help you," Aodhan said. When I gave him some side eye, he went on, "I mean, can't be that hard. Old structures get restored all the time. I reckon we can have it set to rights by early summer, and then you can pack it full of tropical flowers and such."

I nodded toward his handful of cookies. "Perhaps I'll grow some vanilla orchids, and make you a batch of cookies as payment."

He stopped walking. "You would do that?"

I laughed, and pushed open the cottage door. Despite all the cleaning I'd done earlier, the place was still a mess.

"I found the mail here," I said, then I remembered it in my back pocket. "This is it," I said, and placed the fragment where I'd found it.

"Interesting," Aodhan said. "Why would an old farm's cottage have bits of chain mail lying about? This must be connected to the sword."

"I suppose it might be." I removed the chain mail to a safer location above the hearth. "Help me unstack these crates?"

He did, and soon enough that stack of crates was laid out across the freshly-swept floor. We began sorting through them, though there was no more mail to be found.

"Are these clothes your ma's?" Aodhan asked as he held up a yellow jumper.

"My aunt's, most likely," I replied. "Shove that one toward me? I think that's the one the mail fell out of. It was next to the table."

"Here you are," Aodhan said, as he pushed the crate toward me.

I pulled off the dust cover, and looked at things I hoped were my mother's. The top layer was clothing, just like the other four crates, although these clothes were of more muted colours. Aunt Donna had always dressed like a rainbow in human form, which is how I knew the bright yellow and green clothes belonged to her. Near the bottom of the crate, I found a large, fluted clam shell.

"Is that a real shell?" Aodhan asked. "It looks more like artwork than something dredged up from the ocean's floor."

"The sea hides many treasures," I murmured, then I shook my head and wondered where that had come from. I carefully opened the shell, and revealed a black velvet-lined interior. Resting on the velvet was a delicate gold chain, from which dangled a single teardrop-shaped pearl.

"Whoa," Aodhan said. "That's amazing. Pearls don't usually get that large."

"I wonder if this is Mama's." I laid the pearl on my palm. It was at least three centimetres long, the largest I'd ever seen by far. "Da never mentioned keeping any of her jewellery."

"Meri, I'm going to say something, but I don't want you to hit me."

"Why would I hit you?"

He glanced at the pearl, and said, "Everything we find points to the sea. The mermaid stories, the sword, and now this."

"How does a sword point to the sea?" I demanded.

"The Atlantean-looking sword that was found in a river?" he countered.

"That river is freshwater." I cradled the pearl in my palm, wishing it could tell me all its secrets. "What are you saying? That there really is a Kilstiffen, and my mother is down there?"

"I don't know." He peeked inside the crate. "Want to sort through the rest of this for clues?"

"All right." I replaced the necklace in its shell. "Let's see what else we can find."

Close, Yet Hidden

The crates in the cottage didn't give up any more hints, ocean-themed or otherwise, and it wasn't long before we closed up the cottage and Aodhan returned to the surf shop. As for me, homework was what was in my future. One of Sister Mary Katherine's assistants had dropped off my assignments on Friday afternoon, and I spent the rest of the day completing them. I may have missed some class time, but there was no way I'd let my marks suffer over what had happened back at the Cliffs. As for my reputation, that had long since been destroyed.

Sunday morning dawned clear and warm, which was a shame since I was yet again stuck home alone. Well, Kevin was home, but he was wrecked from whatever he'd got up to the night before, so he didn't count. As for Da, he'd either already gone out to his boat or hadn't yet returned from wherever he went last night. I hoped it was the former.

I wandered around the house, picking up and setting down at least a dozen projects. Nothing in the house was interesting, not after finding the chain mail and pearl in the cottage. Eventually, I sat at the dining room table and texted Aodhan.

Meri: What're you up to?

Aodhan: I'm about to take the boat out on the first tour of the day.

Meri: Do you have many booked today?

Aodhan: Three. We go around the bay, buzz the Aran Islands.

Aodhan: You should come, when you're allowed on water.

I grimaced, and wondered if I'd ever be out on Aodhan's boat again.

Meri: That would be nice.

Aodhan: What are you doing today? Want to hang out at the shop?

Meri: I don't want to keep you from your work. Have a good day.

Aodhan: I'll text you after the last tour.

I set down my phone and leaned back in my chair. It was just as well that Aodhan was too busy to come over. He'd been neglecting both the shop and his classes while we embarked on these mad searches for gold keys and Atlantean swords, and while I enjoyed his company, I was starting to feel guilty. It would be a shame if his grades or livelihood ended up suffering over my mistake at the Cliffs.

I gazed about the dining room, wondering what to do with myself. The room itself was grand, and it was by far the largest room in the house. I used to wonder why any one family would need such a large room just for eating, but Da had explained that when this was a working farm, the hired hands ate with the family. There was an old-fashioned hearth and grate at the far end, which was where prior generations of Murphys had done all the household cooking, and a fair bit of the washing. An iron bar spanned the top of the hearth, and the hooks still held a dusty old kettle and a few iron cauldrons. The sight of it made me appreciate modern times more than all the vaccines and indoor clothes dryers combined.

My family hadn't cooked over the hearth in decades, thanks to my grandfather giving my gran the gift of a new kitchen back when they were first married. According to Da, she'd balked at the idea, but Granddad had built on the addition with his own two hands and installed the best appliances he could afford, all of it as a wedding gift to her. By all accounts Gran had loved it, and the house's daily operations had relocated to the new kitchen almost immediately. The old hearth was left to dust and cobwebs, and the spacious dining room slowly became little more than a space for storage.

Space was all the room had, nowadays. Once there had been a table that ran the length of the room and could easily sit ten, or twelve if everyone got on well. That table had been long since relegated to the shed—not the cottage I'd cleaned out, but one of our many other unused outbuildings—and we now had a simple round table that lived in the kitchen. It worked out quite well for Da, Kevin, and me.

The room still had a few odd bits of furniture. There were three desks, assorted mismatched chairs, several bookcases, and a drafting table shoved against the far wall. Add to that a selection of steamer trunks and several generations' worth of bric-à-brac, and the place looked ready for an estate sale.

"Maybe that's what we need," I muttered. "We could sell off all this useless stuff, and start fresh. Most of this junk hasn't been touched since Mama was here."

I sat straight up in my chair. What if my mother *had* touched some of these items? What if some of this junk was hers?

I crouched before the nearest chest and flung it open. I'd never looked inside any of these chests, and I couldn't imagine what I might find. This one turned out to be filled to the brim with cloth. Thinking that the cloth was laid atop more delicate items, I removed bolt after bolt of it, all of it in varying weaves and patterns. By the time I reached the bottom, I'd cleared it out so efficiently there wasn't even a spare thread left in the corners. I turned to the next chest; it was filled with more cloth. The third was only halfway full, but with lace and a few old newspapers. And so Da found me, sitting on the floor amid empty chests and heaps of paper and fabric.

"What's all this, now?" he asked.

I looked toward Da's voice. He was frowning at the mess I'd made.

"I-I was just wondering where all this stuff came from," I said. He grabbed a chair, spun it around, and sat near me.

"The short answer is that we come from a long line of farmers, and farmers tend to hoard supplies," he began. "The longer answer is that some times were good, and some were lean. No matter how good things got, we never forgot what it was like to want, so we kept everything what had some use left in it. These particular trunks once belonged to your grandmother. She was a seamstress, and she always bought up all the cloth she could get her hands on, when the price was right." He picked up a yellowed newspaper from the last trunk, glanced at the headlines, and set it back down. "What are you searching for, Meri girl?"

"Something of Mama's," I replied. "There's just so little left of her. Sometimes it's like she was never here at all. I'm sorry for all this." I gestured at the mess I'd made. "I'll clean everything up."

"Don't worry about it." He stood, and said, "Come with me."

I followed Da into his bedroom. It was the second largest room in the house, being that it was meant for the head of the family. I watched as he approached his wardrobe and pushed it aside, revealing an open space in the wall.

"Is that a secret passage?" I asked.

"More of a hidey-hole," he replied. "On occasion, a body needs to keep things close, yet hidden." He dragged a few wooden crates out from the hidey-hole, and pulled the dust cloth off the first. Inside the crate were stacks of neatly folded shirts.

"As for what I needed to be kept close…" Da sniffed, then he grabbed a handkerchief from his pocket and wiped his face. "These are your mother's things."

"Oh." I sank to my knees next to the crates. "Are they all filled with clothes?"

"Mostly." Da awkwardly sat on the floor beside me. "There's also some books, and a few other odds and ends. Everything she left behind. I packed it all up and set it here." He smiled, but I saw the tears welling up in his eyes. "After all, she'll need all of this once she returns to us."

"Are her bracelets here?" I asked, remembering their fish scale pattern.

Da shook his head. "She took them with her when she… When she left. This is all that remains."

"This isn't all of it," I said in a rush. "At least, I don't think so. I found a pearl necklace in the cottage."

"Big fat pearl, the size of a sheep's eye?" Da asked, and I nodded. "Aye, that was Calliope's."

"I can go get it, and put it with the rest," I said as I started to rise. Da stayed me with a hand on my arm.

"Keep it. The pearl was always meant for you, and now it's yours." Da looked over the three crates. "Did you find anything else out back?"

"Um, yes, a bit of chain mail. But that couldn't be Mama's," I added.

"Why couldn't it?" Da countered. "Let me know when you're ready to hear that story, and I'll tell it."

"All right," I said, while my mind was whirling. I couldn't believe that chain mail was really Mama's! Why had she even owned chain mail? It's not like people actually wore that stuff any more. It's not like she was a knight.

I remembered the sword. Perhaps she was a knight, after all.

I shook my head. Best to leave off any speculation until I had more evidence in front of me. I tugged the dust cloth off the next crate, and saw the books Da had mentioned.

"What did Mama like to read?" I asked.

"You'll never guess." A pregnant pause later, he said, "Mysteries! She especially liked the ones where the detective had a cat. Loved cats, your ma did."

I laughed. I liked mysteries, and cats, too.

MURPHY'S MANIACS

I'd dreaded going to school many times in the past, but never so much as I did the Monday after my unplanned school holiday. So much had happened over the past week that sitting in classes seemed horribly mundane.

As I walked to The Saints, I thought about the past few days of searching for clues about my mother, all the way from the top of Slieve Callan to my own home. As I replayed them in my mind, I tried convincing myself that Aodhan's notions about my mother were so much nonsense. Of course, there was no sunken city under the sea, and if there was, it was a prehistoric settlement or something similar. And if a city had sunk centuries ago, no one, least of all my mother, would be living there now.

My newly practical stance didn't account for the sword at the museum, or the bit of chain mail I found in the cottage. And why had the pearl necklace been hidden out there? It was an odd place to leave a piece of jewellery, especially since Da had kept the rest of her things in his bedroom.

Aodhan had said the sword and pearl were clues, but what were they pointing toward? The sea, which Aodhan wholeheartedly believed? While that made sense, I had a hard time agreeing with him. My mother couldn't have been at sea all this time. Could she? Add to those clues the fact that Da was not shocked when I found a scrap of chain mail in the cottage along with the story behind it he promised to someday tell, and I was thoroughly baffled. What story could he be waiting to tell me that centred on my mother wearing chain mail?

I couldn't stop thinking about the sword. The way the blade had reflected blue in the light, and the carvings on the handle that matched Mama's bracelets, and how those carvings had resembled fish scales... or, as Dr. Fitzsimmons had pointed out, the scales on a merrow's tail. No matter how hard I tried, I couldn't get that sword out of my mind. MacCreehy had said mermaids were called merrows in the old days...

A person cut across my path, nearly knocking me over. I began to excuse myself, and saw that I was nearly all the way to school. I'd been so lost in my thoughts I hadn't realised where I was. At least this latest bit of lost time was only around ten minutes, and I hadn't ended up in the water.

I looked up and saw the school's grey stone façade looming over me, and the rows and rows of pointed windows glaring down at me like so many disapproving stares. I clutched my book bag, and debated running away.

"Meri!"

I turned and saw Aodhan jogging toward me. So much for running. "Why don't you drive to school?" I asked. I resumed walking, and he fell into step beside me.

"I did. I parked and came looking for you."

"Well, you found me."

He grinned. "Of course I did. Your last period is study hall in the library, correct?"

"Correct, you stalker."

"Wonderful. We can cut out and meet my uncle."

I stopped walking and stared at him. "What in the world makes you think I'm leaving study hall to meet with one of your relations? And why would I want to meet him, anyway?"

"Oh, right, I forgot to tell you about him. He's one of the garda, and he remembers when your dad rescued your mother out on the beach way back when."

I stood there blinking at Aodhan, feeling the blood drain from my face and pool in my knees. "He does?"

"I rang him on Sunday night and we talked all about it. He's going to haul out the original reports for us. We can pop by and have a look at them for ourselves." Aodhan moved closer, and continued, "This is what we needed, Meri. Not rumours and fairy tales, but an objective report on where your ma came from. Maybe something in the paperwork will give us an idea about where she might have gone."

"So Da really did find a strange woman on the beach," I mumbled. "Aodhan, do you know what this means?"

He laced his fingers with mine. "I have an idea."

"You two! Separate yourselves!"

I looked up and saw Mr MacCreehy scowling at us. For a moment I didn't understand why, then he looked pointedly at our hands. I'd become so used to being close with Aodhan that his casual touches hardly registered any more.

"Sorry, sir," Aodhan said as he withdrew his hand from mine.

"Mr Sullivan, I trust you have a doctor's note to explain your absences last week?" MacCreehy demanded.

"Yes, sir, of course I do, sir," he replied. "I will bring it to the main office before my first class."

"See that you do." MacCreehy looked down his nose at me. I took a step back. "Are we feeling a bit more grounded today, Miss Murphy?"

"Yes, sir," I said. "I am very happy to be back at school."

"And what did your father say about what happened at the Cliffs?"

I swallowed. "H-He was very glad I wasn't hurt."

"You can tell me if he was cross with you," MacCreehy added.

"He wasn't," I blurted out. "Just concerned, is all."

MacCreehy gave me a look that said he knew I wasn't telling the whole truth. Instead of interrogating us further, he waved Aodhan and me toward the school's entrance.

"It's almost like he wants you to be in trouble with your father," Aodhan said.

"As if I would ever confide in him," I muttered.

"Hey." Aodhan opened the school door and held it for me. "What'd you do with your finds from the cottage?"

I tugged at my collar, revealing the pendant's gold chain. "The mail's in my bag."

"Good idea, to keep them with you. See you at lunch, Meri," Aodhan said once we were inside the school.

Ignoring how my pulse quickened, I said, "See you then."

I didn't see Aodhan at lunch as we'd arranged, all because Sister Edward devised a brilliant plan for me to earn some extra credit in mathematics to offset my absences the week prior. She even let me eat my lunch while I worked, and was most impressed when I finished my exercises in half the allotted time. At this rate, I would have no problems obtaining my leaving certificate, and leaving all of County Clare behind.

Was that still my dream? I didn't know if it could it be, now that I'd finally found some real clues about my mother's life, and her disappearance. What if more were still waiting to be found? And what if we did find her, what then? Would she want to recreate her life with me and Da and Kevin, or would she tell us all to move on and forget about her? What if she had moved on already? And what if she was really, truly gone?

I shook my head and took a deep breath. Of the many things Da, Kevin, and I avoided discussing, the possibility that Mama had never returned because she had passed on was the most off-limits of all. Add to that the fact that Da had packed away all her belongings and was convinced that she would eventually return to us... However, those crates in the hidey-hole didn't tell me where she'd been all this time, or why she'd left us in the first place. I wondered if Da even knew, or if he'd only made up a few stories as a salve for his wounded heart.

Soon enough, it was last period and I was due in study hall. I found Aodhan waiting for me in the corridor outside of the library, leaning on the wall next to the doors. "I have a plan," he said without preamble.

"A plan to study?" I asked hopefully. When my sciences professor, Sister Nora, had heard how well Sister Edward's extra credit scheme had played out, she assigned me two essays due by Wednesday's class. I wanted to get started on them straight away.

"Sorry about missing lunch," I added. I'd seen him skulking in the corridor outside my mathematics classroom.

"I was lost without you. Anyway, I have a plan to get out of here." Aodhan leaned closer, and continued, "Father Flaherty's minding the students today, but he's always busy grading and such. Never raises his head from his work, that one. We'll walk in all casual, sign in, and leave through the back of the library."

"Is this a good idea? What if we get caught?"

Aodhan shrugged. "We can always say we were wandering the aisles looking for a book. We're supposed to be studying, after all."

"We can't just actually study, and meet your uncle after school lets out for the day?"

Aodhan shook his head. "Shift change is at three, and then he has some time off. If we don't go today, we'll need to wait two weeks until he returns."

I bit my lip. As much as I didn't want to sneak out of school, I wanted to read those reports for myself. I needed to know what had really happened when Da found Mama on that beach. "All right, let's do it. But if we get caught, I'll tell everyone you were kidnapping me. I need to preserve my innocence in this matter."

"Kidnapping? Really?"

"Really."

Aodhan sighed. "Kidnapping it is. See you in the stacks, Meri."

Aodhan grabbed his bag and entered the library, and after a moment, I followed. I signed in at the front desk, and said a quiet hello to Father Flaherty. He mumbled an acknowledgment, never raising his gaze from his desk. Just as Aodhan had predicted, Father was up to his eyeballs in paperwork. I did not envy him.

I walked calmly past where Aodhan was seated at one of the long research tables, and wandered through the stacks. I found myself in the poetry aisle, and trailed my fingers across the volumes of Byron and Yeats.

"You like poetry?" Aodhan asked when he came up behind me.

"Yeats is one of my favourites."

"Me, I'm more of a Rilke guy."

"Really?" I turned to face him, the surfer with the deep, deep eyes. "What's your favourite piece?"

"It's a secret," he replied. "There's a time and place to share poetry, and sneaking out of school isn't it. Now, over a nice dinner..." We turned a corner into the next aisle, and almost bumped into Sister Mary Katherine.

"Hello Meri, Aodhan," Sister said. "Can I help you find something?"

Aodhan froze, and I blurted out, "Sister Nora assigned me two essays due by Wednesday!"

"Essays on science?" Sister Mary Katherine asked. I nodded furiously. "That's an odd assignment. Have you any idea what to write about?"

I looked from her to Aodhan and shook my head. "No, Sister. The topics are up to me, and I really don't know where to start."

"Well, then." Sister tapped her chin with her forefinger. "You could write about an Irish scientist. What about Robert Boyle? Or maybe a feminist icon, such as Marie Curie?" Sister winked. "I know you young girls like to be called feminists these days."

I blew out a breath, feeling more relieved than I'd expected. Truth be told, I was at a loss as to what I should write about, and those were two good suggestions. "Thank you, Sister. I'll start there. If I get a good grade, I'll need to thank you again."

"No thanks are needed. It's my job to help you succeed." Sister turned to Aodhan. "And what can I help you with?"

His cheeks paled and then reddened. "Ah, nothing. I was just following Meri."

Sister patted his hand. "I appreciate your honesty. Now I need the both of you to get your books and find a seat. Study time is about to start."

"Thank you, Sister," Aodhan and I said in unison. She walked toward the circulation desk, and disappeared after she turned a corner.

"My heart has never beat so hard in my entire life," I said once she was out of sight. "Is anyone else lurking about?"

"I hope not." Aodhan scouted both ends of the aisles. "We're alone, for now."

That was a relief. "Tell me, surfing poet man, how are we going to make our daring escape? Sister Mary Katherine knows we're back here."

"She's just left." Aodhan jerked his chin toward the main entrance, and I saw Sister step out to the corridor. "We just need to wait until Father Flaherty gets distracted, and then we'll make a break for it."

"What on earth will distract him in the library?" I wondered out loud. As if on cue, Father Flaherty got up from his desk and went toward the reference section.

"That," Aodhan said. "He triple checks every fact he reads, and he does it old school, with encyclopaedias and almanacks. Let's go."

I followed Aodhan toward the back of the library. At the end of the last row, behind some shelves of out-of-date periodicals, was a door. Aodhan pushed it open, and we hurried down a poorly lit staircase toward a second door. On the other side of that door was freedom.

"That was a neat trick," I said as we stepped out into the student car park. "How many times have you cut out this way?"

"What, you think I'm admitting to that? Come, love, the car's this way."

We got inside the car and Aodhan drove us to the garda station. The station's car park was near empty; it must have been a slow day for crime. After we parked, we entered the station, and the man at the front desk pointed us toward a corridor that led to several offices. We went to the third door on the left, and Aodhan knocked on the open door. The man behind the desk looked up and smiled.

"Aodhan, good to see you," he said.

"Hello, Uncle Mark," Aodhan replied. "This is Meri, the friend I told you about."

"Hello," I said. I raised my hand in a halfhearted wave, then thought the better of it. I'd never been in a garda station before, and even though we were just visiting, my nerves were on edge.

"Good to meet you, Meri," Officer Mark said. "Please, have a seat."

"Thank you, Officer," I said.

He smiled. "Call me Mark."

I returned his smile, and felt some of my anxiety dissipate. Aodhan's uncle didn't look how I'd pictured a member of the garda, which was world-weary and scowling. He was Aodhan's mother's brother, and just like Aodhan, his eyes were bright and he laughed easily. Truth be told, he reminded me of an older version of Aodhan. It made me wonder what Aodhan's father had been like. His parents must have made quite the pair.

"Here we are," Officer Mark said as he withdrew a folder from a drawer and set it on the desk between us. "These are all the reports we have in the archive concerning one Calliope Murphy." He glanced at me, his brows drawn low and forehead creased like an accordion. "It's been a long time, Meri. Why are you looking into this now?"

"I need something of her to hold on to. Something real." I traced the edge of the folder, and continued, "You must have heard the stories. Brian Murphy was so drunk he picked up a woman on a beach and thought he rescued a mermaid. Old man Murphy's wife left him, he claims she swam back to her mermaid palace." My voice cracked at the end. Aodhan touched my forearm, but I shrugged him off.

"I don't need those stories. These reports talk about my real mother, not some bit of trashy gossip. Can't you see why I need that?" I asked, rather desperately.

Officer Mark's forehead creased further, fast becoming a critical mass of creases. "Name one reason why I shouldn't ring your father right now and tell him what you're doing."

"What makes you think I'll keep this from him?" I countered. "If your terms are to tell my father that I came here wishing to know more about my mother, I'll ring him for you myself."

He sighed, and pushed the folder toward me. "It's all in there. I'll give you some time to read it over."

Mark left the office, leaving Aodhan and me alone at his desk. I opened the folder and rifled through the pages. There had to be twenty sheets of paper inside, ranging from interviews to copies of newspaper reports, far more information than I'd anticipated. For the first time since Mama left us, I felt I might actually see her again.

"There's so much in here," I said. "How will we ever make sense of it all?"

"Let's read them chronologically, oldest to newest." Aodhan flipped through the paperwork, noting the dates. After a moment, he pulled out a sheet and set it on top. "I think this is the report from when he rescued her."

I swallowed. "Here we go."

The first report was an official garda statement, complete with a government seal at the top of the page. It was dated June seventeenth, and the narrative was as follows:

Local fisherman Brian Murphy came to the station at approximately three in the afternoon, accompanied by a woman he claimed to have rescued at sea. Murphy had called in the woman's location to the Coast Guard, but when search and rescue arrived at the location, the woman was gone. Officers then contacted Murphy and requested that he and the woman report to the station for questioning to rule out the filing of a false report.

Per Murphy, he found the woman on one of the beaches below the Cliffs of Moher that are only visible during low tide. She appeared to be in some distress, alone and with no food or other supplies. She was initially resistant to board Murphy's craft, which was when he contacted the Coast Guard. Once the tide started to come in, she changed her mind. He collected her onto his boat, and gave her dry clothing, food, and water. Murphy is a lifelong resident of the area, and claims to have never before set eyes upon this woman.

The woman in question has advised that her name is Calliope Kearney. She stated that she was unfamiliar with this part of Ireland. Kearney claims to have family in the area, but denied being a local resident.

"Kearney," I murmured. "I never knew her maiden name."

"Calliope," Aodhan said. "Such a pretty name."

"Da always said it was a fitting name, because of her voice." I flipped to the next page. "Here, there's more."

Kearney claims that she was out on the water when she was picked up by a current and swept out to sea and then onto the beach where Murphy eventually found her. She appears to be of sound mind, and grateful to Murphy for his assistance. Kearney is of below average height and has an unusually athletic build. Her hair is blonde and ends just past her waist, and her eyes are blue. Kearney is either unable or unwilling to produce the names, addresses, or contact information for herself or any living relative. This investigation is ongoing.

"Seems she was a real woman after all," I muttered, then I started on the next report. It was on the same official paper, and was dated October twenty-second.

This officer made a routine check on a woman who was rescued from a beach below the Cliffs of Moher a few months prior, and learned that Calliope Kearney has made plans to marry her rescuer, Brian Murphy. Further, the Coast Guard are not pursuing Murphy for making a false report, since Kearney was indeed stranded at the time of his call to the Guard. All appears to be well between those involved. This case is considered closed.

"See there?" Aodhan said. "True love is what it was."

"Look, here's another report. It's from May fifth of the following year." I pushed the sheet toward Aodhan and we read it together.

A man called S. MacCreehy came to this station seeking information regarding his missing adult daughter, Aoife Ni Ceithearnaigh. When questioned why his daughter bore a different surname from him, MacCreehy explained that Ni Ceithearnaigh is her mother's name. He claimed that Aoife had been boating on Liscannor Bay with her family, where they were taking holiday, but had somehow been separated from the rest. Neither Aoife nor her craft have been recovered as of the date of this report. When questioned why the Coast Guard was not alerted to her disappearance, MacCreehy advised that they were, but he did not have the report information on his person. Follow up calls to the Coast Guard made by this office revealed that no such report had been filed.

MacCreehy described his daughter as being in her early twenties, of short stature but "built as a warrior should be", and having blonde hair and blue eyes. He did not present a photograph of her likeness, only a general description. A thorough investigation was done, including the canvassing of local hospitals and morgues, but no trace of MacCreehy's daughter was found. Being that the woman in question is an adult, and that no evidence of foul play had been uncovered, this investigation is closed and shall only be reopened should new information be presented.

"Why is that report even in here?" I looked up, and found Mark hovering nearby. "I think this one might be in the wrong file."

"Is it?" Mark set the initial report next to the last one, and indicated the physical descriptions of my mother and this Aoife Ni Ceithearnaigh. "The descriptions of Calliope and Aoife are nigh on identical. And MacCreehy claimed that his daughter, this Aoife, had been washed into Liscannor Bay, and Calliope said she'd been swimming and got scooped up by the current."

"But what about the names? My father has always referred to my mother as Calliope, not Aoife, and this MacCreehy gave a different surname."

"Ni Ceithearnaigh is the older version of Kearney," Aodhan said. "Means descended from warriors." I raised my eyebrows, so he elaborated, "Not my fault my Irish is better than yours."

I frowned, and shuffled through the paperwork. Da had always claimed Calliope was what he called my mother, and never once had he claimed it was her actual name. He'd also never once mentioned her maiden name. Was my mother Calliope Kearney, or was she this Aoife Ni Ceithearnaigh?

Amidst the reports and official garda forms, I found a photograph of my mother that must have been taken soon after Da found her. Her hair was tangled, she was pale as death, and looked like she hadn't eaten in a week. But she was smiling, and she looked happy. Da had always said that when he and Mama were together, they were happy.

"Did you show MacCreehy this photograph?" I asked.

He shook his head. "If you check the dates, you'll see that Mac-Creehy came by about a year after your father brought in Miss Kearney. We called round to the Murphy house and asked her if she was any relation to MacCreehy, and she denied it." Mark paused, and added, "I remember her being pregnant at the time. Must have been with your brother?"

"Yes. He's a few years older than me." I touched the photograph of my mother. "Why is there no statement from my mother? There must have been more of an investigation than just this narrative. Wasn't anyone curious as to where she'd come from?"

"She did give a formal statement that included more details, but it's gone missing," Mark replied.

"You're certain she gave one?" Aodhan asked.

"I am, because I remember the very day Brian Murphy brought her in." Mark looked at me, gave a sad smile. "It's not often a fisherman rescues a lovely woman from a beach, and brings her down to the station. Tends to stick out in one's memory."

"I'm sure." I regarded the professional Officer Mark in his pressed uniform shirt. "My father says your family used to poach oysters alongside mine. Any truth to that?"

Mark's eyes went wide, then he laughed. "Aye, Meri, that happened. Seems the Connors and Murphys of the world have been up to no good together for some time now."

"I'm not up to no good," I said. "This is a legitimate investigation."

"Quite legitimate," Aodhan added, ever ready to defend my honour. "I know all of this happened a while ago, but do you remember anything else about Meri's mother?"

"One other thing that I've always found odd about this case—other than how your ma was found and all—was this MacCreehy fellow," Mark continued. "He was hell bent on finding his daughter, and even though this was a dead end, he returned to the area around seven or eight years ago. He settled nearby and got himself a job, and to my knowledge, he's never mentioned this missing daughter of his since then."

"Do you think he could be related to my mother?" I asked. "And me?"

Mark shook his head. "I don't know, but you may be better off without knowing about that skeleton in your closet. There was something off about that one. As soon as he started talking, I knew he wasn't telling the whole truth, but he was tight-lipped and stuck to his story. He must have a good education and some kind of credentials too, being that he ended up working with children."

"Wait," Aodhan said. "Are you saying that this S. MacCreehy of the missing daughter is also Seamus MacCreehy, headmaster at The Saints?"

Mark nodded gravely. "That is exactly what I'm saying."

Aodhan flopped back in his chair. "That can't be a coincidence."

I looked over the reports, wishing I could make heads or tails of this new information. "If it's not a coincidence, then what does it all mean?"

"That, lass, is something I've been wondering for many years." Mark withdrew a large manila envelope. "I can't let you take the originals, but I've made copies of all the reports and photographs. If you find something that may lead us to your ma, give a holler and we'll be there to help however we can."

"Thank you." I shook Mark's hand. "I really appreciate your help in all of this."

"You're very welcome." Mark's eyes twinkled, and he added, "Aodhan made it clear that this is important to you, and therefore it's important to him. Since he is my favourite nephew and all, I figured I had to help."

"I'm your only nephew," Aodhan said. "But thanks all the same."

Aodhan and I gathered up our coats and the envelope, and left the garda station.

"That was enlightening," Aodhan said once we were outside.

I hugged the envelope to my chest. "I know so much more now. I even have a new photo of her." I looked up at Aodhan. "Thank you. I'd never have known any of this if it wasn't for you."

Aodhan ducked his head. "My uncle, too. He helped the most."

"You both did." We walked toward the car. "I suppose our next move should be to scrutinise these reports."

"But what of MacCreehy?" Aodhan asked. "What do we really know about him? I fear he may have some vital information. Perhaps we should pursue that."

"How would we get it? He hates all the students, so it's not like we can ask him a few questions hoping he'll share what he knows. Besides, he is well aware of the fact that I'm Brian Murphy's daughter."

"Then we'll have to figure out a different way." We got back to the car, and Aodhan tore out of the station's car park as if he was a criminal.

"Did you know your grandfather was a poacher?" I asked suddenly. "Before I mentioned it earlier."

Aodhan's gaze slid toward me, a terrifying move on account of how fast he was driving. "Did your dad tell you that?"

"He did," I replied. "I asked how he knew who you were that time you walked me home, and he told me that he knew your parents. And that your grandfather and mine used to poach oysters together."

Aodhan smiled and settled lower into his seat. "See that, Meri? We were meant to be together."

"Because we're both descended from thieves?"

"Thieves who worked together," Aodhan amended. "We can start that up again, you know. Not the poaching, but we could have a gang."

"And what would we call this gang?" I moved sideways in my seat and watched his profile. "Sullivan's Sailors?"

"Murphy's Maniacs," he replied, and we laughed. We reached the top of my driveway, and Aodhan stopped the car.

"Would you like to stay for dinner?" I asked in a rush. "We've plenty of leftovers from this weekend."

"I would, but I'm expected at the shop." Aodhan squeezed my hand. "Thank you for the offer, though."

I ignored the sharp pang of disappointment in my belly, and smiled. "See you at school tomorrow."

"Aye, then." He squeezed my hand again. "Tomorrow."

A Party?

On Tuesday I made sure I got to school extra early, not so I could catch up on assignments or start on the essays assigned by Sister Nora, but a for project of my own. I had the photocopied reports from Aodhan's uncle stashed in my bag, and I wanted to use the library's copy machine to make a second set. This way, I could research and make notes on one set, while the originals—well, original to me—would stay pristine. As research plans went, mine still had a bit of fleshing out to do, but that was all right. It was a start.

Actually, it was more than a start. I couldn't remember the last time I'd learned a new bit of information about my mother from anyone other than Da, and now I had specifics like her maiden name, and dates and times to work with. Finally, I had more insight about my mother than what my memories and a few photographs, all of which had faded with time, could provide. I had actual facts, and not just my father's drunken ramblings.

I also knew that there was more to Mr. MacCreehy than met the eye. He was working out to be the villain of the piece, and here I'd always thought he was nothing more than a cranky office worker.

Try as I might, I couldn't remember him behaving in any way other than as the school's headmaster toward me, and I don't think he'd ever once spoken to Kevin or Da; at least, they'd never mentioned any conversations they'd had with him to me. But the school trip to the Cliffs of Moher had been MacCreehy's pet project every year, and when I finally participated in the outing, he had made sure to be on the same bus I'd chosen. He'd been right there when Kelsey tossed a drawing of a mermaid at my head, and when I almost went over the edge and into the sea. He also got angry whenever Aodhan was near me, more so than my own father did. It made me wonder if there was more in Aodhan's family's past, and mine, than a few filched oysters.

I smiled when I thought of Aodhan, and suppressed a giggle as I pictured him dressed like a cartoon thief in black trousers and a watch cap whilst poaching oysters in the dark of night. I was still grinning like a fool when I entered the library and saw Kelsey and Sarah standing at the circulation desk.

"Well, look who it is," Kelsey said. "First she fakes sick for a week home, then she skips out of yesterday's last period."

"W-What do you mean?" I asked, as my face went hot. Before yesterday I had never, not even once, skipped class or stayed home unless I was legitimately ill. Kelsey and Sarah skipped classes as if it was the latest fashion trend.

"We all saw you drive off with Aodhan," Sarah said. "What he sees in the likes of you, I'll never know."

I opened my mouth to give them a piece of my mind, then I saw the librarian, Sister Geneve, emerge from the stacks. Deciding not to engage with those two tormentors, I plastered my best teacher-pleasing smile across my face and approached Sister with my folder.

"Good morning, Sister," I said. "Would it be all right if I made some photocopies?"

"I don't see why not," she replied. "Will they be for a project of yours?"

"Yes, they're for a research project I'm working on," I replied. "Thank you, Sister."

I turned toward the office, but halted when Sister Geneve touched my arm. "Are you feeling a bit better after your time off, Meri? You're not letting those old stories go to your head, now, are you?"

I heard Kelsey mutter something under her breath, but I ignored her. "Yes, I'm feeling much better. Thank you again."

I continued ignoring Kelsey and Sarah as I walked past them and into the library's office. The photocopy machine was a hulking piece of machinery, and over the years more than a few of my essays had been sacrificed to its capricious nature. As I set up my papers and placed them on the feed tray, I spied the flashing digital panel and had an idea.

The copier was also a scanner, and it could make an electronic document of whatever I copied and deliver it right to my email address. Then I'd not only have my paper originals, but an electronic file that I could potentially add to over time. The file could assist me with internet searches and the like.

"Brilliant," I muttered as I keyed my home email address into the digital touchscreen. Less than five minutes later, I had my photocopies, and the originals stashed in my bag, and I was taking my seat in my first class of the day. I couldn't wait to check my email and see how the digital copies had turned out.

My classes went quite well that morning, not that I paid them much attention. It was secretly thrilling to have that folder of garda reports in my bag, and all that new and factual information about my mother within arm's reach. And factual is just what it was; while I would never accuse Da of lying to me, everything he'd ever said about Mama was softened by his desire to spare me the worst of it. That tactic had been fine when I was a child, but now I wanted nothing less than the truth. I could handle it. At least, I hoped I could.

When it was time for lunch, I filed into canteen services with the rest of the students. While I waited, I saw Aodhan queue up for his own lunch. I paid for my sandwich, found an empty table and sat. A bare minute later, Aodhan claimed the stool next to me.

"What's the what, Meri?" Aodhan asked. His tray held two sandwiches, a roll, a bowl of soup, and a slice of pie.

"What, you didn't get a carton of milk to wash it all down?"

He grinned. "Perhaps I will, later."

"Good to know. Anyway, I've some ideas about our next steps."

"What sort of ideas?" he asked.

"Genealogy, for starters," I replied. "Now that we have a few surnames to work with, we can go online and look up some family trees."

As if on cue, Mr. MacCreehy strode into the cafeteria and scanned the room. When his gaze landed on my and Aodhan's table, he scowled.

"You think he really has anything to do with it?" I asked. Aodhan glanced over his shoulder at MacCreehy, then he turned back to his food.

"I've no idea," he replied around gulps of soup. "But that's another thing for us to figure out, yeah?"

"Yeah." I tore the crusts off my sandwich and reduced them to crumbs. "Where should we do our research?"

"The shop's got a great Wi-Fi signal," Aodhan said. "Fancy keeping me company while I do some work this evening?"

I smiled, the prospect of hanging out with Aodhan after school warming me like a hot cup of tea. "I can do that."

I met Aodhan in the student car park after the school day ended, and after he folded his incredibly long legs into his car, we drove to the surf shop. Aodhan let me out near the front door, then he went to park the car. Since the last time I'd visited his business I'd been a bit distracted, I took the time to check out the shop's main room.

The interior of the shop was filled with bright and colourful displays; if anything, it reminded me of an ocean-themed amusement park. When I first entered the shop, I was met with clothing racks and shelves filled with shirts, sneakers, and boat shoes. An area off to the left had a display of mannequins wearing wet suits and swim goggles, and the back wall held an assortment of surfboards laid out on horizontal shelves. The colours were arranged from light to dark, and seven more boards hung from the ceiling arranged like a rainbow from red to purple. The shop was so cheerful I understood why Aodhan spent so much time at work. The shop was happiness made real.

"Hello, Sandy," a man said to me. When I didn't respond, he continued, "Nice of you to stop by again."

"You must have me confused with someone else," I said. "My name isn't Sandy."

"Isn't it?" he countered. "Last time you were here you were chock full of sand."

My stomach twisted in knots. I realised the man must have been in the shop last Thursday, and that he'd been the man behind the counter. Worse, he'd had an eyeful of me at my worst. Before I could hide behind one of the surfboards, Aodhan arrived.

"Meri, this is Lorcan," Aodhan said, as he strode through the front door. "He's the shop manager. He also thinks he's funny," Aodhan added.

"I *am* funny," Lorcan insisted.

"Funny looking doesn't count," Aodhan said.

Lorcan smirked. "Nice to formally meet you, Meri. Let me know if this one bothers you," he added, nodding toward Aodhan.

Aodhan laughed as Lorcan returned to his spot behind the counter, then he turned toward me and spread his arms wide. "What do you think of my shop? Does it make you want to catch a wave?"

"Not exactly," I said. "I can't even swim. If I went out on one of those boards, I might lose it entirely."

"The boards have tethers," he said. "And you'd have me looking out for you, though we should probably start you off with a few basic swimming lessons."

"Swimming?" I looked out the front windows toward the sea. It was high tide, and the waves crashed against the sea wall. "In the ocean?"

"That's how we do it around here. Come on. The office is this way."

I followed Aodhan up the stairs. At the top was a mural of The Great Wave Off Kanagawa by Hokusai. It was reminiscent of the current scene outside, and reinforced my desire to never, ever go swimming.

"When did that go up?" I asked. I was certain I would have noticed something that dramatic the last time I was there.

"Lorcan put it up just yesterday."

"He paints?"

"Nah. It's stick-on wallpaper."

"Oh." I stepped closer to the mural, noted the paper's seams. "How long has Lorcan worked here?" I asked.

"Since the beginning," Aodhan replied. "He was the shop manager under Dad. Here we are."

Aodhan led me into the back office, and got me set up at a table with my laptop. He claimed a chair behind a rather impressive looking desk and turned on the computer. A moment later he set to work opening up ledgers and accounting software.

"Checking the day's sales?" I asked.

"What? Oh, yes," he replied. "I like to make sure we're profitable, look for trends, see what stock's selling well and needs to be reordered, things like that."

"Such the businessman." While my laptop powered up, I opened a copy book and scrawled "genealogy" across the top of a blank page. "What name should I start with?"

"Maybe our own surnames, just to get a feel for it," he suggested. "I'm going to forage for snacks. Be right back."

Searching our own names was a very smart place to start on this leg of the quest. I began with Aodhan's surname, Sullivan.

According to the first site I clicked on, Sullivan meant "little dark eye" in Old Irish. A misnomer if there ever was one, being that Aodhan's eyes, while brown, were so bright and expressive. They weren't even that dark of a shade. I kept clicking around the internet, and eventually I landed on a folklore site. It claimed that the Sullivans of Kerry were noted for taking merrows as lovers.

"I was not expecting that," I muttered.

"Not expecting what?" Aodhan asked. He'd returned with an armload of food, and set out two bananas, a loaf of bread, a few bags of crisps, and a tin of biscuits. While I stared at the heap of food, he disappeared again, and returned with two bottles of water.

"Is this all you could find?" I asked.

"Oh, there's more," he replied with a grin. "This all is just for starters. Find anything interesting?"

"Only that Sullivans are known for hooking up with merrows." I turned the laptop toward him. He scanned the screen and laughed softly. "Is that what this is all about? Looking for a bride, Mr. Sullivan?"

"Meri, you're the one who keeps insisting we're just friends," he replied as he opened the biscuit tin. My throat went tight and my eyes burned, so I grabbed a bottle of water and twisted it open. I don't know why Aodhan's words had affected me so; we weren't an item, that much was true, and I was the one who kept saying I didn't want to be anyone's girlfriend. Friendship was all I was interested in, no more, no less.

As I sipped from the bottle, I thought of the photograph of my mother I'd got from Aodhan's uncle. She'd looked so happy, gazing at my father as if he was her world. I know that she had been his everything... And then she left.

What if Aodhan and I became something more that friends, and I had to leave him someday? How would he cope? How would I cope? Worse, what if he left me?

I shook my head. I am a basket case.

Aodhan eyed me as I guzzled my water and had my internal debate over my motivations, as he shovelled biscuits into his mouth as if he hadn't eaten in a week. I ignored his inquisitive stare and turned the laptop back around.

"What should we search for next?" I asked. "MacCreehy?"

"That, and Kearney," he replied. "And Murphy."

I frowned at that last bit, and typed in MacCreehy. There weren't nearly as many results as there had been for Sullivan, and soon enough I was on a genealogy site.

"Oh," I said, after I'd read over the page. "The original MacCreehy was a saint. He killed a monster along the shore."

Aodhan snorted. "That does not fit our MacCreehy in the slightest."

I read a bit further. "There's a church named after him. Kilmacreehy. It's in ruins." I gave Aodhan a look. "I know how you like those tumbled down structures."

At that, Aodhan laughed out loud. "Perhaps we'll have a look at it next weekend. What name should we try next?"

"Let's check Mama's maiden name," I said as I typed in Kearney to the same genealogy site. After I read the article, I said, "Kearney means what you said back at the garda station, 'descendant of Ceithearnach', who was a warrior."

"Warrior," Aodhan murmured. "It is looking more and more like your mother really was a soldier of some sort. Makes sense, what with the sword they dredged up from the river, not to mention the chain mail you found in the cottage."

I'd instantly known that sword was associated with Mama. I entered my own surname, and learned that Murphy was derived from the Gaelic *muir*, which meant "sea" and *cadh*, which meant "warrior".

"Seems your house is packed full with warriors," Aodhan said.

I stared at the screen. I'd never wondered what any surname meant, and now I knew that both of my parents' surnames mentioned warriors. "I suppose that since Da's a fisherman he is a type of sea warrior."

"Then it stands to reason your mother would seek him out," Aodhan said. "Warrior to warrior, like to like."

"She didn't seek him out. He found her stranded."

"Maybe she was waiting for him."

"I never thought of that." All of the rumours, and Da's own half-soused tirades, tell how he'd rescued Mama from that beach. What if she'd somehow known of him already, and had arranged for him to find her?

"Aodhan?" called a woman's voice. "Are you up here?"

"We're in the office," he yelled. A moment later, a woman stepped into the room. She had brown hair, a bit silvered at the temples and pulled back in a bun, and while her eyes were green, they were as bright as Aodhan's.

"We?" she asked as she entered, then she saw me behind my laptop. "Oh, hello."

"Meri, this is my mother," Aodhan said. "Ma, this is Meri Murphy."

"A pleasure to meet you," I said.

"You as well," she replied. "Are you two working on some homework?"

"Yes, we're in The Saints Academy together," Aodhan replied. His mother's mouth quirked, and I imagined that she realised he hadn't answered her, but decided to let it slide for the time being.

"Well, then, don't let me interrupt," she replied. "Remember, the party is tomorrow night at seven sharp." She paused, and added, "Why don't you bring Meri?"

"A party," I repeated. I hadn't been to a party in years. "What is the party for?"

"My stepfather's birthday," Aodhan said. "Happens every year around this time."

"Much as all birthdays are yearly events," she said. "Meri, tell Aodhan it'll be fun."

"I'll go if Meri will go," Aodhan said.

I glanced between Aodhan and his mother. "Am I really invited? Are you sure?"

"Of course you're invited. I am not above bribing my son to attend family gatherings," she added. "I'll leave you two to your studies. Wonderful to meet you, Meri."

"You too, Mrs Sullivan."

Aodhan's mother looked like she'd swallowed a bug, then she composed herself and left us. As the door shut behind her, I figured out what I'd done.

"Och, her name isn't Sullivan anymore," I said. "I'm a daft idiot."

"Happens all the time," Aodhan said. "My stepfather never adopted me or my older sisters, so that makes me the last Sullivan in the house. It's unusual that we don't all have the same name."

"Well? Are you going to tell me her name, or do you just want me to embarrass myself again?"

He leaned back in his chair and rubbed his chin. "Let me think about it."

"Aodhan," I squealed, and he held up his hands in defeat.

"Dumhach. Ma's name is Bridgette Anne Dumhach."

"Dumhach," I repeated. "I can remember that." I scrawled it under the list of surnames I'd started earlier. "So about this surname research we're doing."

"What about it?"

"Do you see a pattern here? Because I've got nothing."

He stood and leaned over the table, reading the list upside down. After a moment he sat down in his chair, and said, "I think these clues all point to your ma being a warrior, and I think what we really need to find out is what she was fighting for. Maybe that will tell us why she left." I must have looked as stricken as I felt, because he added, "Are you still up for that?"

"I am, but that's as dead an end as could be," I replied. "According to Da, one morning he woke up, and she was gone. There was no fight with Da, no note left behind... It was like she'd never lived with us."

"Perhaps it wasn't her choice to leave."

"I... I guess maybe it wasn't."

"Did anyone ever file a missing person report?"

"The guards wouldn't take one," I replied. "They said it wasn't that unusual for a young woman to up and leave her family behind. According to them, it happens all the time."

"Hm." Aodhan tapped his pen against his chin. "I asked my uncle about any missing person report, and he said much the same. I didn't doubt him, but it made me wonder if it had been filed at a different station."

"Her leaving was the beginning of the whole world thinking my father's nothing but a drunk," I said bitterly. "If not for me and Kevin, I bet they'd say he made her up entirely."

"They're just jealous," Aodhan said. "The naysayers and the like. Your parents had true love, which is something that's rare enough on its own."

"That's one way to look at it." I turned my attention back to the laptop. "Where do we think a woman in love would have gone without so much as a goodbye? And why did she leave?"

"If we figure out the where, perhaps we'll also learn the why."

ARCHEOLOGISTS OF QUESTIONABLE INTENT

Wednesday morning at school started out no worse than any other day there. Kelsey and Sarah kept to themselves, and I didn't know if I was glad to be overlooked by those two, or if I should worry about whatever new torments they were plotting to unleash on me. I'd be shocked if it was anything but the second option.

When it was time for my literature class to begin, I entered the auditorium and saw Aodhan seated on the far side of the room. He was looking straight ahead, and his mouth was screwed up so tight I wondered if his superhuman diet had finally given him indigestion. I nodded hello to him, and chose a seat in the back row. After I sat, I glanced at Aodhan again. When he noticed me, he jerked his chin toward the front of the room.

I looked. Then I dropped my pencil case.

Sister Mary Katherine was not in her usual spot at the lectern. Instead, Mr. MacCreehy was standing at the fore of the room, hands on his hips as he looked us over the way a warden would oversee his inmates. Next to him was a long table covered with swords and knives.

I covered my mouth and forced a cough, trying to hide how shocked I was to see Seamus MacCreehy dominating the front of a room he had no business being in. A man who may know who my mother really was, and might know where she'd gone. He might know where she is now. I looked at Aodhan again, and he slowly shook his head.

I suddenly had a feeling in the pit of my stomach that something terrible had happened to Sister Mary Katherine. Good God, I hoped I was wrong about that.

I wasn't the only one who was surprised by MacCreehy's presence. The rest of the students whispered amongst themselves whilst they tried to avoid catching MacCreehy's eye. It wasn't just that the towering man had replaced Sister Mary Katherine without a hint of warning. Mr. MacCreehy wasn't even a teacher; at least he'd never taught a class in all the years I'd attended, even though his title was headmaster. The fact that he'd decided to start teaching my literature class two days after Aodhan and I had visited the guards and gotten those reports detailing how Da had rescued Mama could not have been a coincidence.

Also, why had he brought a veritable armoury with him? The school had a strict no weapons policy, one that he was supposed to enforce.

A thought entered my mind: *Is he planning to use those weapons?*

I got Aodhan's attention and motioned for him to come and sit next to me. He moved to gather his things, then MacCreehy knocked on the lectern for attention.

"Stay in your seats," he ordered, and Aodhan sank back down in his chair.

Well, that was it, then. MacCreehy was here, Sister Mary Katherine was missing, and Aodhan and I weren't allowed to sit together. Things had officially taken a turn for the worse.

God Almighty, what was he planning to do with those swords?

The bell rang, and the room stilled. Every student faced forward. I couldn't imagine what was to come next.

"Good morning," MacCreehy began. "How is everyone today?"

"Where's Sister?" a student in the front row asked.

"She's taken ill, so I am taking over her classes for the day," he replied. The whispering resumed; Sister Mary Katherine was well liked by students and teachers, and we were all concerned for her.

"Settle down, now," MacCreehy said, holding up his hands to quell the room's murmuring. "As you might guess based on the props I've brought along, today's lesson will be all about notable weapons in literature."

MacCreehy surveyed the auditorium. It was so quiet you could've heard a pin drop. "Can anyone name a sword found in literature?"

"Excalibur," someone called out.

"That's an easy one," MacCreehy said.

"Durendal."

"Joyeuse."

A few other ancient names were called out, but since Sister Mary Katherine had been teaching us about early twentieth century literature, we didn't have a lot to go on. The room went quiet, then Aodhan cleared his throat.

"Gáe Bolga," Aodhan said.

MacCreehy nodded. "Gáe Bolga surely is a weapon, and a powerful one at that, but it's a spear."

"It was the spear of Cúchulainn, right?" Aodhan pressed. God, why was he pressing MacCreehy? "Wasn't it made from a sea monster?"

MacCreehy showed his teeth. A beat later, I realized that was his version of a smile. "Aye, the Gáe Bolga was crafted from a monster's bones, and that made it all the deadlier." MacCreehy strode to the table of weapons and selected a sword. He spun around and faced the auditorium, brandishing the sword like an actor playing King Arthur. Cold sweat broke out across my shoulders. I glanced toward the entrance, and wondered if I should claim a headache and flee to the nurse's office while I still could.

"Often monsters—once slain, of course—have their bodies repurposed into weapons that are used to put down other monsters." He completed a few flourishes with the sword, and the edge of the blade reflected blue under the fluorescent lights. "It's what some call the transference of power, with the monster's strength imbued in the weapon made from its remains. Only the greatest of warriors were allowed to wield such treasures."

"Why did they need them?" I blurted out. When MacCreehy fixed me in his gaze, I continued, face hot, "I mean, if these warriors were so great and all, why did they need these enhanced weapons?"

"A warrior's first duty is to the people," MacCreehy replied. "And to keep their people safe, he—or *she*—will use any means necessary."

MacCreehy set down the sword and kept on speaking, but I didn't hear another word he said. My gaze was fixed on the sword he'd brandished at us. It wasn't nearly as ornate as the sword we'd seen at the museum, but the handle was covered with iridescent green scales.

The moment class ended I gathered my things and darted out of the room, fearful MacCreehy would intercept me and want to speak further about monsters and the warriors that killed them. I put my head down and plowed through the crowded corridors, straight past the door to my next class and into the library. I didn't stop until I was in the depths of the stacks in the poetry section. A bare minute after I got there, Aodhan arrived.

"That was an interesting lecture, yeah?" he said by way of greeting.

"You saw the hilt?" I demanded.

He nodded. "You know what we need to do?"

"We must return to the museum and have another look at that sword."

Aodhan grabbed my hand. "Let's go."

Sneaking out of school was much easier the second time around. At this rate, I have a promising future as a criminal.

"Ugh. I am becoming a delinquent," I said.

"It's all right, Meri," Aodhan said as he drove. "We'll just pop in and have a chat with Dr. Fitzsimmons. She was real friendly, remember?"

"There is nothing all right about this," I said. "MacCreehy must know we talked to your uncle. He must know we have copies of the reports. How could he know that? And how did he get a sword like the one at the museum?" I turned toward the side window and bit the inside of my cheek. "Do you think he... Do you think MacCreehy made my mother disappear?" My throat tightened. I bit down harder, and tasted blood. "Do you think he'll do something to us?"

"Hey. Hey!" Aodhan swerved to the side of the road and stopped the car. "Meri, look at me."

I didn't want to, but his tone brooked no resistance. His brows were pinched and his lips thinned as he watched me cowering in the passenger seat. Aodhan blew out a breath, then he placed his hands on either side of my face.

"Listen to me," he began. "I'm not going to lie to you and tell you your ma's fine. Truth is, we don't know how she is, but we're working on that. What I will tell you is that if MacCreehy's done anything to her as soon as we have some evidence I'll call my uncle and the rest of the guards, and he'll be dealt with."

"Thank you," I said. "I hate it when people tell me Mama's fine just to shut me up."

"I'll never try to shut you up, and I'll never let MacCreehy or anyone else hurt you." He drew my face closer to his. "I promise, Meri. I'm with you till the end."

I nodded. "You're my man, and I'm your girl. We'll see this through, right?"

Red stained his cheeks. "Murphy's Maniacs, that's what we are." He pressed his forehead against mine for a heartbeat's time. "Are you all right to go on?"

I placed my hand on top of his. "I'm okay." He drew back, but I held onto him. "I won't let anyone hurt you, either."

Aodhan smiled, and stroked his thumb across my cheek. "I know you won't," he said, then he released me and resumed driving.

"Shouldn't take too long to get there at this time of day. Half an hour, tops."

"I wonder what we'll find at the museum," I murmured. I could still feel where he'd stroked my cheek.

"Answers, I hope," Aodhan said. "Do you finally believe that your ma was a warrior?"

"Why would—" I caught myself, remembered all we'd learned in the last week. "I suppose she might have been. Was your father a warrior, too?"

He frowned hard. "Trust the brilliant girl to add things up."

"What is that supposed to mean?"

"When my dad lived in California, he ran a martial arts studio. He used to win medals, tournaments and such," Aodhan replied. "And before you get any more ideas, you can't help me find him. I know he's not coming back."

"I'm sorry. I was just curious."

He blew out a breath. "I'm sorry, too. He's just hard to talk about sometimes, you know?"

"I do."

We were silent for the rest of the drive. I peeked out the window and saw dark clouds stacking up overhead. I hoped the weather wasn't a portent for things to come.

When we finally got to the center of the village, Aodhan parked the car down the street and around the corner from the museum. I didn't ask, but it seemed like he was setting the car up for a quick getaway. I appreciated that.

We walked down the main road and entered through the museum's front door, and followed the same path through the exhibits we'd taken the week before. Mind you, then we'd looked like casual tourists in our regular clothes, not two students who'd skipped out of class and were still wearing their school uniforms. Now, we stuck out like sore thumbs attached to larger, sorer hands.

Not that there was anyone present to witness us. "Where is everyone?" I asked.

Aodhan turned in a complete circle, and scanned the main exhibit room. There wasn't a single other person in the museum, not even the front desk clerk or a cleaning lady. "I have no idea," he replied. "The hours on the door say it's open. Maybe they're all on their lunch break?"

"Who sends everyone on break at once?" I muttered. I glanced at the customer service desk, where we'd spoken to a very helpful associate. Maybe she'd been a bit too helpful. "This is weird."

"Or maybe it's a bit of luck. Let's get down to the archaeology room and hope that's deserted as well."

It wasn't long before we descended the stairs to the basement level and reached the double doors that led to the research rooms. A quick tug on the handles told us they were locked.

"Now what do we do?" The door only had one long, rectangular window set in it near the top third of it. I stood on my toes and tried to see inside. The lights were on, but that was all I could glean at first glance.

"Can you look for another way in?" I asked.

"On it," he replied, as he jogged down the corridor. "See anything happening in there?"

I stretched until I could just see into the window. Dr. Fitzsimmons was inside, as were three other individuals. I assumed they were having a meeting about some archaeological topic, maybe with that club she had mentioned when we met. I could only see them from their shoulders upward, and really had no idea what they were doing. Then one of the individuals lifted their arm, brandishing the topic of their conversation for all to admire. It was my mother's sword.

I gasped, then I slapped my hand over my mouth and dropped down to a crouch. Aodhan was back in an instant, crouching beside me.

"What is it?" he whispered.

"The sword. It's in there, but there are people all around it."

Aodhan stood and peeked in the window; he was so tall he didn't need to stretch as I had. He was down beside me a moment later. "Did you get a good look at the three new ones?"

I shook my head.

"They're, ah, not normal."

I raised an eyebrow. "Not normal how?"

Aodhan stood, but remained bent at the waist. "Want me to boost you up? So you can see."

I scowled; the last thing I wanted was for Aodhan to help my short, clumsy self get a better look at whatever was going on in there. But the sword was in that room, and I needed to know who those other three people were.

"All right. No funny business."

"Never."

Aodhan moved behind me and gripped my waist, then he hoisted me up so my face was level with the window. I braced my hands against the door, suddenly hoping it really was locked and I wouldn't tumble arse over teakettle into a secret meeting. Once I was steady, I turned my attention back to the room and its mysterious occupants.

"Christ," I whispered.

"Like I said, not normal," Aodhan murmured.

Dr. Fitzsimmons appeared much as she had during our prior visit, dressed as an academic would in a jumper, slacks, and sensible shoes.

Dr. MacElroy was nowhere to be seen; perhaps it was his day off. It was the other three that told me this was no ordinary get together.

The three newcomers were not wearing modern or sensible clothing. Each wore a long chain mail shirt, belted at the waist, over long-sleeved shirts and long pants coloured in brown and green. Two of them were wearing ornate bronze helmets, while the third had removed his and tucked it underneath his arm. I couldn't see their footwear, but I did see round bronze shields strapped to their backs, and swords with fish scale hilts hanging at their waists.

"Aodhan, their swords," I whispered.

"I know," he said. "We have to get them out of there so we can get your ma's sword. We need a diversion."

He loosened his grip, and I slid down to the floor. I twisted around and looked up at him. "What kind of diversion?"

"I don't know. Let me think for a moment."

I glanced down the corridor. "Did you find another door?"

He shook his head. "No, just another staircase back up. Also, that cabinet doesn't have a back, or any shelving inside it. It's just doors, the sides, and a top."

"What possessed you to look inside the cabinet?"

He shrugged. "I was hoping for a secret passageway. No luck, though."

I glanced at the cabinet in question. I'd noticed it the last time we were here, mainly because it reminded me of the cabinets in the storage area behind the science rooms at school. It was also huge, easily one metre high and two across, and, since I now knew it was empty, seemed like a colossal waste of space.

"Boost me up again, a bit higher this time," I said. "I want to see if there are any doors in the back of the room."

"All right, then." We stood, then Aodhan grabbed my waist and heaved me upward with such force I fell against the door. All four occupants in the room turned toward the noise and saw me splayed against the window like a bug on a windshield.

"It's the girl from last week," Dr. Fitzsimmons shouted. "Grab her!"

"Aodhan we need to go!"

We fell to the corridor floor, then Aodhan hopped up and grabbed my hand as we ran toward the staircase at the far end. He moved to ascend, but I yanked his arm.

"They'll just follow us up," I said, then I spied the cabinet. "In there!"

We opened the doors and shoved ourselves inside the cabinet. Aodhan fit himself into one of the corners and pulled me against him, then we pulled the doors shut. We'd no sooner done so when we heard the others burst out of the archaeology room and thunder up the stairs.

I pressed my face against Aodhan's chest, willing myself to stay still. My heart was pounding, and the combination of dust and rank cleaning product residue threatened to make me sneeze. I breathed in the scent of Aodhan's shirt, like fresh laundry powder; somehow, it calmed me, even though I could feel his heart pounding under my cheek. As for him, he pressed his face against my hair and fisted his hands against the back of my jumper. His arms trembled around me, but he stayed silent. Somehow, we both did.

I've no idea how long we stayed like that, but it felt like an eternity. When enough time had gone by without a sound outside the cabinet, I cracked the door and scanned the hall.

"Empty," I whispered. We unfolded ourselves from our hiding spot and crept back to the door. Aodhan tried the handle, and swore.

"Still locked," he said. "And there's no other way off this corridor, save for where the other two went. Come on, let's go back up and see if there's another way down here."

We went back up to the ground floor, and thankfully didn't stumble into any archeologists of questionable intent or sword bearing men in the process. The whole of the museum remained deserted. When we got to the front entrance, we figured out why.

"This is locked, too," Aodhan said after he tried the door. "They've trapped us inside."

"What are we going to do?" I asked.

Aodhan considered the entryway, then he grabbed the umbrella stand. "Cover your eyes."

"Why?" I asked, then he slammed the umbrella stand into the door. Glass shattered as ear-piercingly loud alarms blared.

"Now they'll all come running," I shrieked.

"I'll lead them away," Aodhan said as he pushed the door open. "Get the sword! Meet in the square!"

Aodhan ran out of the museum. I saw him speed down the road as the heavy door closed; he was fast, but could he outrun what were certainly trained warriors? I didn't have time to worry about all of that, not with the sword lying unguarded for these precious few moments. I turned and sprinted back to the basement.

The archaeology room's door remained locked, as doors do. Taking a page from Aodhan's book, I grabbed a nearby fire extinguisher and beat it against the door's handle. The handle broke off before the extinguisher exploded or did anything else wonky. I pushed the door open, strode to the table, and saw it up close for the second time. My mother's sword.

I don't know how I knew it was hers, but I was certain. The scabbard, a plain brown leather sleeve, lay next to it, along with a matching sword belt, and both were as mundane as the sword was fantastic. The blade reflected blue, and the green and gold scaled hilt was as iridescent as an oil slick.

I couldn't not pick up the sword, no more than I could have stopped running toward the Cliffs or avoided walking into the sea. I needed to feel the hilt in my hand as much as I needed to breathe.

I traced my finger along the length of the blade. The metal was cold as ice and smooth as silk. When my hand reached the scaled hilt, I grasped it, the weight of it putting me momentarily off balance. It was heavier than I thought it would be.

"Mama, how did you lose this?" I whispered. "Are you okay?"

Footsteps on the stairs broke me out of my reverie. I grabbed the sword, scabbard, and belt, and ran behind the shelves. With any luck, they'd think whomever had stolen the sword was long gone.

"I know you're in here," growled a woman's voice. "I know you're her daughter. I knew it the moment you recognised the sword."

I crept farther back, and slid the sword into the scabbard; it took three tries on account of my hands shaking, but I got it done. Now that I had the sword, there was no way I was leaving it behind. Dr Fitzsimmons stepped into the aisle between the shelves, wielding a sword of her own.

"Your mother is a traitor, did you know that," she said. "I'm glad she lost her sword. She doesn't deserve it! Hand it over, and prove you're better than her." She paused, and added, "Don't be a coward, now. You're born of a long line of cowards. Be better than them."

She went on, taunting me with how my mother was a coward and a weakling, but all I heard was her speaking of my mother in the present tense. That meant that as far as Fitzsimmons knew, my mother was alive, and she must be nearby.

Also, if Fitzsimmons thought a bit of name calling was enough to rile me up, she'd obviously never spent ten years being bullied at school. I could weather her lame taunts like a champ.

Fitzsimmons came down the aisle, and I backed around the edge of the shelves and around to the far side. My heel bumped against something softer than a bookshelf or wall. I glanced over my shoulder and stifled a scream. Behind me was Dr MacElroy, head lolling to the side and a rope around his neck.

I clapped my hand over my mouth, and nearly dropped the sword in the process. I moved to check his pulse, but hesitated. I didn't want to touch a corpse, but if he was alive he needed medical attention. I didn't know how I'd get him to help; he was too big for me to move, and I already had four people after me. Dragging Dr MacElroy along would only make it easier for me to get captured.

What would Sister Mary Katherine do? That was easy: Sister would have done things methodically, one step at a time. First, check for signs of life, then work out the rest. No use losing your head over things that haven't happened yet, she'd say. She also would never abandon someone in need. I took a deep breath, and touched Dr MacElroy's wrist. He was stone cold.

"I'm sorry," I whispered to his body. I heard Fitzsimmons's footsteps, and resumed creeping down the aisle. Hopefully, she would keep to her present search pattern, and I could slip out the door and meet up with Aodhan. I could see her through the open spaces on the shelf, methodically scanning the area. Her back was to me, and I took the opportunity to move a bit faster.

Then I backed into a shelf, and a heap of boxes came crashing down around me.

"Stop," Fitzsimmons yelled. I ran toward the door, clutching the sword to my breast. Fitzsimmons ran too, her wicked blade out and terrifying. I grabbed a rolling office chair and pushed it toward her. She couldn't evade it in time and tumbled over the chair. I looked back when she screamed, saw red on the floor.

My God, had I killed her?

Fitzsimmons groaned, and pushed the chair aside. Satisfied I wasn't a murderer, I tore up the stairs. Two of the mail-clad warriors were standing in front of the entrance. Had they seen me? Not knowing what else to do, I ran to the far end of the museum and found a fire exit. I pushed open the door as more alarms sounded off, and kept running.

The rain was tipping down outside, from one of those fast moving storms that dumps buckets of water on you in the space of a few minutes. I was supposed to meet Aodhan in the square, but I didn't want to lead the warriors right to him. Since I also couldn't stay near the museum, I put the sword inside my jacket as best I could and slogged through the puddles in the opposite direction of the square.

I crept up and down the warren of streets, circling the museum but staying out of sight. I caught glimpses of the warrior men as they searched for me, or maybe they were still after Aodhan. For a time, I hid in an alleyway, as the rain soaked through my clothes and chilled me down to my bones.

The rainwater was nothing like the sea. Seawater had made me feel strong, and centred, and in control of my surroundings. Even when I'd run toward the Cliffs, or when I'd woken on the beach, I knew the sea wouldn't harm me. Rainwater, on the other hand, sapped my strength and drained my conviction. I felt hope draining from my soul, drop by drop.

I withdrew the sword from my jacket and ran my fingertips over the hilt. The scales were in relief, with the surface an iridescent green and edged in gold. As I traced the edges of the scales, I felt t a measure of strength return. I couldn't give up, not until I found my mother and returned her sword to her. She needed it.

"Mama, what are you caught up with?" I whispered.

After an hour passed with no sight or sound of my pursuers, I emerged and made my way toward the town square. When I approached, I saw a dark figure slumped against the base of the central monument. I froze, terrified one of the warrior men was lying in wait. Then a car motored down the road and in the beam of the headlights I recognised Aodhan.

When he saw me, he leapt to his feet and sprinted across the square, and wrapped me in a bear hug. "I was so worried." Aodhan cupped my chin in his hand, then he moved closer. At the last moment, he shut his eyes, and rested his forehead against mine. "You have it?"

"I have it."

"What took so long?" His arms tightened. "I was sure they got you."

"I had to hide." The hilt was digging into my chest, and I shifted against him. "I thought I killed Fitzsimmons."

He drew back and regarded me. "Did you?"

"There was blood. I-I… I don't think so. She moved, afterward." I gulped. "Aodhan, someone killed Dr MacElroy. I-I saw his body."

He pushed the wet hair back from my forehead. "We'll call the guards about that. Anonymously," he added. "But you're okay?"

"I'm okay."

Aodhan nodded. "Come on. We've a long walk to the car."

"I thought it was by the museum?"

"As soon as I got to the car, I moved it," he replied. "Then I jogged back." He eyed the sword. I clutched it with both hands and pressed it to my chest. "Want me to carry that?"

"No." I held it tighter. "I've got it."

The walk to the car felt like it took forever. By the time we reached where Aodhan had left it, the rain had stopped, but it was long after sunset. Aodhan drove straight to the surf shop. It had already closed for the evening, which saved us having to make awkward explanations to the staff. Aodhan unlocked the front door, and I followed him across the sales floor and up the stairs to the back room.

I sat down on the couch with the sword resting across my lap. Aodhan sat beside me and rested his elbows on his knees.

"I was actually terrified," he said.

"Me too." I shuddered; now that the adrenaline had worn off, I shivered in my cold, wet clothes. "Have you any spare clothes?"

Aodhan looked down at himself. "Christ, yeah. We've got the couch all wet, too."

Aodhan opened the cupboard and dragged out the air mattress. "We can sit on this," he said. I set the sword onto the couch and plugged in the pump that inflated the mattress.

"I don't have anything clean in here," he said, after he'd looked through the cupboard. "Hang on."

"I don't care if they've been worn," I called after him, but he was already heading down the stairs to the sales floor. He came back with a blue shirt emblazoned with the surf shop's logo and a pair of bright pink board shorts.

"Thank you," I said. I pulled off the tags. "I'll pay for these."

"Don't bother. I know the owner." He winked. I smiled, and went to the bathroom to change. By the time I emerged, Aodhan was wearing black track pants and a black short-sleeved shirt. There was a mound of blankets on the air mattress, and he was rooting around in the kitchen.

"I hung my clothes over the shower rod," I said.

"Good idea," he said, then he scooped up his pile of soggy clothing from the couch and went into the bathroom, presumably to do the same. While he did that, I laid the sword across the kitchen table and sat there staring at it.

I could hardly wrap my mind around what we'd done. Not only had we slipped out of school—again—since then we'd committed several criminal acts. Were there cameras in the museum, or outside in the town? Would Aodhan's uncle be by to arrest us? Would they think we had killed Dr MacElroy?

I shook my head. I refused to feel any guilt over the archaeologist's death. Sadness, yes, but not guilt. Nothing Aodhan or I had done had led to his demise. That Fitzsimmons—I strongly suspected she wasn't a doctor of anything—was obviously off her rocker. While I didn't know who had killed Dr MacElroy, my money was on her.

I touched the sword again. The cold metal of the cross guard quieted my mind. Everything we'd done had been worth it. The sword was with me, and I was a step closer to finding my mother.

The kettle whistled. Before I could move, Aodhan emerged from the bathroom and shot toward the kitchen like a laser to deal with it. A few minutes later, he delivered two mugs of tea and a tin of biscuits to the table.

"Thank you," I said. I spied a fresh scrape on his elbow. "You were hurt?"

"It's nothing." He jerked his chin toward the sword. "How's it feel, having a piece of her back with you?"

"Good, I guess." I picked up my tea, and my unsteady hands made the water slosh over the rim of the mug. "I can't stop shaking."

"You're still chilled from the rain." He set my mug on the table and stood. "Here, get under a blanket."

Numbly, I followed Aodhan to the air mattress and let him drape a blanket over my shoulders. He set a kitchen chair next to us with our tea and biscuits on the seat, then he settled himself on the mattress across from me with the sword lying between us.

"It's amazing," he said. "This is real, hard evidence of... Of something."

"It's my mother's, I'm certain of it," I said. "When Fitzsimmons found me in the room, she said she knew I recognised the sword. She called me her daughter. Her daughter! Aodhan, I think that means my mother is nearby."

He nodded. "We've got her sword. Now, we just need to find her."

KEEP MOVING

I woke lying on the air mattress in the freezing cold shop. Apparently, Aodhan hadn't yet fixed it so the heater would come on earlier in the day. I glanced at the couch, and saw it empty. I wondered where he'd got to, then I felt a small movement on the far side of the mattress. Aodhan was sleeping beside me.

That's right, the couch was wet. I didn't mind sharing the air mattress with him. It was his by rights, and how could I really complain when he'd been saving me time and again? Besides, it's not like we were sleeping together. Near one another, yes, but not together.

Technicalities may be the death of me.

Aodhan was still sleeping. I rolled over and admired his long, dark lashes as they lay against his cheekbones. His hair had curled tighter after being drenched in the rain, and it wasn't as shiny as it usually was. I wondered if he used hair products, and if all those flowery shampoos in the bathroom really were his and not his sisters'.

I wondered if he looked like his father.

I wondered if his father was like my mother.

I moved closer and put my hand on his chest; I never would have dared touch him like that if he'd been awake. His heartbeat was steady, sure. Reliable.

My face went hot, and I decided to keep my hands to myself. My movements disturbed him, and he opened his eyes.

"Hi."

"Hi."

"Sorry about this. The couch—"

"I know. It's all right, we've done this before."

He smiled. "Getting to be a bit of a habit."

I shrugged. "There's worse ones. At least we're not doing heroin."

He laughed. "True."

"Where's the sword?"

"Under the couch. Didn't seem smart to leave it lying in plain sight." He rolled onto his side and propped himself up on an elbow. "Meri, we need to talk about what to do next."

I touched his hand, startling him so much he stopped speaking. "Can we worry about that in the morning and stay here, just a bit longer?"

"We can do that." Aodhan reached for me and I went to him, my cheek resting against his throat as his arms came around me. We settled against each other in our nest of blankets, and I refused to think about swords or crazed archeologists or anything but the warmth surrounding me. I wanted to stay in his arms forever.

"Aodhan Lucas Sullivan, get your arse up now!"

Aodhan sat straight up, jostling me awake in the process. We must have fallen asleep again on the air mattress. Blinding sunlight streamed in through the skylight, and I blinked tears from my eyes. Silhouetted in the light was Aodhan's mother, standing over us with her hands on her hips and a face as red as a tomato.

"So this is why you weren't at your stepfather's party," Mrs Dumhach said. "Brought your tart up here instead?"

"Ma, no, that's not it," Aodhan began, but she made a cutting motion with her hand.

"I don't want to hear it. Get dressed and get to school."

Aodhan nodded, then he got up and went into the bathroom. I cowered underneath the blankets, unsure if I should move or stay put.

"I'm sorry," I said, having decided I couldn't let Aodhan shoulder all of the blame. If we hadn't gone after my mother's sword, and been attacked by a band of actual warriors, he would have attended the birthday party as planned. "I know this looks bad, but nothing happened. I'm not like that."

Mrs Dumhach glared at the closed bathroom door. "Aodhan is like that. You can't rely on him for anything. That one's heartless, just like his father was."

Despite her words, I could see the pain on her face. Mrs Dumhach was mad, yes, but more than that she was hurt. "It was my fault he missed the party. Please, if you're mad at anyone, be mad at me."

She fixed me in her gaze. "Is that an invitation?"

"Ma, leave her be," Aodhan said as he rejoined us, his arms laden with his clothes from yesterday. "Meri, your uniform's dried out."

I fled to the bathroom. My clothes didn't look too bad after all they had gone through, though the fabric was a bit stiff. I dressed quickly and pulled my hair back into a ponytail, making myself as presentable as possible with the limited resources at hand. When I emerged from the bathroom, Aodhan was also wearing his uniform, and he was alone.

"Where'd she go?" I asked.

"She went back home," he replied. "Got to get my younger sisters ready for school. She just stopped by here to yell a bit."

"Does she do that a lot?"

Aodhan's throat worked. "Yeah. She does."

"She said you're heartless." I shouldn't have told him that, but the words just spilled out of me. "I wanted to disagree with her, but it's not really my place to tell your mother what to think."

He smiled tightly. "She's been angry since Dad died, and since he's gone, she's only got me to yell at."

"What about your older sisters?"

"Mary went to university three years back, and Anne left a year after her." Aodhan blew out a breath. "So it's just Ma and me missing Dad. We both miss him in our own way."

"She still misses him," I said, thinking about how Da still mourned Mama's leaving him every moment of every day. "Makes you wonder if it's all worth it."

"If what's worth it? Love?" Aodhan shook his head. "Without love, what's the point?"

I snorted. "Saving one's sanity, for one."

Aodhan glanced at me over his shoulder. "Why are you doing all this, nicking swords and digging up old garda reports?"

"To find my mother," I replied. "You know that."

"And why do you want to find her?"

I blinked at Aodhan, and he smirked, because of course he was right. I wanted to find Mama because I loved her, just as I loved Da and Kevin and they needed to get her back, too. I thought about Aodhan's mother, who must have been sick with worry when we hadn't attended the party last night. Had her anger really been relief, knowing Aodhan hadn't come to harm? Were her angry outbursts at Aodhan all because she still loved and missed his father, and Aodhan was all that was left of him?

"So why are you helping me?" I demanded. "You don't love my mother. You've never even met her."

Aodhan smiled. "Oh, Meri. I'd help you with anything."

I opened my mouth, intending a sharp comeback, but my throat went tight as my face went hot. I was glad he was helping me, and truth be told, I'd help him with anything, too.

We were quiet during the ride to school. Aodhan's well-stocked kitchen had produced a box of granola bars, and we'd eaten all of them before we pulled into the student car park. After we got out of the car, Aodhan hefted his duffle bag out of the back seat and put it in the boot.

"Do you have practice today?" I asked, as he locked the car.

"Track," he replied. "Same time as you have choir practice."

"Stalker," I said, but without malice. "Want to eat lunch together?"

There was that grin, and I was almost ready to admit how much I looked forward to seeing it. "Of course I do. Talk soon, Meri."

I kept my head down as I navigated the corridors, wondering if and when I would get pulled into MacCreehy's office and reprimanded for leaving school grounds without a note... But nothing happened, and that was more disconcerting than if I'd been slapped with a formal expulsion. It was as if no one had noticed I'd missed lunch and the entire second half of school yesterday. Or perhaps the school had been instructed to overlook it. Perhaps my obtaining the sword was all part of a larger plan, and by being here, Aodhan and I were playing right into MacCreehy's hands.

Now that's just paranoid.

I made it through my first two classes without incident, and by the time my music class rolled around, I was so relieved I almost skipped into the music room. Choir practice was by far my favourite class. To be honest, there were several times I'd considered dropping out of school altogether, but the choir was what always made me stay. For a few short hours each week, I could lose myself in my singing, riding the high notes and the low as my cares fell away. It was one of the few times I felt at peace.

Of course, choir wouldn't have been half as wonderful without the instructor, Rose Fennimore. She was an actual music producer, and ran a studio in Cork. Some whispered that she taught at our school because she was searching for the next big star, while others thought she was performing community service for some hushed-up incident involving one of her artists. I was just glad she was there.

Rose was always pushing me to take on more solos, but I resisted. I didn't want to be a pop star—at least, I didn't think I did—and I certainly didn't want to garner any more attention at school than I already had. I just wanted to sing. Imagine my surprise when I entered the music room, and Rose looked straight at me and frowned.

"Shit," she said. Rose had never been one to watch her language.

"Hello to you, too," I said. "Sorry I missed last week."

Rose's brow pinched. "Meri, I wanted to have this dealt with before you arrived."

"Have what dealt with?" I looked around the room and saw Kelsey and Sarah snickering in the corner, while the rest of the students were staring at the whiteboard with expressions ranging from confusion to hilarity. I followed their gazes. When I saw it, I dropped my book bag.

Someone had drawn a mermaid across the length of the whiteboard. An often enough occurrence around me, certainly nothing new or shocking. Only, this time the artist had taped a picture of my mother's face over the mermaid's head.

"You!" I spun around and pointed at Kelsey and Sarah. "This stinks of you!"

"What's the matter?" Kelsey asked. "Did we get the fins wrong?"

"Going to cry?" Sarah sneered. "Big crocodile tears, salty like the sea?"

"What is your problem?" I demanded. "That gossip was ancient ten years ago! Of course, I'm not a mermaid's daughter, you daft cows! Why do you keep beating this dead horse? Can't your tiny, tiny minds come up with something new? Is this really all you think about, me and my missing mother?"

"She's not missing, she took off," Kelsey said. "Or your drunk old man knocked her off his boat."

I was across the room in an instant, my hands fisted in Kelsey's shirt. "Insult my father again and you'll be the one going over."

"You really think you're special, don't you?" Kelsey sneered. "You're not the only one whose mother's gone."

Kelsey's admission shocked me into silence. Even though we'd been schoolmates for ages, I knew next to nothing about her, or her family. "What do you mean, gone? Did something happen to your mother? Did she die?"

"If only. She was a slag, like yours."

I tightened my grip on her shirt. "Say that again."

"Meri." Rose put her hand on my arm. "These two aren't worth it. You know they aren't. I'll alert the administration and they'll be punished."

I jerked free of her. "Do whatever you like with them. I don't care what happens."

I stalked toward the whiteboard and ripped down my mother's picture, then I grabbed my bag and made for the door.

"Where are you going?" Rose demanded.

"I'm not feeling very musical."

I moved through the corridors like a ghost, quiet and unseen. Or maybe others had seen me, but the word had already got out: the Murphy girl's finally lost it. She's ready to take that flying leap into the sea. Steer clear of that lunatic.

Eventually, I arrived at the athletic field. I found a seat in the bleachers, and watched the team as they queued up for sprints and other exercises. When the lads took a water break, Aodhan spotted me.

"Who's the stalker now?" he asked as he sat beside me. I remained silent. "What happened?"

"Kelsey and Sarah drew up one of their famous mermaids," I replied. "Only this time they used a picture of my mother for her face."

"I hate those two," Aodhan said. "How'd they get a picture of your ma?"

I unfolded the paper and smoothed it across my knees. "This is one of the pictures from the garda files," I said. During the half hour since I'd stormed out of the music room, I'd pieced together where the picture came from. I couldn't help feeling that this was partly my fault. Maybe I deserved it. "I photocopied all of the papers in the library, but the copier keeps a digital image. I must not have cleared its memory after I was done."

Aodhan draped his arm around me. I leaned my head against his shoulder. "We're not having a very good day, are we?" he asked.

"No, we certainly are not." I closed my eyes and took a deep breath. "Do you like school?"

"Yes. No. It depends on the day." He was silent for a moment. "Most of the days are okay, but every so often someone makes a comment about how I'm only good at sports because my father was an award-winning athlete, and if only we could get a few more ringers like me on the team we'd win all our matches. Once, another school tried to get me disqualified. Said having me compete was an unfair advantage.”

“That’s horrible,” I said. “That one should have been disqualified, for unsportsmanlike behaviour.”

Aodhan snorted. “They swept it under the rug, just like they do with all the other nasty comments that get made about me. Don’t want to upset anyone by causing a scene.”

“I know that act all too well. ‘Oh, Meri, what they did wasn’t so bad. Can’t you just move on?’ Meanwhile, they’ve never moved on from tormenting me.” I tore at the corners of the photocopy. “My earliest school memory is Kelsey distracting me so Sarah could push me over. Skinned both my knees, but everyone said it was an accident. A misunderstanding. Here we are all these years later, and we’re still having misunderstandings.”

“Those two have really made you hate it here, haven’t they?”

“Every day, for as far back as I can remember, they’ve been after me. Why?”

“I wish I knew. I’ve always thought they were born wicked.”

Born wicked. If Kelsey and Sarah had been born bad, did that mean Aodhan and I’d been born good? What about my mother, the woman who might be a warrior? Why had she really left us? A good woman wouldn’t leave the man she loved and her small children, not unless there had been something bigger at stake.

What in the world could be more important than your family?

“I don’t know what to do about all this,” I whispered.

Aodhan squeezed me against him. “We keep moving, that’s what we do. A wise man once said when you find yourself going through hell, it’s best to keep going.”

I leaned back and regarded him. “Did you just quote Winston Churchill?”

"More of a paraphrase, but yeah." His brow pinched. "Was that too weird?"

"No, it wasn't. And you're right." I sat up straight, and decided to take the next step. "I don't care about Kelsey and Sarah and their games. We have the sword, that's what we need to work on. We will keep moving, no matter what those two do. They aren't important right now."

"Agreed. What do we do next?"

"We need to talk to my father. I'm ready to listen to him now."

READY TO LISTEN

I waited by the car for Aodhan to shower and change after practice. He met me wearing not his uniform, but the track pants and tee shirt he'd slept in the night before.

"Couldn't stand those rained on clothes for another moment," he explained when I gave him a look. "Jealous?"

I made a face and placed my hand on the door handle, then something behind Aodhan distracted me. There were three white cars with yellow and blue detailing parked near the school's front entrance.

"Are those garda cars?" I asked. Aodhan turned around. As he did several uniformed guards exited the school and descended the steps. In their midst was Mr MacCreehy.

"Yeah. Wonder why they're hanging around with MacCreehy?"

Before I could reply, Mr MacCreehy spotted us. His face twisted into a scowl as he stalked across the car park.

"Aodhan, we've got to go," I said.

"He's already seen us," Aodhan said. "If we take off we'll look guilty."

"Guilty of what?" I demanded.

"Whatever he's already decided we did," Aodhan replied. "It's okay, Mer. We'll just talk to him for a bit."

"You two," MacCreehy yelled. "Where do you think you're going?"

"Home for lunch, sir," Aodhan replied. "I've done it several times, have clearance on account of my age. The necessary form should be in my file. Why? Has the policy changed?"

"What's changed is that the garda need to question each and every student currently enrolled in the academy," MacCreehy replied. "It seems two of our students left school grounds yesterday and caused a disturbance at a museum."

"Two students from The Saints?" Aodhan said, his voice breaking at the end. "Must be a case of mistaken identity, sir. We've all been taught better than that."

"That's what I said, but they have the video surveillance," Mac-Creehy said. "The criminals are wearing our uniforms. One of the deviants looks much like you, Miss Murphy."

My heart was in my throat while my stomach plummeted to the ground. Some hapless person had found Dr MacElroy's body, checked the surveillance footage, and now Aodhan and I were about to be arrested. We would go to prison for a murder we had no part in, and I would never find my mother or return her sword and dammit we were innocent!

MacCreehy moved toward me. "Come along now, dear. Let's talk to the garda together."

"No," I whispered. Then I sang, "*No, no, no.*"

MacCreehy stopped moving. Something in my brain clicked, and I kept on singing.

"*We don't need to talk to the garda,*" I sang as Aodhan gaped. "*Aodhan and I are innocent. It makes sense. We're innocent.*" I looked at Aodhan. "*We're leaving now.*"

MacCreehy scowled and flailed his arms, but he remained rooted in place. "How dare you use a song against me! I'll have your throat for this, girl!"

"*No, you won't,*" I sang. "*I say to you, don't. And you won't come after us.*"

Aodhan came around and opened my door. "Get in," he said, as he shoved me inside. By the time I'd shut my door, Aodhan was behind the wheel and we were squealing out of the student car park.

"Do you have any water?" I gasped. My heart was hammering against my ribs and I couldn't catch my breath.

"Here."

Aodhan handed me his bottle from practice, and I gulped the tepid water. He shifted gears, then he reached over and rubbed my back.

"You okay?"

"I think so." I scrubbed my face with my hands. "Aodhan, are we going to jail?"

"If we do, can you sing us out of it?" he countered. "What was that back there?"

"I don't know." I stared at my hands. "I knew we couldn't go with him. All I wanted was for him to let us drive off. I don't know why I sang."

Aodhan's hand paused on the back of my neck. "I'm glad you did. Still on to your dad?"

"Yes." After the display I'd put on in the school's car park, I needed to talk to my father more than ever.

"Will your dad be home now?" Aodhan asked. "If he's out on his boat, maybe we should go to the docks."

I shook my head. "I promised him I wouldn't go back to the sea. I need to make good on that."

"Right, then."

Aodhan drove like a madman down the narrow roads, flying over the hills like a banshee. "Have you ever been in a wreck?" I demanded after he careened around a bend in the road.

"Not yet. Why? Don't trust my driving?"

I remembered what his mother said about him being unreliable. "Do you and your mother get on at all?"

He sighed. "Yes, and no. When it's just her and I we're great. When it's us and my older sisters, we're a force to be reckoned with." He paused. "But when my stepfather gets involved, things get weird."

"He was your father's best friend?"

"Yeah. And he and Ma have two girls, my younger half-sisters. Funny thing is, he never misses an opportunity to remind me that they're my *half*-sisters. As if I'm the outsider." He snorted. "I was there first."

I used to wonder if Da wouldn't be better off if he moved on and found someone new. After hearing these details about Aodhan's home life, I reckoned that Da was fine the way he was.

Screw that. Da was not fine the way he was, none of us were. As I rode in Aodhan's car, throat raw and heart thudding, I resolved to find out what really happened to my mother, even if it took the rest of my life to do so. I needed answers, not excuses.

It wasn't long before we reached my house. After we parked, Aodhan grabbed his duffel bag from the boot and followed me inside. I led him through the side door into the kitchen. We found my brother sitting at the table, eating a sandwich.

"Why aren't you in school?" Kevin asked by way of greeting.

"We need to talk to Da," I replied.

Kevin glanced between Aodhan and me. "Are you pregnant?"

"No!" I snapped.

"Wouldn't be mine," Aodhan added.

"Then what do you need him for?" Kevin asked.

"We need to talk about Mama."

Kevin set down his sandwich. "This is because of what happened at the Cliffs, isn't it?"

"No," I replied, while Aodhan said, "In a roundabout way, yeah." When I glared at Aodhan, he continued, "Listen, before last week you were Meri Murphy, the quiet girl with the pretty voice. Now the sea calls to you and you steal swords."

Kevin's eyes narrowed. "You went to the sea again?"

"You're more concerned with that than me stealing a sword?" I countered.

"Swords have a way of popping up 'round here." Kevin frowned. "The sea, Meri. Why'd you go?"

"I didn't mean to," I said. "The waves, they pulled me there."

Kevin stood and put his plate in the sink. "I'll go down to the docks and get Da. Don't leave."

Kevin left without another word. Aodhan said, "Your family really has the market cornered on secrets. I used to think mine kept a ton of stuff from me, but this is beyond the pale."

"What did they keep from you?"

"My ma wanting to marry my stepfather, for one," Aodhan replied. "They kept me and my sisters in the dark about their relationship until a week before the wedding day."

"How old were you?"

"Eleven."

I almost said he was lucky he'd had a mother when he was eleven, then I pursed my lips and swallowed my short comeback. It wasn't Aodhan's fault he'd been luckier than me, and had grown up with both of his parents for longer than I had. After all, his father had died while mine still lived.

Perhaps I was the lucky one.

"I'm going to change," I said. "Help yourself to the fridge. I know you must be starved."

"What makes you say that?"

"You're always starved."

I left him to it and went into my bedroom, and stood staring into my closet. Kevin was probably already at the docks, which meant that now he and Da both knew I'd been sneaking around and investigating Mama's life and eventual disappearance. There was no going back now; either Da and Kevin would support me and we'd all be in this together, or I'd keep on sneaking about without them. God help me if it was the latter.

After I picked out a new set of clothes, I took everything into the bathroom and had a quick shower. When I reentered the kitchen, I found Aodhan standing over the sink eating a slice of bread.

"Are we out of plates?" I asked.

Aodhan looked toward my voice, and almost choked on his bread. "You're wearing a dress."

I glanced down at my clothing. I was wearing a long blue dress decorated with tiny orange flowers scattered across it. The neckline was high, and the pearl pendant was safe and hidden against my breast. I'd had the dress forever and never worn it, but I'd bought it because it reminded me of something my mother would have worn. After learning how Da had preserved each and every one of her possessions, including all of her clothing, I was certain of that fact. He'd treated all those old clothes and books as if they were sacred. To him, I suppose they were.

"So what if I'm in a dress? You see me in my uniform skirt five days a week."

He shook his head. "That manky plaid skirt is nothing compared to what you have on now."

"My skirt is not manky." Before I could further defend my clothing, Da strode into the kitchen, Kevin hot on his heels. His eyes were glassy, and he swayed a bit on his feet, and I worried he was too drunk to be of any help. He looked from me to Aodhan and nodded.

"I take it you're ready to listen now," Da said, his voice clear and steady.

"Yes, Da," I said, relieved he was sober. Sober enough, at least. "We're both ready."

THE TRUTH ABOUT CALLIOPE

I bustled about the kitchen, making tea and setting out what few snacks we had on hand; since Da's last market trip Kevin and I had eaten almost everything, and the press was looking rather bare. As much as I didn't care for acting the waitress, the focused activity gave me a few moments to settle my thoughts. Besides, Da needed the tea to offset whatever he'd been drinking earlier.

Once the tea was done and delivered, Aodhan and I sat at the table with Da. Kevin leaned against the counter, watching us like a sentry. Da nodded to Kevin, who then retrieved the bottle of whiskey and four glasses. He set all of it in the centre of the table.

"We'll start with a drink," Da said as he arranged the glasses in a row.

"None for me, thanks," Aodhan said. "I'm in training."

Da nodded. "Where do you want me to begin the story?"

"At the beginning, preferably," I replied. "Actually, we recently learned a bit about how you and Mama first met."

I pulled out my folder with the photocopies of the police reports and slid it across the table. Da spread out the reports in front of him, pausing to touch the picture of Mama.

"Where did you come by all of this?" he asked.

"My uncle, sir," Aodhan replied. "Officer Mark Conner."

"Bridgette's brother," Da said, and Aodhan nodded.

"He remembered when you found your wife and brought her to the station."

"We had to go to the station," Da said. "The Coast Guard threatened to charge me with filing a false report." Da muttered something about bureaucrats under his breath, then he looked over the paperwork.

"Aye, this is what happened," he said, after he'd read the first report. "She was on the beach, and I saw her from on deck. She needed help, and I helped her." He cleared his throat. "At least, that is what we told the guards."

"You mean these reports aren't accurate?" I asked.

"They are, but we omitted quite a few details," he replied. "For instance, Calliope had been stranded on that beach for some time before I convinced her to get on the boat with me."

"How long was she there?" I asked. "And how did she survive, all alone on a beach?"

"I... I don't remember how long she'd been there," Da admitted. "It had been a few days, at least. Still, she was stubborn as a mule and refused to let me help her. The first time I came across her, I ended up tossing her some water and leaving her be."

"You just left her there?" I demanded.

"She threatened to cut my head off if I set foot on that beach," Da replied. "Went on about how people were after her, about how she couldn't bring me into whatever she was caught up in. So I gave her the water and I left, fully intending to call services and let them know there was a stranded mad woman what needed help."

"But you didn't do that."

"No, I didn't." Da fingered the handle of his mug. "I couldn't get to sleep that night for thinking about her, and how she'd been singing. It was her song what drew me toward that beach in the first place. I heard it when I was still quite far off, an impossible distance for one wee woman's voice to travel. But even though your mother was small, her voice has always been large."

"You really did fall in love with her voice first."

"Aye, that I did, and I woke the next morning knowing I had to help her. First, I called the Coast Guard and notified them of her location, and then I went straight back to that beach. That time I was prepared, and brought her food and blankets. She hadn't done well overnight, and she finally let me drop anchor and join her on the beach. We spent some time talking, then the tide started to come in, and only when the waves were lapping at her toes did she agree to get on my boat." Da paused to sip his tea. "And here we are."

"Was she wearing this?" I withdrew the pearl pendant from underneath my dress, and Da nodded.

"Yes, she was wearing the pearl," Da replied.

"If you don't mind my asking, which beach was she on?" Aodhan asked.

"One of the narrow strips below the Cliffs, near the old fort," Da replied. "When I asked her how she got there, she just smiled and said she was a good swimmer."

"More like an Olympic swimmer," Aodhan said.

"Did you know a man was looking for her? Or someone we think might have been her." I put the missing person report Seamus Mac-Creehy had filed about his supposed daughter on the top of the pile. "Could this Aoife have been Mama?"

"Aoife," Da repeated, rolling the name about on his tongue.

"I thought Ma's name was Calliope," Kevin said.

"No, I called her Calliope," Da replied. "As for her true name, she made me forget it long ago."

I bit my lip; how on earth could a man intentionally forget his wife's name? I left that question for another time, and asked, "So is the Aoife in this report also Mama?"

"If it were, that begs the question of what she was doing between the time when this MacCreehy fellow lost her, and I found her," Da replied.

"Is that MacCreehy the same bloke what runs the school?" Kevin asked.

"According to the guards, he's one and the same," I replied.

"That one's not right," Kevin continued. "I remember when he came on as headmaster. He used to take over random classes and go on about legendary weapons and warriors. He was obsessed with the music classes, too. Talked about mermaids a lot, but he had a different name for them."

"Merrows," I said.

Kevin snapped his fingers. "That's it."

"He told me about merrows on that school trip to the Cliffs," I said. "Said their children are called the merrowkin. As if I was a merrow's child."

"Get that daft notion out of your head," Da said. "Your mother did not have a fish tail, and I'd know more than anyone."

"Then why did he bring that up?" I asked.

"Like Kevin said, he's off," Da replied.

"Was Calliope from Kilstiffen?" Aodhan asked.

Da looked at Aodhan and cocked his head to the side. "What do you think you know about Kilstiffen, then?"

"I know it's out below the sea, and surfaces every seven years," Aodhan replied.

"So you mean to tell me you think there are people living at the bottom of the sea?" Da laughed. Kevin hadn't moved from his post at the counter. "How do they breathe down there?"

"I've heard it call me," Aodhan said, and Da stopped laughing. "Just like it calls Meri, and how Calliope called you. I bet you've heard it too," he added, nodding toward Kevin.

Kevin swallowed hard. "I don't hear it. Not anymore. Not since…"

"Keep your secrets," I said, the words tumbling from my mouth. "For now, at least. This doesn't need to be a group therapy session."

"I don't think we can afford secrets any longer," Kevin said. "It's almost time."

"Time for what?" When both Da and Kevin were silent, I continued, "Is the city rising? Is that why Mama's back?"

"Back?" Da leapt to his feet, knocking his chair over in the process. "Have you seen her?"

"No, sir," Aodhan said as he opened his duffle bag. "We found this." He withdrew the sword and set it across the table. Da and Kevin stared at the sword as if they'd seen a ghost.

"It's hers, isn't it?" I asked. "I knew the moment I saw it. The hilt, it's just like the bracelets she used to wear."

"Aye, this is Calliope's sword." Da traced the length of the blade, then the flame-shaped cross guard. "I'm surprised you recognised it."

"I haven't seen it since the day she left," Kevin said. He stepped forward and peered at the sword. "The last time I saw her, she was dressed for battle, carrying this sword. I tried to go with her, told her I'd fight too."

"You saw her leave?" I asked.

"Aye. Broke my little heart."

"Why didn't you ever say you saw her go?" I demanded.

Kevin bowed his head. "She made me promise not to tell. To this day, I wish I'd followed her."

"I would have gone with her too, if only she'd have let me," Da said.

"But where did she go?" I demanded, exasperation getting the better of me. "And if you knew, why didn't you go after her?"

Da looked at Kevin, then he slid glasses of whiskey toward Aodhan and me while Kevin claimed one for himself. "Remember how I said there's no way a city could be at the bottom of the sea?" Da asked. "What I have to tell you now is a fair sight stranger. Even the athlete will need a drop or two before we're done here."

"What are you going to tell us?" I asked.

"Where your mother really came from."

A Proper Gang

We sat around the table, holding our glasses of whiskey and waiting for Da to continue telling us where my mother came from. Well, three of us were holding our glasses; Da had already downed his first measure and quickly poured himself a second.

"As I've told you, I found your mother stranded on a beach below the Cliffs of Moher," Da began, gesturing with his glass toward the police reports. "What you did not know is that she was in hiding from her own people."

"Then MacCreehy—or someone—really was searching for her," I said.

"So it would seem." Da rolled the glass between his hands. "What the reports also do not mention is what she was wearing."

"Wasn't she wearing the mail?" I asked, hoping Da hadn't come across her starkers.

"Aye. She was." Da leaned back in his chair and closed his eyes. "She was wearing armour. Not the flashy metal plate you see in movies and the like, but hardened leather topped with that lovely chain mail. I knew straight aways she was a person of some importance, since her mail was gold."

I set the scrap of chain mail I'd found in the cottage in the centre of the table. "It's so pretty, isn't it?"

Da fingered the golden rings and smiled. "Aye, that it is. Just as beautiful as your mother."

"The three we saw at the museum wore silver mail," Aodhan said, which led to us informing Da and Kevin of everything that had happened at the museum, and later at the school. We omitted the part where Aodhan and I had slept together on the air mattress. Once that was done, Aodhan said, "Maybe they were like infantry, and your ma a general."

A general. I touched the golden flames that made up the sword's cross guard. "Did she have this sword with her on the beach?"

"Aye, and a round shield on her back. She was so lovely, standing there on the beach with the sun winking off her golden mail. You can imagine why I hailed her."

"And then what happened?" I prompted.

"Once we got past the point of her telling me to leave her be for fear of losing my head, she told me she was on the run and asked if I could hide her. I helped her on to my boat, and we concocted the tale of her being lost at sea. I went so far as to make up a name for her—Calliope, as you well know—and that was the name she gave when we went to the guards to give our statements. I never thought it would be so easy to start a new life."

"Easy to start, but not so easy to keep," Kevin muttered.

"Less easy to keep when you fall in love, too," Da said. "I threw a wrench in her plans."

I sat back in my chair. It had never occurred to me that Mama had been on a mission, and her falling in love with Da might have derailed it.

"Can you tell us why she needed to hide?" I asked.

Da tossed back his second whiskey. "Here's the part where you'll think I'm crazy. You've heard of Kilstiffen and that it's at the bottom of the sea. That's true, and yet it's not." Da grabbed the whiskey bottle, but I covered his glass with my hand.

"After you tell us," I said.

He set down the bottle. "All right, then. Do they still teach the old tales of the Tuatha dé Danann, and how they went underground?"

"You mean the bargain with the Milesians?" Aodhan asked.

Da nodded. "That's the one; the Milesians were to get Ireland above ground, and the Tuatha dé Danann kept what's below. Kilstiffen is a doorway or portal, if you want to call it such, between our land and the one underneath. My Calliope was one of the portal's guards, tasked with keeping our worlds separate. To hear her tell it all was as it should be until a new military leader came to power, one who wished to use the portals for his own ends. Of course, most of those who lived in the city wanted to maintain their way of life and didn't support him. One by one, he ousted those who opposed him and set about building himself a new army. I'd bet my boat that man was Seamus MacCreehy."

"How did he do that?" Aodhan asked. "If his own people weren't interested in supporting him, where did he get followers?"

"The jumpers," I said, and Da nodded. "All those poor souls who went over the cliffs and were never found, whose families said they weren't depressed or unhappy. They all went down to Kilstiffen."

"And now that the seven year mark has come again, there's been an increase in jumpers," Kevin added. "It's been all over the news. The ones jumping, that is."

"Seven years?" I asked. "What's that got to do with anything?"

"The portal opens naturally every seventh year," Da replied. "Something about keeping a balance between our world and the one below."

I did a bit of maths in my head. "You met Mama twenty-one years ago, didn't you," I said, and Da confirmed it. "And she left seven years later."

"Aye, Meri girl, that she did." Da fingered the edge of his glass, but he didn't refill it. Not yet, anyway. "She'd promised to return to me during the next breach, but she didn't. Ever since then I've had no idea if she was alive or dead, but this," he paused to touch the sword, "this gives me hope."

Seven years ago, I'd been ten, and I remembered when Da hadn't come home for days; he'd been gone so long Kevin and I had started calling the local hospitals. Eventually, the guards dropped him off at the top of the driveway, with a stern warning for him to watch himself lest he end up with a permanent seat in the drunk tank. I'd always wondered why Da had suddenly turned the corner from drinker to drunk, and now I knew. Mama hadn't come back, and he'd been in mourning. He'd thought he'd lost her for good.

"Why did she come above in the first place?" Aodhan asked. "I get that she wanted to stop MacCreehy and all, but wouldn't that have been easier to do down in Kilstiffen?"

"The city within the portal doesn't rise and fall all on its own," Da replied. "The king has a key that opens and closes a special gate; without it, Kilstiffen stays put. Calliope stole the key and hid it somewhere above."

Aodhan slapped the table in triumph, jostling the glasses and spilling whiskey. "I knew the key was important!"

"Do you know where she hid it?" I asked.

Da shook his head. "She never told me, which was just as well. The more who know a secret, the more likely it is that the secret will be exposed."

"True." I regarded Mama's sword; the sunlight coming through the kitchen window was angled just so, and the blade shone like blue fire. "We must get her sword back to her. She's too vulnerable without it."

Da's brows lowered. "You believe all of this?"

"Of course I do," I said. "It's a relief, really, knowing I'm not crazy. Well, maybe I am, but not because of Mama."

"Have you any idea where her sword was found?" Kevin asked.

"Near where the Shannon meets the River Fergus," Aodhan replied. "By all accounts, it was just lying atop the riverbed, not silted over in the slightest. Couldn't have been there for very long."

"She must be nearby," I said. "Da, where would she go?"

He exhaled and ran a hand over his hair. "I can check a few of her old haunts tomorrow, and I will check them alone. Hear me out," Da said when I began protesting. "Those after her are very dangerous, and I can't have you getting tangled up with them. The last words I ever spoke to Calliope were an oath to keep you and your brother safe."

I opened my mouth again, but Kevin shook his head slightly. I decided to play along, at least for the moment. "What will you do if you find her?"

Da shrugged. "I'll begin by saying hello. That's how we started the last time. It'll do for the second." Da placed his hand on mine. "I know that's not what you want to hear, Meri girl, but what did you expect? That I wanted you to run off after her, and perhaps get tangled up with an army from down below?"

"I understand," I said, then I looked at Aodhan. "I think we'll be in a good bit of trouble for leaving school as we did."

"And there's the—" Aodhan began, but I shook my head. I didn't want to tell Da about the guards visiting our school. Not yet.

"The what?" Da prompted.

"The test. In maths," Aodhan replied.

Da glanced at the clock on the wall. "If you go back now, you should arrive just after lunch. If the school decides to make a case of it, we'll handle it then." Da squeezed my hand. "You are just like your mum, you know that? Kevin is cautious like me, but Calliope never thought twice about running toward danger rather than away from it."

"I've never run toward anything," I began. "I've always hidden away... But I ran toward the Cliffs last week. I guess something broke in me, then."

"Or something fell into place." Da smiled, and I saw tears well up in his eyes. "And now you may have found her again. You never gave up."

"I couldn't. I need her. We need her back here."

"Aye, Meri girl. That we do."

"You'll tell us what you learn tomorrow, when you go looking?"

"I surely will. As for now, I do need to finish up my workday. Give an old man a lift, Kevin?"

Kevin opened the kitchen door and held it for Da. "After you, old timer."

Da and Kevin left for the docks, leaving Aodhan and me sitting at the table with Mama's sword lying between us.

"Want to return to class?" I asked.

"Not on your life."

"Right then. What's our next move?"

"You tell me. You're the leader of our gang."

"You can't be a gang with just two," I said, then my phone chimed.

"It's a text from Kevin," I announced, then I tilted the screen toward Aodhan.

Kevin: Shannon Pot

"Looks like Kevin's our third," Aodhan said. "Now we've a proper gang."

"Does he want us to do a bit of cooking?" I mused.

Aodhan shook his head. "The source of the River Shannon is called the Shannon Pot."

Meri: The river's source?

Kevin: Yeah. It's one of Ma's shortcuts to below.

Kevin: Don't tell Da!

Meri: I won't. Thank you!

Kevin: Be safe.

I set down the phone and regarded Aodhan. "There's our move."

The Shannon Pot

One thing I hadn't realised while I was texting Kevin is that the Shannon Pot is in County Cavan. Not only was that a three-hour journey by car to the north and east, it was almost all the way to Northern Ireland.

"It's early yet, so we may as well make the trip today," Aodhan, the eternal optimist, said. "If for no other reason than we need to get this sword back to your ma as soon as we can."

I rubbed my hands up and down my arms. "But we'd be going so far. I've hardly ever been outside the county."

Aodhan shrugged. "You were bound to leave Clare again sooner or later. May as well be for a good cause, yeah?"

"What about your shop? Can you really be away from it for two days in a row?"

"I wasn't scheduled yesterday and I'm not scheduled tonight, since I'm supposed to be at practice. My workload's pretty light this time of year."

I glanced at the kitchen clock. It was almost noon. "I don't want you to miss practice on account of me."

"And I don't want you to miss out on possibly finding your mother on account of me."

"What about our classes?" I pressed.

"What about them?" When I didn't reply, Aodhan continued, "What, you want to go back to school and get interrogated by the guards, and then have to answer to MacCreehy? Or see what fresh hell Kelsey's drummed up?"

I opened my mouth to protest further—but Aodhan was right. I didn't want to return to The Saints. I was only arguing with Aodhan because returning to school would be the right thing to do. Well, right for who? Not me, or Da, or Kevin, and it certainly wouldn't be doing right by Mama. More than anything, I wanted to keep searching until I found her, or at least until we came across the next clue.

"All right, you've convinced me. Hang on while I find a jumper."

"Wonderful. I'll check the kitchen for supplies."

While Aodhan packed up snacks for the ride and filled our water bottles, I slipped into the dining room and checked the hutch for money, and got the shock of my life. My envelope was empty.

It had never, not once in all my years of going to it, been empty. Sometimes there was more money than others, but there had always been something. Now, when I truly needed the cash, the envelope was so barren there wasn't even dust in the corners.

I crumpled up the envelope and threw it to the floor. Da had been out drinking before noon, so he clearly had money of his own to waste, but I had nothing. Now, when I really needed it, I had nothing.

"It's not fair," I muttered.

"What's that?" Aodhan called from the kitchen.

"Just thinking out loud." I took a deep breath and dashed a hand across my eyes. I was the one who wasn't being fair. This was money Da had earned, not me. I had no rights to it, and he didn't have to share any of it with me. I had been visiting the hutch more often of late, what with Aodhan and I ordering takeaway as we did. Aodhan had offered to pay for my food more than once, and I knew he wouldn't mind footing the bill for whatever expenses came with this trip to County Cavan. I, however, wanted to pay my own way. What's more, even though the envelope had been empty, I still had plenty of money. I picked up the crumpled envelope off the floor, then I went into my bedroom and opened the cashbox hidden in my closet.

I dragged out the box and popped open the lid. As I stared at the neat pile of euros, I had a pang of doubt. I'd saved this money to eventually leave Clare, and I'd long since resolved to only use it for that or other truly important things. Since I was closer than I'd ever been to finding my mother, this qualified as important. Besides, what with Aodhan's shop and the possibility of finding Mama, it didn't look like I'd be leaving Clare anytime soon.

Wait—had I just decided to stay in Clare because of Aodhan?

I counted out twice as much money as I thought we'd need, then I slammed the lid on the cashbox while also mentally slamming the lid on that thought. If I remained in Clare after I left school—and that was a very big if—it would be my choice, and it wouldn't be because of some boy. Not even if that boy was Aodhan.

Jumper in hand, I stomped into the kitchen and saw Aodhan standing over the table as he packed up Kevin's lunch cooler. "Hey, Mer," he said when he saw me. "I found this lunchbox, so I made us some sandwiches for the ride. That way, we won't waste time trying to find something to eat."

And, my heart melted. Just like that, Aodhan made staying on in Clare seem not so bad, after all. "That was very thoughtful of you. Want to get going?"

"Surely."

Funds in hand and snacks sorted, Aodhan and I were on the road a few minutes later. I probably should have changed entirely instead of just grabbing a jumper and putting on my hiking boots, but for the first time in fourteen years—twice seven; it occurred to me then that Da had reckoned time in sevens ever since he'd met Mama—there was the very real possibility I could end up standing face to face with my mother. For an occasion that momentous, a dress was certainly in order.

"Don't fret so," Aodhan said. "You look great."

My face went hot as I slunk down in my seat. "Whatever that voice is from the sea is, one thing's for certain. It has addled my brain. I never used to think out loud."

"You've always done that. It's just that you mumble, and most aren't close enough to hear you."

I glanced sidelong at him. "And you always are?"

"Seems that way, eh?"

After a long and uneventful drive—save for Aodhan's reckless speeding—we arrived at the Shannon Pot; or rather, we parked near the metal gate that marked the beginning of the footpath that led to the site in question. It was a packed earth walkway, which was a welcome surprise. I'd been afraid of a repeat of our near fruitless hike as we pushed our way through the brush on Slieve Callan.

We exited the car, and I awkwardly fastened the sword belt around my hips. "Well, this is a bit obvious," I said, staring down at the sword. It was so long the tip of the scabbard dragged in the dirt, and heavy enough to make me list to the side.

"Is wearing a sword even legal?" Aodhan asked. "Perhaps we should leave it in the car."

My fingers closed around the hilt. "I don't want to leave it behind."

"Here, let's put it in my bag," he said. I hesitated, then I unbuckled the sword belt and handed it to Aodhan. Once it was secure in his duffle, he slung the bag across his shoulder. I'd wanted to be the one to carry the sword, but the duffle bag was a good idea since the sight of two teenagers wandering about the countryside with a massive weapon could garner us unwanted attention. Besides, it was heavy, and Aodhan was stronger than me.

We set off down the footpath, and soon enough we were standing on the shore of the Shannon Pot. It was a round pool about fifteen metres across, and it was fed from below by an aquifer; I'd had plenty of time during the ride up to do some research about the location on my phone. The pool's surface was calm, and it was surrounded by some low trees and shrubs. It was a nice spot, a place where normal families came on weekend outings to get some exercise or maybe have a picnic. Despite the picturesque view, both the vegetation and the water were silent on the subject of my mother and portals that may or may not lead to an undersea kingdom.

"There's nothing here," I said. We'd cut class and driven clear across the country only to reach another dead end. I clenched my fists and swallowed hard. "I-I can't believe it."

"Don't be so quick to judge," Aodhan said. "Let's take a walk 'round the edge."

He started walking, and I fell into step beside him. It was an easy path, which was wonderful since we'd spent so long stuck in the car. If nothing else, we got to stretch our legs a bit.

"If this is one of her shortcuts, how did she use it?" Aodhan mused.

"The sites I looked up said there's a chamber in the limestone below," I said. "Divers have mapped the entrance, but not the chamber itself. It's been deemed unstable and was never fully explored." I stared at the pool's glassy surface. "That's it, then. The way below must be through that chamber."

"Huh. It's literally below." Aodhan held his arm out in front of me, blocking my way. "Hang on. I hear people."

We retreated behind the shoreline trees, and watched as five warriors moved through the underbrush on the opposite side of the pool. They were dressed identically to the ones we'd run into at the museum the day prior, and all of them were armed with swords and shields. I grabbed Aodhan's shirtsleeve, wanting to draw him farther away from that lot, when I caught movement out of the corner of my eye. Several metres away from the group of warriors, another was emerging.

It was plain that this sixth person was a warrior as well, what with the leather armour she wore and the bronze shield strapped across her back. The newcomer's gender was betrayed by her slight form and long, plaited hair. But even though she was smaller than the others she wasn't weak; in fact, she carried herself with the confidence of one who'd fought and won many battles. Then I caught a glimpse of her gold mail skirt, and my breath caught it my throat.

A triangle-shaped patch of mail was missing over her left hip.

"It's her," I whispered. "Aodhan, that's my mother."

Aodhan squinted at her. "Are you sure?"

"Yes." I opened my mouth to call out to her, but Aodhan clamped his hand over my face. He shook his head and nodded toward the others.

"We're outnumbered," he said.

I pulled down his arm, and asked, "How do I tell her I'm here?"

Before he could reply, Mama raised a crossbow and fired at the group of five. One of the warriors fell, tumbling headfirst into the water. The splash alerted the other four, and they drew their swords. Another fell with a bolt protruding from her neck; they were down to three. I glanced at Mama and saw her duck behind the brush and out of their sight.

"Stop her," yelled one of the warriors. Mama stepped out from her hiding spot and set one foot in the water, her crossbow trained on him.

"Move, and it will be your last," Mama growled. The warrior hesitated, then my mother fired a warning bolt and dived into the pool, disappearing under the surface.

"No," I shrieked; after all this time I found her—I actually flipping found her—and after the barest moment she's gone again? Before I even got to speak to her? No.

No.

My shouting alerted the other warriors to our presence. Two stormed down the right side of the shore while the other took the longer route on the left, cutting off our escape.

Aodhan grabbed my arm. "Meri, we've got to go!"

"Not without my mother," I said, then I stepped into the pool. Cold water flooded my boots. "Dammit, I can't swim!"

Aodhan rearranged the duffle bag's strap across his chest. "I can, well enough for both of us." He grabbed my hand. "Go. I'll be right behind you."

I did the only thing I could do. I jumped in.

The Wormhole

I leapt further into the pool, with Aodhan splashing down beside me a moment later. We were still close to the shore, and the pool's waters only reached my hips. My dress was floating around me like a blue target. The frigid water chilled me, making my legs heavy as stone.

"S-So cold," I said.

"Got to keep going to stay warm," Aodhan said as he moved past me.

The remaining warriors bellowed for us to get back onto the shore, but we ignored them as we moved farther into the pool. We only made it a few more steps before the bottom dropped out from under us, and we hurtled through the icy water.

The water was so clear I could see as well underneath as I did on the surface. I could also hear a song, the vibrant, lilting notes surrounding me like a soft breeze. The song was familiar, like a dream I couldn't quite remember. And who in the world was singing underwater?

While I wondered where the sound originated from, we kept falling, and as we fell away from the surface the light was swallowed by the depths. The water got colder the farther down we went, deeper and deeper into the darkness. Eventually, there was a pinprick of blue light in the distance.

Aodhan swam toward the light. I grabbed his arm, and he pulled me along. My lungs should have been burning from lack of air, and I should have been having a panic attack from being underwater for so long. But I was calm. At peace.

Is this what drowning feels like?

We swam closer to the light, and finally saw the woman singing: my mother. Calliope; or rather, Aoife. Mama. She was floating just above the bottom of the chamber, her arms stretched out on either side of her, her mouth open and her song all around us. Suddenly I understood that it was her song allowing us to breathe, and that she was the one keeping us safe from the crushing weight of the water.

Mama saw me. I smiled. She shot through the water like a torpedo and grabbed my neck.

Thief!

I'm no thief!

Then how did you get this? Mama yanked the chain from my neck. *This isn't yours,* she said, shaking the pearl in front of my nose.

Mama, it's me! Your daughter!

Mama stilled. *Meri?*

It's me, Mama! I found the necklace in the old cottage. I've been looking for you!

Oh, Meri. Mama embraced me, and even though we were in the cold, dark water metres under the surface, I was happy. At long last, I'd found her. Then she drew back and frowned.

Meri girl, you must swim on, my lamb. I can't keep up this song and fight off the others.

But we've come to help you!

Never you mind helping me, Meri girl. This isn't a safe place.

I've missed you. Da and Kevin have, too.

She touched my cheek. *I've missed you, too. We will be together again, but not this way.*

If not this way, then how?

Mama's song ended, and she pressed the pearl into my hand. I gripped it as I felt the weight of the water against me, flattening my lungs and crushing my bones. Then she sang a single high note, and I was spiralling away from her. Aodhan grabbed my legs, and as we spun I saw the three remaining warriors from above hurtling past us in the opposite direction, straight toward my mother. I stole a final glance at her, so tiny in the distance.

Soon, my love.

I broke the surface of the water, splashing and sucking in great lungfuls of breath that were at least half liquid. Aodhan looped his arm underneath mine and swam us to the rocky shore. Once we were on land, I turned on to my side and spluttered up the last of the water while Aodhan rubbed my back.

"She sent me away," I croaked. "After all this time, after I finally found her, she sent me away."

"She did that because it wasn't safe," Aodhan said.

"You could hear her?"

"Yeah. The song, what you said to each other with that mind meld, everything." Aodhan cleared his throat. "I think this was as far as she could send us."

"We're only at the shore."

"Meri. Look around."

When we'd surfaced, I'd assumed we were still in the Shannon Pot. I took in our surroundings and saw that the surrounding meadow and tree lined shore were gone. Instead, we were huddled on the edge of a rectangular pool that appeared to have been carved from bare rock. I licked my lips and tasted salt. Any Irish could tell you that the River Shannon was fresh water.

"She sent us to the sea?"

"I think we're on Inis Mór." Aodhan craned his neck, getting a better look at this new, rugged landscape. "Yeah, they do cliff diving here."

I looked up at the cliffs. There weren't as high as Moher, but they were awfully far up from the water. "Why in God's name would anyone dive from up there?"

"Same reason as I surf. For the thrill of it." He looked from the cliffs to the pool. I could just see him calculating which spot was best for diving. "This pool's called the Wormhole. Fancy, eh?"

"Fancy." I sat up and regarded the grey stone that surrounded us. "Why would she send us here?"

"I don't know why she sent us here in particular, but she did this for you." Aodhan wrapped his arm around my shoulders and dragged me against his chest. "You saw how those others were after her. She was all by herself. She said couldn't look after us and fight them at the same time, and I believe her." He glanced at my throat. "Do you have the pearl?"

I opened my palm, revealing the pendant. The clasp was broken, but I supposed that could be repaired. My heart, not so much. "It's fine. Where's the sword?"

Aodhan swung the duffle around. "Safe, just like us."

Not like my mother.

"We didn't even give Mama back her sword," I said, remembering the warriors speeding toward her in the water.

Aodhan squeezed my shoulder. "We'll take care of that when next we see her."

We climbed up from the edge of the pool and followed the tourist signs until we reached the port, and the ferry dock. The ferry, in turn, brought us back to Doolin. As the boat chugged across the waves, I stared into them, desperately hoping to see my mother again. We'd found ourselves a seat near the back of the ferry, and I wiggled my toes in the sea breeze. I'd taken off my boots in the hopes they would dry out a bit before we reached the mainland.

"For our next adventure, I'd prefer it if we didn't get soaked every day," Aodhan said. He'd removed his runners and was wringing out his socks, and getting a few curious glances from other ferry riders. "Or maybe we should invest in a few waterproof packs. That way, we can always have dry clothes on hand."

I gave him some side eye. "You're already planning our next adventure? I can barely handle this one. I may not make it through a second."

"You're doing great, Mer," Aodhan said. "But we do need to sort out your swimming lessons."

Aodhan resumed seeing to his footwear, and I watched the clouds. He'd been trying to distract me with talk of adventures and swimming lessons, and while I appreciated his efforts, they hadn't worked in the slightest. All I could think about was tracking down Mama again; she'd lived in Clare for seven years, surely someone other than my father would have an idea of where she'd go, or with whom she might associate. I wracked my brain, trying to remember every single person who'd ever claimed to be friends with Mama, and remembered something that had been said recently at the Cliffs of Moher.

Once we reached Doolin, we went ashore with the rest. Unlike the rest who hurried into town, Aodhan and I took a moment, and we stood alongside the docks looking out over the sea.

"It's so beautiful," I said, staring at the waves. "I feel foolish for avoiding the sea all these years."

"You had your reasons," Aodhan said. "Where should we go next?"

"We need to go back to Moher," I said. "Cara will know what to do."

"Who is Cara?"

"She's the medic at the Visitor Centre. She helped me after... Well, you know. I think she may know how to reach my mother, and how to get down to Kilstiffen."

"How on earth can she do that?"

"She said something about secret mermaid meetings. Said she could sneak me into one."

Aodhan nodded. "Let's get going, then."

A Right Traitor

A odhan and I tended to experience good and bad luck in equal measures. The bad luck was that we'd left his car in County Cavan, and since it hadn't appeared alongside us on Inis Mór, we assumed that was where it remained. Hopefully, it wouldn't get stolen or towed away before we could figure out a way to retrieve it.

Our bit of good luck came in the form of a shuttle bus that ran between Doolin and the Cliffs of Moher every hour on the hour. Once we'd boarded the next scheduled departure, it was only a thirty-minute ride to the Visitor Centre. That gave me plenty of time to explain to Aodhan who exactly Cara was, and why I thought she could help us.

When we arrived at the centre, we disembarked with the rest of the tourists and headed inside the main building. It was a half hour till closing time; we'd made it by the skin of our teeth. We walked right past the displays about the environment and Moher's archeological and cultural history—though Aodhan did gaze longingly at the restaurant—as we went straight to the first aid room.

"Should we knock?" I asked.

"Would you knock if you'd been hurt?" Aodhan countered as he pushed the door open. Cara was seated at her desk, making notations in a small book. When she saw us, she stashed the book in a drawer and stood.

"Hello there," she said. "I remember you. Meri, is it?"

"Yes, and this is Aodhan," I said. Aodhan waved. "I'm sorry to burst in like this, but do you remember how you said I could talk to you?"

"I do." Cara's gaze moved to Aodhan and back to me. "Would you like to speak alone?"

"Aren't we alone?" When Cara looked pointedly at Aodhan, I said, "Oh, he can stay. Have you ever heard of Kilstiffen?"

She tilted her head to the side as her brows pinched. "Kilstiffen? Why, yes, there's an exhibition about it in the Legends of the Cliffs area. Has something happened near the display?"

"No, I mean real Kilstiffen," I said. "I saw my mother earlier today, and I think that's where she's going."

"I thought your mother had been gone for fifteen years."

"Fourteen. But she's recently returned, and we need to help her. Do you know the way there?"

"To Kilstiffen? The city at the bottom of the sea?"

"Yes, that's right."

Cara nodded. "All right. Wait here."

About thirty minutes later, Aodhan said, "Cara turned out to be a right traitor."

I frowned at him, but he was correct. "Sorry."

"It's all right, Mer. We'll find our way out of this."

I appreciated Aodhan's optimism, but we'd really stepped in it this time. When Cara had left Aodhan and me in her office, we thought she'd gone for help to get us down to Kilstiffen, or at least hand over a map or a set of directions so we could go there on our own. She went for help all right, but it was help to get "two teenage pranksters away from the paying visitors".

Like Aodhan said, traitor.

When Cara returned, she'd been accompanied by two park representatives. They escorted Aodhan and me into a smaller, greyer office, and as luck would have it, also in attendance was the ranger who'd been present during our school trip. Of course, he recognised me as the potential jumper who was also Brian Murphy's daughter. That same ranger took a peek inside Aodhan's duffle, and almost had a heart attack when he saw Mama's sword. That was when the park officials called the garda, along with our parents.

Aodhan's mother beat the garda by twenty minutes.

"I just can't believe the two of you," Mrs Dumhach said as she paced across the security office. "First, I find you in bed together, and now you're skipping class and terrorising people with a sword!"

"We weren't 'in bed'," I muttered. "Not like that."

"It was really just an air mattress," Aodhan said, rather unhelpfully.

"Where did you get a sword? No, no, don't answer that. I don't know if my heart can take it." Mrs Dumhach crossed her arms over her chest and shook her head. "It's that school. I know it is. Did you know that two of your classmates were being questioned by the garda on school grounds, and they attacked the headmaster and ran off?"

Aodhan and I froze. The only sound in the office was of Mrs Dumhach's heels clicking against the floor. "Why were the guards at The Saints?" Aodhan asked.

"Something about a theft at a museum. When I was at The Saints, it was an excellent school, but now it's full of criminals and delinquents. Both of you have obviously felt their influence." She stopped pacing and faced Aodhan. "I don't know what I'm going to do with you. Lucas would have known."

Before anyone could say anything further, Da entered the office. I leapt to my feet and blurted out, "I didn't mean for any of this to happen!"

Da smiled, albeit a bit sadly. "I know you didn't, Meri girl," he said, his voice steady and his eyes clear. Thank God he had sobered up after lunch. "Come along, now. We'll get this sorted out and I'll take you home."

"We're going too, Aodhan." Mrs Dumhach held out her hand. "Give me your car keys. You've lost your driving privileges."

"Ah, the car is in County Cavan," Aodhan said.

"What?" Mrs Dumhach shrieked, as she glared at me. "You home wrecking harpy! What have you done to my son?"

"Who are you to call me a home wrecker?" I shot back. "You wrecked your own home long before I came along!"

"How dare you," Mrs Dumhach began, her hands trembling. "You...you—"

"That's enough, from both of you," Da said, his voice booming in the small office. "Meredith, you know better than to speak to your elders in such a manner. And as for you, Bridgette, I remember your youth well enough to be certain you should not be throwing stones."

Mrs Dumhach purpled. "I'll not listen to the likes of you on proper behaviour, Brian Murphy. Come along, Aodhan. For all I care, your car can stay in Cavan, and you're still grounded."

"No, Ma." Aodhan remained seated.

"What do you mean, no?" Mrs Dumhach demanded. "You are my child living in my house, and you will obey me!"

"I'm not a child," Aodhan retorted. "I'm eighteen, and I own my own business. You can't punish me like I'm a kid!"

"As long as you live in my house, I can!"

"Then I'll live at the shop."

"You cannot do that!"

"Why can't I?" Aodhan countered. "I'm the sole owner of the shop. I can do whatever I want with it."

"But it's no place to live," she began, but Aodhan waved it away.

"Like home is? With your husband refusing to acknowledge me? I've been sleeping at the shop every night for almost two years. When did you even notice that?"

Mrs Dumhach pressed her lips together as her eyes welled up. Da coughed, and it startled her, as if she'd forgotten he and I were there. "Fine. Keep house with your tart in the back of a shop. I want your property out of my family's home by tomorrow evening."

Aodhan nodded. "Very well."

She turned and stormed out of the office, shoving one of the guards in the process. Da stood and nodded toward the door. "All right then, Meri girl. We'd best be on our way, the sooner the better. I'll have a word or two with the officials."

Da ambled toward the front desk and spoke to the ranger and the guards. While he signed a few forms, Aodhan leaned close to me.

"We have to get the sword back," he whispered.

"But how?" I whispered back.

Da returned, standing over us like a mountain. He had Aodhan's duffle bag slung over his shoulder, and his car keys jangled in his hand. "We can leave now. Aodhan, would you like a lift into town?"

"Yes, sir. Thank you, sir."

The three of us were silent as we walked through the visitors' centre, with the employees' gazes following us all the way to the door. I didn't see Cara skulking about, which was just as well. I don't know if I could have been civil with her.

"Sorry I yelled at your mother," I said to Aodhan.

"Don't fret, Meri," Aodhan said. "She did yell at you first."

"Maybe after she calms down a bit, I'll write her an apology letter."

"That's more like it," Da said over his shoulder. "Perhaps bake her an apology cake, too."

My shoulders slumped. "Yes, Da."

Once we got to the car, Da put Aodhan's bag in the boot, then we piled inside. I looked toward the sea, but a warning glare from Da made me face forward.

"Meri, you may have just used up your last bit of fortune," Da said as he pulled onto the main road. "The guards have agreed to not press any charges against either of you, though truth be told, I don't know what they could get you on. And you're both banned from the Visitor Centre, and the nearby trails."

"Forever?" I squeaked.

"Not forever, but for the next five years. Once that's passed, you can petition the management to have the decision overturned." Da glanced in the rearview mirror. "Aodhan, I took the liberty of signing on your behalf. I hope you don't mind."

"I don't. Thank you, sir."

"How will we ever get Mama's sword back?" I asked.

"It's in the boot," Da replied. "I slipped it into Aodhan's bag while they weren't looking."

"You stole evidence?" I demanded. "What if they realise it's gone and they question you?"

"If anyone ever comes 'round looking for it, I'll say it's a family heirloom." Da flexed his fingers on the steering wheel. "So. You went to the Pot."

"Da, we saw her there, in the water. Mama."

He swallowed hard. "Did you. How... How is she?"

"Like a badass warrior queen," Aodhan said. I twisted around and glared at him. "Sorry," he mumbled.

"She was fighting a bunch of other warriors, with a crossbow," I said. "We tried to follow her, but she sang us away."

"Ah, her voice," Da said. "I dream of her voice almost every night."

"Da! Open your eyes!"

"What? Oh." He made a show of concentrating on the road. "When we get home, you'll tell me everything, yeah?"

"We will. Promise."

"Aodhan, I understand that you're a business owner and a legal adult and such, but we do have a bit of room in our farmhouse if you'd like to stay with us, at least for a day or so," Da said. "I'd even wager that Kevin will assist you with collecting your belongings."

"Really?" Aodhan said. "That would be wonderful."

"There are, however, rules you must abide by," Da continued. "There are not, nor will there ever be, any air mattresses in my home."

"Da," I squeaked. Now I knew he'd heard at least some of Mrs Dumhach's complaints. "I told you it wasn't like that!"

Da's gaze slid toward me, then back to the road. "I trust both of you understand my meaning?"

"Yes sir, of course," Aodhan said. "No air mattresses, not ever."

"I've never been so embarrassed in all my life," I muttered.

"Imagine how I feel," Da said.

"I do appreciate your offer, Mr Murphy," Aodhan interjected. "I swear on my dad's memory that I will uphold your rules, every single one of them. Thank you for all your help today, really."

Da sighed. "No thanks are needed. You and Meri have just confirmed that my Calliope is still alive, and that she's here in Ireland. I need nothing more."

Gold Bars And Shepherd's Pie

K evin did indeed offer to drive Aodhan to his family's home so he could collect his clothes, sports gear, and various other possessions. I imagine my brother helped further by carrying a few bags and boxes, or perhaps he offered a bit of moral support. Kevin was always ready to lend a shoulder, or an ear, when needed.

While they were gone, Da went to the market to pick up some ingredients for dinner, and I set up Aodhan's room. How funny that I already considered it his room, when he had yet to spend a night in it. Our old farmhouse had plenty of spare bedrooms, and since it was at the edge of the village, we also had plenty of privacy. Add to our remote location the old fields and overgrown gardens that surrounded the house, and we also had our share of solitude. It meant that we could largely do what we wanted without fear of nosy neighbours or curious passersby. It was the perfect place to hide a rogue warrior from Kilstiffen, especially if that rogue happened to be the king's daughter.

The farm had been in my family for generations. Back when Da was young, he'd had notions of opening one of those farm to table restaurants, and of growing as much of the produce as he could right here on the farm. It was why he'd followed in his uncle's footsteps and become a fisherman, so he could have access to the freshest possible salmon, char, and sea trout, though he'd never gone after freshwater fish. Even in his ambitious days, he'd been content to leave the coarse fish to the hatcheries. But then he'd gone out alone on his boat one day, and heard a woman singing in the distance...

Well, you know the rest.

Da returned from the market, and we fell into a familiar rhythm as we prepared dinner. "Da, I have to tell you something," I said.

"Are you pregnant?"

"Da!" My peeler clattered into the sink as I faced him. "You know I'm not! Why does everyone keep asking me that?"

"Perhaps it's because you turned up in bed with Aodhan."

My shoulders slumped. "Did you hear everything Mrs Dumhach said?"

"I heard enough." He wiped his hands on a towel. "What do you need to tell me?"

"Did you hear her mention the students that eluded the garda at The Saints?" I asked, and he nodded. "That was Aodhan and me, but it didn't happen the way she said."

Da began slicing vegetables, but very slowly. "What did happen?"

"The guards were there at school, but Aodhan and I never talked to them. We were in the car park, and MacCreehy came up to us and acted like he wouldn't let us leave. So I told him in a song to let us go."

Da stilled. "You sang, and he obeyed you?"

"He did! And then, at the Pot, Mama sang us away." I looked at my reflection in the window above the sink. I swallowed, and watched a tear leak out of my eye. "I sing all the time, but I've never done anything like that. It... It comes from her, doesn't it?"

"It does." Da pulled me against him, and for a moment I was a small child again, and the only thing in the world that would make me feel better was a hug from my da. "It's nothing to be afraid of. It's something natural to your mother's people, and now to you."

"I'm like her?"

"Aye, Meri girl. You are so much like her." Da wiped my cheek with his thumb. "I wish Calliope were here so she could help you with this."

"I hope we find her soon," I said into Da's woollen jumper. "I need her so much."

"Aye. We all do."

We broke apart a moment later, and returned to our tasks. "Meri?"

"Yes, Da?"

"Why were the guards at The Saints?"

"The museum, the one where we found Mama's sword. An archaeologist was killed there." I stared at the knife in my hand. "I saw his body."

"Did you see who killed him?"

I shivered, remembering his ice cold skin. "He was dead long before we got there. I-I touched him, and he was already cold."

Da grunted. "Good. Time of death is a good ally for the innocent."

"Perhaps. MacCreehy said they had us on surveillance."

"That was probably a lie," Da said. "If the guards knew your identity, they either would have picked you up at the Cliffs or they'd be here now. No, Meri girl, I don't think that's a worry for the top of our list. Not today, anyway."

"Are you sure?"

Da smiled at me. "I'm never sure, but I do have a great deal of hope."

That was one thing about Da, he always had hope enough to spare. By the time Kevin and Aodhan returned, Da and I had just finished preparing dinner.

"How did it go?" I asked when Aodhan stepped into the kitchen. I glanced into the front room, and saw a few suitcases and bags heaped up near the door. Aodhan's entire life with his family, reduced to a few bits of luggage.

"No one was home, so it went quite well," Aodhan replied. "I know my stepfather's at work right now, but Ma must have taken my little sisters out on some errands." His throat worked, and for a terrible, heart-stopping moment I thought he would cry. Then he smelled the food.

"What's all this, then?" Aodhan wandered further into the kitchen; trust that boy to always be thinking with his stomach rather than his brain. "You've made... potato muffins?"

"They're shepherd's pies, but I cooked them in muffin tins," I replied. I'd piped out the mashed potatoes before broiling them so they looked like cupcakes. "That way we each have our own individual servings. I also roasted some cabbage wedges and carrots for a side dish, and of course, there's bread."

Kevin entered the kitchen, and stopped dead when he saw dinner resting on the hob. "Da, why did you let her do that to the pie?"

"It's cuter this way," I said.

"Da," Kevin pleaded.

"Meri was in charge of dinner, and I only did what I was told," Da said. "I did, however, make my special onion gravy for the pies."

Kevin grunted, then he helped himself to two of the pies and half the pan of gravy. Da only shook his head, and I got to filling up the rest of the plates.

"You get your talent for cooking from your dad," Aodhan said after sampling a spoonful of gravy. "Don't you?"

"Da is the best cook in Ireland," I said. "He used to cook all the time, before... Before he got too busy on his boat. Here you are," I added as I set a plate in front of Aodhan.

"Thank you," Aodhan said. "All of you," he added.

"A friend of Meri's is always a friend of ours," Da said. "Now let's eat while everything's still hot."

We tucked into our plates, making small talk and passing rolls as if Aodhan and I hadn't been traipsing across the country earlier today as we chased magical warriors, and my mother. What's more, my mother was one of those magical warriors.

As I chewed my food, I thought about Mama. She'd been both beautiful and fierce, brandishing her crossbow and taking out two of the others before escaping into the pool. And her voice... I'd never heard anything like it.

No, that wasn't true. I'd heard a similar voice many times, in recordings of my own singing. And earlier, when I'd sung at MacCreehy until he let us leave school grounds. What else was my voice capable of?

"If Mama is some kind of super powered warrior general, what does that make Kevin and me?" I looked across the table at Da. "What does that make you?"

"In hiding," Kevin answered without looking up from his plate.

"That's enough," Da said.

"Well, aren't we?" Kevin challenged. "You're pretending at being a drunk who's lost his mind, and Meri and I are just going through the motions of life. Yet for all your antics at the pub, we've got plenty of money, more than any half-pissed fisherman should be able to bring in."

I winced; Kevin's words were accurate, but harsh.

"Perhaps Da couldn't do more," I said. "Were you sworn to silence?"

"More like I lived in fear that they may come and take my children away like they'd taken my wife, and that I'd die alone," Da said. "Can we discuss this after dinner?"

I started to say that no, we could not discuss things after dinner. I'd already been waiting fourteen years for answers, and I didn't want to wait a moment longer. Then I remembered Da's words, that he'd been living in fear that something might happen to me or Kevin. He had lived with that fear all this time, all to keep his family safe. In light of his sacrifice, the least I could do was let him finish his meal.

"That seems fair," I said at length.

The rest of dinner was uneventful. We ate in silence, with even good-natured Aodhan keeping his thoughts to himself. As for me, I was so anxious I could hardly eat.

After the dishes had been washed, dried, and put away, I made tea and we all retired to the sitting room.

"I promised that we would tell you everything that happened to us at the Shannon Pot," I began, and Aodhan and I proceeded to tell Da and Kevin about the warriors tracking Mama, how she'd fought them, and how we'd jumped into the water after her. My voice cracked when I described how she'd sung us away; Aodhan squeezed my hand, and finished off the story from our arrival at Inis Mór to getting the guards called on us by Cara the Evil Medic.

"You told Meri about the doorway below Shannon Pot," Da said to Kevin once we were finished, proving that he'd missed nothing.

Kevin shrugged. "I didn't think they'd take off and go immediately."

"Yeah, well, you know me. Crazy Meri Murphy." After we'd all stared into our mugs for a few moments, I asked, "Are we really in hiding?"

"No. Yes." Da got up, grabbed the whiskey, and topped off his tea. "I always assumed that if I played the part of the drunk whose wife had left him, they would assume that I believed it all a legend." He turned the whiskey bottle around and scrutinised the label. "Perhaps I played my part a bit too well."

"Who are 'they'?" I asked.

"The ones Calliope was running from," Da replied. "The ones who think they can keep the portal open at all times."

"Why would anyone want to do that?" Aodhan asked.

Da shrugged. "For the same reasons any fool does such things. They create a plan that they believe will make them powerful, and that power then leads to money, influence, and whatever else they think they want."

"Power," I repeated. "But what they really want is control."

"What better way to control others, than to have a line straight to their children?" Aodhan asked.

I darted into my bedroom and retrieved the folder of police reports, and set the one concerning MacCreehy and his missing daughter in front of Da. "Have you ever spoken to Seamus MacCreehy?"

Da shook his head. "I know he became the school's headmaster the year before Kevin started attending The Saints. I've never once seen him in person."

"That's odd in and of itself," I said. "Everyone in this town knows everybody else, save for you and MacCreehy."

"Maybe there's a reason for that," Aodhan said. "Maybe he thinks you'll recognise him, and somehow warn Calliope."

"How could I warn her when I haven't seen her myself in over fourteen years?" Da asked.

"He doesn't know you haven't seen her," I said. "You're on your boat every day. Maybe he assumes you're meeting her somewhere out on the water."

"If only I were." Da traced the photocopied picture of Mama that had been taken the day he'd brought her to the garda station. "These warriors you encountered at Shannon Pot. Was MacCreehy among them?"

"He wasn't," Aodhan said. "I get the impression he's not a warrior so much as someone who gives orders."

"Are you sure about that?" I asked. "He had all those swords that time at school."

Aodhan grunted. "Yeah, there's that."

I glanced at Kevin, and asked, "What about the money?"

"What about it?" Da countered.

"Kevin's right," I said. "We've always got plenty of money stashed about, yet you're a fisherman who works alone. How many fish could you possibly catch without anyone to help you?"

"And how much are you selling them for?" Kevin added.

Da ran a hand through his hair. "The money is from your mother. Her family is well off, and after we were married, she went to her father and demanded her dowry." He laughed to himself. "She came home with gold."

"Gold coins, like pirate treasure?" I asked.

"Worse. She returned with actual gold bars. It took us a donkey's year to find a bank what would accept them."

I sat back against the cushions. "If we're rich, why don't we have a maid?"

Da gave me a look. "Afraid the broom'll give you a splinter, now?"

"Wait," Aodhan said. "First you said her family was well off, then you said her dowry was actual gold bars." He whipped out his phone and started typing. "Says here a standard gold bar is four hundred troy ounces. The current spot price for gold is one thousand twenty-eight point thirty-three, and multiple that by four hundred…" Aodhan stared at his screen for a moment. "Exactly how many bars were there?"

"It took ten men from her world to carry them," Da replied.

Aodhan flopped back against the couch. "Wow."

"We have gold bars. Great. So what are we going to do now?" Kevin asked. "We know Ma's nearby, and we know there are people after her. How can we help her?"

"First, we need to find her," I said.

"Maybe we just need to track down the ones who're after her," Aodhan said.

"What do you mean?" I asked.

"Well, they may be after your ma, but after what we saw earlier, it's plain that she's after them too," Aodhan said. "Perhaps we should hang around the docks tomorrow and keep an eye on whoever's keeping an eye on you, Mr Murphy."

"I don't know if that's a good idea," I said in a rush. "What if I try to jump into the sea again?"

"I don't think you will," Aodhan said. "You were fine on Inis Mór, and after that at the Cliffs. You were fine when we rode the ferry to Doolin, too."

"Huh." Aodhan was right; I'd spent hours on or near the sea and hadn't once felt its call. "I wonder if Mama's song gave me a sort of immunity."

"Maybe it did," Aodhan said. "Besides, you won't be alone. Kevin and I will be there, and we won't let you hop into the waves. Will we, Kevin?"

"I suppose not," Kevin said. I stuck my tongue out at him.

"What do you think, Da?" I asked. "Can we come to work with you tomorrow?"

Da drained his mug in one gulp and refilled it straight from the whiskey bottle. "This'll be a right disaster."

We all went to bed shortly after we'd finalised our plans to go down to the docks with Da the next morning. Neither Da nor Kevin thought it was a particularly good idea; Da because of the danger posed to his children and Aodhan, and Kevin due to the early hours Da kept. Kevin hadn't risen earlier than ten since before he'd taken his transition year.

As for me, I thought our plan was brilliant, and an excellent way to get a leg up on whomever was behind Mama having to leave us all those years ago, with the added benefit of paving the way for her return. That confidence didn't lend well to sleep, and I found myself staring up at my ceiling well after midnight. Finally, I gave up and went to Aodhan's room.

Aside from an abundance of dilapidated garden rows and neglected sheep pens, living in an old farmhouse meant that on those rare occasions when we had overnight guests, everyone got their own room. I'd set up Aodhan's on the second floor, a door down from Kevin, so he could have his privacy but not be too far from the rest of us. As I crept up the stairs and across the corridor in the dark of night, I wished I'd put him next to my own room.

I stared at his closed door for what felt like an hour. More than anything, I wanted to talk to him, but he needed as much sleep as he could get before we set out tomorrow. For that matter, so did I, and if I had an ounce of sense, I'd turn right around and return to my own room. If there is one truth about me, it's that when it came to Aodhan, I didn't have any sense.

I knocked softly on his door. I didn't have to wait long for an answer.

"Yeah?"

I cracked the door. "It's me. May I enter?"

"Yeah."

I entered the room and carefully shut the door behind me, then I faced Aodhan. He was sitting up in bed, an open book in his lap. I assumed it was from the bookshelf on the far side of the room. "I, ah, couldn't sleep."

"Me neither." Aodhan shut the book and moved to one end of the bed, then he drew back the blanket. "Pull up a pillow. We can be insomniacs together."

I took a step toward him and froze. I'd just snuck into a boy's room in the dead of night. Earlier I'd been adamant to both my father and Aodhan's mother that nothing had happened between us, and here I was, standing in front of him in my pyjamas.

"I should go," I said.

"If you like, but I promise there's no air mattresses here."

He smiled. I laughed. Thus disarmed, I sat on the foot of the bed, my back against the wall. Aodhan tossed me his pillow and moved so he was leaning on the wall beside me.

"I never realised your house is so big," he said. "It's hard to tell from the front, but you've got all these grand rooms. I should have figured it was big, what with the gardens out back."

"I should give you a tour," I said. "I'd forgotten that you've really only seen the kitchen and part of the garden."

"The kitchen is the best room in any house."

"With the way you eat, if you ever stop running or surfing you'll end up weighing twenty stone. Thirty, maybe."

"Then I'd better not stop."

We smiled at each other, then I remembered we were sitting next to each other on an actual bed. I rubbed my sweaty palms on my legs and stared at my lap.

"I got you something," he said.

"You did?"

"Yeah, I found it in my room when I cleared out my stuff." Aodhan leaned over and grabbed something from the bedside table. "Hold out your hand." I did, and he dropped a gold chain onto my palm.

"What's this for?" I asked.

"The pearl," he replied. "It's not as fine as the one from the cottage, but I figured that since the clasp broke on the other chain, you needed a new one."

I poked the chain in my palm, feeling the smooth links. "Thank you, Aodhan. I really appreciate this. And you."

He blushed, thus becoming the most adorable person to ever exist. "Do you have the pearl? I can help you put it on."

"I do."

I withdrew the pearl from my pocket and threaded it onto the chain, then I handed it to Aodhan and lifted my hair. After he fastened the chain, his fingers lingered on my neck.

"Thank you," I said. "Again."

He brushed my hair over my shoulder. "You're welcome. Again."

"I'm glad you're here," I said at length. "You don't have to be, though. This is my family's problem, and I've just been dragging you along, and now your mother is so mad—"

"Meri. It's all right." He put his hand on mine. I repositioned my hand so he wouldn't feel my clammy palm. "I'm here of my own free will, and I'm glad to be."

I closed my eyes and leaned my head back against the old floral wallpaper. If Aodhan stayed much longer, we'd probably have to re-decorate to a more masculine theme.

Good God, even my stray thoughts were trying to distract me. What girl worries about redecorating the first time she's on a bed with a boy? And not just any boy. Aodhan.

Actually, he's eighteen. He's a man.

I opened my eyes just wide enough and watched Aodhan. He was examining my hand where it lay in his, rubbing his thumb across my fingernails. There was so much I wanted to ask him, but I didn't want to start that just yet. We had unfinished business to see to, and that needed to get done before we could address what was growing between us. After all, what if this was nothing more than friendship?

Aodhan laced his fingers with mine and squeezed. If this was just friendship, he was the best friend I could hope for.

I swallowed hard, and asked, "What do you think will happen tomorrow?"

"Honestly? I haven't the foggiest. But it will happen to both of us, and we'll figure it out together."

My gaze dropped to our entwined hands. "I guess we will."

CAVES

"Meri! Kevin! Aodhan! Time's a wasting," Da bellowed up the stairwell. The sun hadn't yet risen, but according to him, that was the best time to get out on the water. As if fish could tell time. "Five minutes or I'm leaving without any of you."

I dragged myself out of bed and stumbled toward my closet. Luckily, I'd had the forethought to lay out my clothes the night before, or who knows what I would have ended up wearing.

Four and a half minutes after Da's wake-up call, I entered the kitchen wearing jeans, a jumper layered over a long-sleeved knit shirt, and my hiking boots. Those boots had served me well on Slieve Callan and at the Shannon Pot, and I hoped they'd continue bringing me good fortune. I supposed I was becoming a bit superstitious. Then again, after all of the weird events that had happened as of late, it was only to be expected.

Aodhan thundered down the stairs a moment after me, clad in a blue athletic suit and matching runners. Kevin was standing at the counter wearing his usual beat up jeans and denim jacket, managing the coffee. I was glad he'd thought to brew a pot. Da was standing in the centre of the room with his arms crossed over his chest, clad in the first few layers of his fisherman's gear. I knew he kept his waterproof hat and jacket, waders, and heavy gloves on his boat. I hoped he had a spare set for whomever ended up on the boat with him.

"The lot of you are no early risers," Da said, shaking his head. "Get moving. The fish won't wait for us to catch up."

The four of us went out into the pre-dawn darkness and set out for the docks. "Want me to drive?" Kevin asked.

"Not today," Da replied. "I always walk to my boat. If there really are people watching me and I arrive by way of the car this morning, they may become suspicious."

"I may fall asleep on my feet, thus making me much easier to spot," I muttered. Aodhan elbowed me, presumably so I'd quiet down. Kevin passed me a travel mug filled with coffee, which did a better job.

The harbour was a short walk down the hill from our house. The rain was holding back, but the air was frigid, thanks to the bone-chilling wind blowing in off the sea. Despite the icy wind, several others were already on their boats, and called out greetings to Da as he ambled past. When we got to Da's boat, we stood next to the ramp in a loose circle, squinting and shivering in the pre-dawn darkness.

"We're here. What's next?" I asked.

"I'll go on the boat with Da," Kevin said. "That way, I can spot anyone spying on us from the water. You two keep watch here on land, and call me if you see anything."

"That will also keep Meri off the sea, and safer," Aodhan added.

"All right, then," I said. "You two on sea, and us on land." I turned to go when Da caught me in a bear hug.

"Stay out of the water," Da said. "If you hear singing, don't go near it. Even if it sounds like your mother, stay away. If you hear singing, grab on to Aodhan and don't let go."

"I will, Da." I squeezed him tighter than I had since I was a wee thing. "I promise."

We parted, and Da turned to Aodhan. "Keep watch over her," Da said.

"I will, sir," Aodhan said. "I promise."

Da and Aodhan shook hands, then my father and Kevin boarded the boat.

I watched Da and Kevin on the boat, sympathising with my poor confused brother, scratching his head as he eyed the controls. I remembered how clueless I'd been when I was out with Aodhan on the surf shop's boat.

After a few minutes, Aodhan and I wandered away from where Da's boat was moored. We walked the length of the horseshoe-shaped docks and back again. We hung around the harbour for the better part of an hour, long after Da and Kevin had set off, and didn't find a single thing out of the ordinary.

"If anyone's watching your dad's boat from the harbour, they're invisible," Aodhan concluded. The rest of the fishermen were gone, and there wasn't another person as far as I could see. "The rest of the boats have set out. We're the only ones left here."

"What should we do now?" I asked. "We can't just keep pacing up and down the docks. If anyone is watching Da, the two of us hanging about will be too obvious."

"Agreed," Aodhan said. "But where to? I don't think anything will open up for a few hours yet."

"Still, I'd rather not skulk about in the dark any more than necessary." As the words left me, I saw a white car with a familiar yellow and blue pattern roll slowly past the docks.

"Do the garda often patrol the harbour?" I asked, nodding toward the vehicle. Aodhan glanced at it, his shoulders stiffening.

"I really don't know," he replied. "Maybe it's on their route? In any case, I think we'd best be gone before they return."

"But where should we go?"

"Hmm."

Aodhan rubbed his chin, then he halted and did a full rotation as he took in our surroundings. "What do we know so far? The Tuatha dé Danann are below, we're up here, and Kilstiffen is what keeps us apart. Whoever your mother was fighting wanted to bring everything together. And what do we think MacCreehy wants?"

"I'd wager he's in the camp that doesn't want above and below separate anymore, and therefore he's not on my mother's side," I replied. "Which is complicated by the fact that Kilstiffen should be rising soon, and that the key remains missing." I considered our experiences with Kilstiffen's warriors at the museum and at the Shannon Pot. "Have you ever seen warriors like those before?"

He didn't ask for clarification. "Outside of a movie or documentary? Never."

"Yet we've encountered them twice in two days. Do you think Kilstiffen rises in stages, thus allowing their warriors to come up to the surface a few at a time? Maybe the key is only needed for the final stage."

"Perhaps. It would also explain why we're encountering them now, and haven't before." Aodhan regarded me for a moment. "Although, we would have been ten and eleven the last time they were about. Would we really remember a few blokes wearing odd kits?"

"Maybe not, but that's not what I'm wondering." I tapped my chin with my forefinger. "How are they getting around now? The ones at Shannon Pot couldn't navigate the water as well as my mother, and I haven't heard any of them sing. They must have a different route between worlds."

"Maybe they use the sea?" Aodhan offered, then I remembered the water-filled caves below the surface of Shannon Pot.

"Caves!" I snapped my fingers. "I'll bet you they're using caves to come up."

"That makes sense," he said.

"But the question is, which caves? Da won't be happy if we go poking about the sea caves again."

"There are plenty of caves to be had right here on dry land." Aodhan whipped out his phone and keyed in a few things. "There's one nearby that lay undiscovered until less than one hundred years ago. People that have been inside have called it right magical. Want to go have a look?"

"You know I'm going to say yes."

While the harbour was within walking distance of my house, the cave in question was not. Since buses wouldn't start running for some time yet, and taking Aodhan's car wasn't an option, I sent a text to Kevin.

Meri: Where are the car keys?
Kevin: Why do you need those?
Meri: We need to borrow the car.
Kevin: For...?

Meri: We're looking for ways below.

Kevin: Caves?

Meri: How much are you not telling me?!?

Kevin: In the basket near the hot press. Grab the bolt cutters from the garden shed.

Meri: Why would I need those?

Kevin: To get into the cave.

JEWEL OF THE SEA

Aodhan and I returned to my house and set about assembling an amateur spelunking slash warrior hunting kit in his eminently useful duffle bag. Once that was done, I grabbed the keys from the basket, and Aodhan drove Da's car to the cave he'd looked up earlier.

"How did you know about this cave?" I asked, as Aodhan navigated the dark and twisty streets.

"To use your term, it's a tourist trap," he replied. "We get plenty of tourists in the shop, and some leave behind brochures about other spots. This cave seems rather popular with those travelling by coach."

"Aren't those tours usually made up of older folks?"

"Yeah, usually."

"Interesting, that some travel agent has them out visiting surf shops and crawling around caves."

Aodhan shrugged. "Just because you're on in years doesn't mean you can't have adventures. My father was still winning martial arts and surfing competitions in his fifties."

I nodded, not wanting to debate the average tourist's athletic ability, but I did wonder if any of them had ended up going over the Cliffs.

Soon enough, we found the sign for the cave in question. We parked in the designated area and walked down the path that led to the entrance. Since it was hours before opening time—and sunrise; how I loved bumbling about in the dark—the entrance was locked. Kevin had been spot on with his suggestion of bolt cutters. Not to mention that if we waited for the site to open, I don't think those working in the ticket kiosk would have been too keen on what we were up to.

"Do you think there's an alarm?" I asked. "Or surveillance cameras?"

"This all looks pretty rustic to me," Aodhan replied, and I did not disagree. The entrance, a stacked stone doorway topped with a massive lintel, was dug into the hillside. It looked more like a root cellar than a tourist attraction. The entry itself was closed off with a glorified metal garden gate secured by a heavy chain and padlock.

"Still, just because it looks old and shoddy doesn't mean they don't have alarms," I pressed. "I really don't want to get picked up for breaking and entering."

"Only one way to find out." Aodhan took the bolt cutters out of his bag, then he used them to snap the gate's lock in half. It took him three tries before the weathered hunk of metal gave way. Aodhan pushed the gate open, the metal creaking ominously against its hinges.

"It's like we're extras in a cut rate horror movie," Aodhan muttered.

"Don't the extras often perish early on?"

"Um. Yeah."

"Wonderful." I peered into the entrance. It was pure blackness. "Think there're any lights down there?"

"I've got that covered." Aodhan stashed the bolt cutters in his bag, and withdrew a torch. "This was in the car, right underneath the driver's seat. Serendipity at its finest, right?"

He grinned. I rolled my eyes. With the gate open and torch ignited, we entered the cave.

Our first bit of fortune was when we found the actual light switch. The torch was nice and all, but I preferred navigating an unknown and underground location with as much overhead lighting as possible. However, this lighting was of the sterile florescent variety usually found in doctor's offices and government facilities. We moved down the too-bright corridor, turned a corner and were in the cavern's entrance. The overhead lighting did not extend to the natural areas, which was a disappointment.

"And we're in the dark again," I said.

"No problem," Aodhan said as he reignited the torch.

"I hope there're new batteries in there," I muttered. Exploring a damp and dark cave filled with unknown objects and possible armed warriors was not my idea of fun.

Our second bit of luck presented itself when we emerged from the natural area into a tunnel that the cave's administrators used as a staging area for the guided tours. It resembled a massive drain pipe, with curved metal walls covered in racks of maps and hard hats earmarked for visitors.

"Now this is brilliant," Aodhan said as he donned a bright blue hard hat. The colour was a near perfect match to his track suit. The whole effect on him was that of a tall, slender blueberry. "We might not have chain mail like those sneaky warriors, but at least we've got these."

I wondered how a hard hat would fare against a sword, or a crossbow bolt. God willing, neither of us would find out.

Properly outfitted with hard hats and clutching maps of the cavern, we continued on and descended deeper into the earth. Stairs had been cut directly from the living rock, and I imagined they were a good deal more stable for exploration than skidding across the cavern's natural floor. Alongside the stairs was a crude railing that appeared to have been cobbled together from old iron pipes, thick with rust spots and layers of enamel paint. It didn't look nearly as stable as the stairs, and was anyone's guess if we'd be safer using the railing or avoiding it altogether.

"How far down have we gone?" I asked as we started on our fourth set of stairs.

"I'm not sure," Aodhan replied. "This all seems like a gentle incline, so not too far."

I realised that we might ultimately descend as far under the earth as we'd been above it at the Cliffs of Moher, and that was more than a bit unnerving. The stairs were damp but not slick, in spite of the pools of brackish water that had collected on either side of the walkway. Every few metres, we passed random holes in the floor that led somewhere deep and dark. Then we turned a corner and were again bathed in wonderful overhead lighting.

"Oh thank God," I said. "I was afraid we'd end up at the bottom of one of those gaping holes on the stairs."

"I'm sure they're not very deep." Aodhan sounded confident, but I had noticed him giving the holes a wide berth.

We descended further along, and soon learned that while the lights illuminated the lower portion of the stairs, they did not extend to the cave proper.

"All of this light then dark is giving me a headache," I said. "Why isn't the whole place illuminated?" I hoped that the lack of consistent lighting wasn't a signal that fortune's well was running dry. Aodhan ignored my complaints and re-ignited the torch, moving forward without missing a beat.

"Evidently, running track fosters all sorts of confidence in oneself," I muttered.

"Actually, the surf shop is what drives me," Aodhan said. Damn it all, I have got to stop thinking out loud.

"How so?"

"Well, first of all, there's the actual act of surfing," he continued. "You need patience to wait for the right wave, and let the others pass you by. Once the perfect wave forms, you need the proper skills to catch it. And when you're riding the wave, it is exhilarating. Nothing else compares." Aodhan glanced at me. "I can teach you to surf, if you'd like. After all of this is buttoned up."

"I don't even know how to swim."

"I already said I'll teach you. We can have lessons in a pool instead of the ocean, if you'd prefer it that way."

I bit the inside of my mouth to keep from saying how I was scared we might not see the other side of this adventure. I'd hardly admitted that to myself, and I really didn't want to admit it to Aodhan. "What else about the shop drives you?"

"Keeping it afloat. Selling goods and lessons and boat tours, and turning a profit. Keeping my father's memory alive." He paused, and the only sound was our footsteps against the stone floor. "Sometimes I think I'm the only one who cares that he's gone."

I touched his forearm. "That's not true. I care, and I'm someone."

Aodhan halted, then he smiled the most heartbreakingly sweet smile. "You're not someone, Meri. You're *the* one."

My breath caught in my throat. Had he meant that? And what did he mean by "the one"? As in, I was his one true friend, or something more?

I opened my mouth and closed it, gasping like a fish trapped on dry land. I wanted to ask him to explain exactly what he'd meant, but now wasn't the time. If he said I was his one true love, what then? Would we end up snogging in a cave when we were supposed to be searching for my mother? And if he'd meant we were nothing more that great friends, then I would be stuck down here with him in a dark, frigid cave knowing that we'd never be anything more than that.

I cleared my throat, and asked, "Can... Can we not talk about that right now?"

"If not now, when?" When I remained silent, he continued, "I've tried to talk to you so many times, but you always shut me out." Aodhan shoved the torch under his arm and took both of my hands in his. "Please, Mer. Don't push me away."

"I don't mean to push you away. Really, I don't, but I can't do this. Not yet, not until this mad search is behind us." I moved closer, staring up at him in the darkness. "If you promise to wait until this is over, I will promise to have that talk with you."

"One thing at a time, then?"

"One thing at a time."

"All right, then, Mer." The corner of his mouth curled up, then he squeezed my hands. "I promise."

We watched each other for another moment, then he removed his hard hat and mine, and set them on the cavern floor. I began asking what he was doing when he wrapped his arms around me and rested his forehead against my hair. I stiffened, then he skimmed one hand down my back whilst the other cupped the nape of my neck.

"I don't know what I'd do without you," he said.

"Me, either." I closed my eyes against the darkness, slipped my arms around his waist, and relaxed against him. I'd never felt that close to anyone, not when we'd been pressed up against each other while hiding at the museum, or even the times we'd held each other at the shop. Maybe having that talk wouldn't be so bad.

"I'm going to hold you to that promise."

"I won't break it."

Aodhan gave me a final squeeze before he stepped back, and replaced my hard hat on my head. "Don't want you accidentally getting any sense knocked into you."

"Or you," I said, tapping his hard hat. Our embrace left me feeling warm and bubbly, and I smiled as I peered into the darkened cavern. "Is there much further to go?"

"I believe we've reached the main feature." He shined the torchlight onto his map, then he moved the beam around the cavern until it illuminated a massive stalactite. The stone was a pale sandy hue, and was made up of dozens—maybe hundreds—of slender stone columns all bonded together. It was several metres long, and dangled from the cave ceiling like a colossal carved stone chandelier. "That's something, eh?"

"More than something," I replied. I could hardly believe such a magnificent formation was natural. "Is there anything else down here? Anything like a passageway, or a door?"

"Let's have a look." Aodhan swung the beam across the chamber, illuminating rocks, a pool of standing water, and more rocks... and the curved edge of an object situated on the cave floor.

"Wait, go back," I said. "Train the beam on that stone directly below the stalactite."

"That makes it a stalagmite," Aodhan said.

I glared at him. "But look at the shape of the bloody thing!"

"All right, all right."

He slowly moved the beam around the stalagmite. It was a long series of curves, with one end being much higher than the other. In fact, the taller end was made up of several curves, then the whole feature tapered into a long, undulating length of stone that lay flush with the cave floor.

"If I get the light on it just right, it looks like a woman lying there," Aodhan said. He swung the beam around the chamber again, bringing it to rest on the stalagmite. "Do you think it could be a statue? Everything else in here appears natural, but that one's uncanny. It's so lifelike."

I leaned over the railing, straining for a closer look. It really did look like a woman lying on her side and propped up on her elbow, from her long hair to her straight back, and on to her tail.

Her tail.

"It's a statue of a mermaid," I said. "Aodhan, it's a merrow."

Aodhan blew out a breath. "Guess that means we're in the right place. Come on, let's find a way down to the floor so we can get a better look at this merrow."

We slowly and carefully navigated down the walkway, and when the steps reached their end, we clambered under the railing and down to the bedrock. It wasn't as slippery as I'd feared, but then again wet rock wasn't what I was afraid of encountering down in the depths of the cave.

When we got to the statue, Aodhan and I circled around her, and it was definitely a her. Whilst on the viewing platform we'd been looking at the back of her head, and now that we could see her entire body, we could say without a doubt she was a merrow. It was as if she was a real woman who'd been made up to look like stone. Everything about her was perfect, from the fringe of her eyelashes to the creases on her knuckles. And the pattern of scales on her tail was an exact match for the hilt of my mother's sword.

"Fascinating," Aodhan breathed. "Think she's a relative of yours?"

I shuddered. "I don't know if that would be a good thing."

A third voice said, "Come on, then. I'm not that bad."

I froze. So did Aodhan, his immobile hand directing the torch's beam at the merrow's tail.

"Was that you?" I whispered, desperately hoping that ventriloquism was one of his talents.

Aodhan shook his head. "Wasn't me."

"I'm sitting right here."

Aodhan swallowed hard, his Adam's apple bobbing up and down, then he raised the torch to the merrow's face.

"Och, that's bright," she said, raising a hand to shield her eyes. Talking and moving stone, then. What fun.

Aodhan removed his hard hat, and said, "Ah, hello. I'm Aodhan, and this is Meri. We're, um, looking for a way below." My eyes went wide, and I shook my head. "We may as well ask," Aodhan said. "We're all here in this cave together. Might as well be friendly."

"I like you." The merrow winked at Aodhan. He smiled. This must be what losing one's mind felt like. "But you're not one of our kind," the merrow continued.

"Our?" Aodhan repeated.

"Aye. The girl and I are merrowkin."

Aodhan dropped the torch.

"Nice to meet you," I said in a rush. I wondered if Aodhan was right, and this insane talking statue could actually help us. "What's your name?"

She sat up a bit straighter and tossed her hair over her shoulder. "You may call me Tourmaline, Jewel of the Sea."

"That's not your real name!"

"If your name can be Merry, then I can be called Tourmaline."

"She's not merry as in Christmas." Aodhan had retrieved his torch and was trying to illuminate the area without blinding anyone. "She's Meri, short for Meredith."

"Meri, short for Meredith, is it?" Tourmaline regarded me. "Then you're Aoife's girl."

I gasped. "You know my mother?"

"Aye, she is one of our greatest warriors," Tourmaline continued. "She alone first stood up to Seamus MacCreehy, and told him that the worlds are kept apart for a reason. When even the king believed Seamus's plan was the future of Kilstiffen, only Aoife saw him for the madman he is."

"Why are the worlds kept apart?" Aodhan asked.

"Safety, of course," she replied. "Those below cannot survive for very long once they venture into the modern world above, and the same goes for those above who head beneath the city. Mortals who spend too much time with the Fair Folk tend to suffer in strange and unusual ways."

"Like Oisín," Aodhan said.

"Oisín?" I repeated.

"He spent three years in Tír na nÓg, but it was three hundred up here in the mortal world," Aodhan explained. "It's an old folktale."

"Brains and brawn," Tourmaline said. "This one's a keeper, Meri girl."

I was so rattled when Tourmaline used my parents' pet name for me, I forgot to ask her to quit flirting. Instead, I asked, "Is that why my mother left above? Did she stay up here too long?"

"Merrowkin can come and go as we wish," Tourmaline said. "It's why we're tasked with keeping the portals secure."

"Then every merrow isn't a mermaid," I muttered.

"Of course not," Tourmaline said. "Not everyone is lucky enough to have a tail."

I took a deep breath and looked around the cave. "Are you guarding a way below, Tourmaline?"

She nodded. "That I am, though it won't lead you to the heart of Kilstiffen, only the edges. And there's a toll to be paid before you may pass."

"A toll? What kind of toll? Does my mother pay a toll each time?" I demanded.

Aodhan touched my shoulder. "Relax. We've handled every other situation we've been thrown into over the past week. We can handle this." He faced the merrow. "What is the toll?"

She smiled, rather deviously, if you asked me. "As you can plainly see, I've little need for possessions here. I have water, the stone, and plenty of visitors every day. What I crave are experiences."

I swallowed. Hard. "What kind of experiences?"

"Experiences that I will remember for some time, that I can play back and forth in my mind long after they've ended. Powerful experiences." Her gaze moved between Aodhan and me. "I'd like a kiss."

"Can't we just give you the bloody torch instead?" I blurted out.

"I have light." She gestured toward a lighting rig installed above the steps and the viewing platform. Though currently dark, when switched on, it must light up the cavern as bright as the sun. "What I need is touch."

"No." Aodhan stepped back from the merrow and shook his head. "Absolutely not. I don't know what goes on wherever you're from, but here in Ireland in the twenty-first century we don't force people to—"

I lunged forward and pressed my mouth against Tourmaline's, my hard hat clattering to the cavern floor behind me. Her lips were smooth and cool, and firm. I suppose that wasn't really surprising, since she was a statue and all, but she wasn't hard like stone. Her mouth was soft and yielding. Kissing her was... nice.

After I felt that my face had been mashed up against the merrow's long enough, I drew back and glanced from Tourmaline to Aodhan. She was wearing a smug grin, and Aodhan's eyes were open so wide I thought they might fall out of his head.

"Was that enough?" I asked.

"Oh, it was more than plenty," Tourmaline replied. "So much so I'll give you a gift along with your passage."

She held out her hand. On her palm rested a plain copper key.

"Is that the key to Kilstiffen?" Aodhan asked.

"It's one of them," Tourmaline replied. "If you want to enter the city, it's best to have a key to the gate."

"If that opens the gate, what opens the portal?" I asked.

"Brilliant girl," Tourmaline said. "There is yet another key, one wrought of fine, pure gold, that can open the portal, and that key alone is what makes Kilstiffen rise and what causes it to return again below. Also," she leaned closer to us, as if sharing a great secret, "The key in question has been missing for over a score of years. Any idea where it might be, Meri girl?"

"Why do you keep calling me that?" I demanded. "That's what my da calls me, and... and my mother."

"Who do you think I heard it from?" Tourmaline countered. "Whenever Aoife speaks of her brave daughter, she calls you her Meri girl. And you've a Kevin lad for a brother, no?"

I backed away from Tourmaline and bumped into Aodhan. He set his hand on my shoulder and squeezed. "You really know her," I said.

"I do, and now I'm honoured to also know her daughter." Tourmaline extended her hand again. "Go on, take the key. You've more than earned a peek at the city."

"I didn't think there would be more than one key," Aodhan said as he accepted the key. "All the stories only mention the one."

"There are many copper ones in and about the portal. The gold is unique."

"Wait, is Kilstiffen a city or a portal?" I asked.

"It's both," Tourmaline replied. "The city around the portal is where those who guard the way dwell."

"Then the legends are true. One of them, at least." Aodhan directed the torch's beam farther down the cavern. "That's the way, I take it."

"It is," Tourmaline confirmed.

Aodhan adjusted his duffle bag. "All right, then. Thank you for your help, Tourmaline."

"I haven't yet given you my gift."

We halted. "The gift isn't the key?" I asked.

"The key is to get you in and out. This," she produced a tiny wooden whistle, "will get you help when you need it."

"You think we'll need help?" I asked. I took the whistle and stowed it in my jeans pocket. "And how do I use it?"

"Surely you've seen a whistle before," Tourmaline said. "Just put it to your lips and blow."

"Yeah, Mer," Aodhan said. "Just blow."

I glared at Aodhan. "Will we need anything else?" I asked Tourmaline.

"Need or not, you must go on, quickly now," she said. "I'm only being so kind because you're Aoife's child. Seamus's followers are searching for you even now, and they'll be here soon enough."

We nodded, and moved on down the cavern. When I glanced back over my shoulder, Tourmaline was gone, replaced by an ordinary lump of stone.

"I can't believe you kissed a merrow," Aodhan said.

"Neither can I."

Below

We followed the tunnel through the cavern as it wended its way deeper into the earth. I'd expected the passage to get narrower as we went further down. Instead, the rough blasted-rock tunnel opened up to a large natural chamber. I checked the map, but it didn't record anything beyond the main chamber. While that wasn't surprising, I did wish we had more than Tourmaline's word to go on.

Something else I didn't expect was how beautiful this lower section of the cavern turned out to be. The torch's beam revealed striated tan and red walls, smoothed down by untold eons of water flowing over them. At the far end of the chamber was a wooden stockade fence. In the centre of the fence was a wooden door, the rough planks a stark contrast to the undulating rock. Being that there was no wind or rain in the cavern—at least, we hadn't come across any storms or other atmospheric events—the wood wasn't as weatherbeaten as the old fence in my back garden. Nevertheless, it was plain to see that the door was old, wearing its years of service as a portal as plain as the pattern in the grain.

"I reckon this is what the key is for." Aodhan approached the door and ran his fingertips over the planks. "I wouldn't have thought it would be a wooden wall."

"What did you think it'd be like?"

He shrugged. "Something more imposing. Stone, perhaps? Here's the lock." Aodhan withdrew the copper key and fit it in the keyhole. "You have the whistle handy?"

"What for?"

"Just in case."

I patted the lump the whistle made in my front pocket. "Whistle is at the ready."

"All right. Here goes nothing."

Aodhan turned the key. The door opened soundlessly. The passage beyond the door was dark, but a greyish light illuminated the far end of the chamber. Aodhan extinguished the torch and reached for my hand.

"We can't have any light?" I asked, not that I was scared of the dark. Whatever was lurking in the dark, now that was another story. "Not even the torch?"

Aodhan shook his head. "We don't know what's down there. I'd like us to be as inconspicuous as possible until we know more."

"All right, then." I laced my fingers with his. Together, we pressed onward.

The walk toward the light took longer than I'd expected; wherever that light was shining from, it had to be inordinately bright. The cold, damp passage that we travelled through didn't make the walk any more pleasant. As we walked, I dragged my fingertips against the wall, wondering if Tourmaline and the cavern were made of the same stone, when a mutant cave slug reared up and attacked me.

"Quiet," Aodhan said when I yelped, then he investigated the wall. "It's just some slime, probably from all the water that drips down from the surface."

"That was disgusting," I whispered.

"Be grateful it wasn't a randy merrow looking for more kisses."

I bumped him with my shoulder. "You're just jealous."

He bumped my shoulder in retaliation. "I'm not. I just..."

"Just, what?" I prompted.

"I wanted to be your first kiss."

My throat tightened, and for a moment I couldn't catch my breath. I'd wanted that, too. Aodhan noticed my struggles, and rubbed my back. "What's wrong, Mer?"

"I didn't kiss Tourmaline because I wanted to kiss her," I began, my breath coming in short gasps. "I wanted to keep moving forward, and it seemed silly for us to be held up over a stupid kiss. Since you obviously weren't going to do it, I did, so we could get on with it." I looked up at him. "I suppose that's not a very good reason to kiss someone."

Aodhan tilted up my chin, and stroked his thumb along my jaw. "What is a good reason? To kiss someone, that is."

"Because you want to. Because you can't stop thinking about them." I touched his hair. "Because you're always wondering if their hair is as soft as it looks, and you really want to touch it."

"All excellent reasons." Aodhan tucked a piece of my hair behind my ear, then he bent his head and kissed me. Kissing him was nothing like kissing Tourmaline. With her, her lips had been soft and cool, and it had been a perfectly nice experience. Aodhan's lips were not cool or soft. They were warm, and chapped, and he pressed them to mine as if I was the most important person in the world.

When we parted, he rested his forehead against mine and grinned. "We skipped our talk."

"I suppose we can have it later," I said, as I stroked the soft hair at the nape of his neck. "Second kisses can be special, can't they?"

"They surely can. Should we carry on? Or stay here and talk a bit more?"

"Let's get on with this." We could talk later, and I was certain he would bring all this up again. He kissed my forehead before he released me, and we continued our walk toward the mysterious brightness. Soon enough, the passage brought us to the edge of a cliff. Below it was another large chamber extending out into the darkness. The light was emanating from whatever was going on below the cliff's edge. We approached the edge, looked down, and immediately scuttled back and out of sight. Below us were dozens—maybe hundreds—of armed warriors.

We hid behind a rock outcrop, my heart racing. "There's a whole army down there," I said.

"What are we supposed to do now?" Aodhan asked.

Hell if I know. I took a breath and centred myself. "We could start by observing them. Maybe we can learn what they're about, or figure out who's in charge."

Aodhan nodded. "Right. Let's have another look."

We moved closer to the cliff, and I peeked over the edge at the assemblage. There were both men and women present, and they were arranged in some kind of military formation, with each group being two warriors across and six deep. Every person was wearing the same leather and chain mail uniform, and their feet were clad in heavy armoured boots. Their uniforms were less posh versions of what my mother had been wearing at the Shannon Pot; maybe Aodhan was right about her being a general.

I put thoughts of my mother aside, and scrutinised their weapons. Each warrior had a sword belted to their waist and spear borne upright in their left hand. From our vantage point, it gave the lot of them the appearance of several enormous spiky caterpillars.

"There are so many," I said. "I thought Seamus had a raggedy little army."

"So did I, but there's nothing little or raggedy about this," Aodhan said, then we were distracted by a sound toward the back of the cavern.

"Someone's back there," I whispered.

"A lookout, maybe?"

"If they were a lookout, they would have raised the alarm by now. Maybe it's someone who can help us."

"Who would help us down here?"

"Tourmaline did. Perhaps she sent another merrow to aid us?" I turned toward the shadows, and called, "You may as well come out. We've already heard you."

Two warriors identically dressed to those below the cliff stepped out from behind the rocks. "Who are you?" Aodhan demanded as he stood and thrust me behind him.

The men were silent, and our shouting had no effect on them. They grabbed Aodhan and then me by our shoulders, and dragged us away.

Badass Warrior Queen

"Where are you taking us?" I demanded, not that the warriors acknowledged me. The one dragging me stared straight ahead, jaw slack and eyes unfocused. What was focused was his big, meaty hand on the back of my neck, squeezing me like a vise grip as he pushed me onward.

"Something's wrong with them," Aodhan said. "It's like they can't hear us."

"They'll hear me, all right." I dug my heels in, trying to become so much dead weight. The warrior retaliated by hefting me onto his shoulder like a sack of potatoes with my legs and arms dangling far above the floor, all without speaking or breaking a sweat. I beat my fists against his back, and still got no reaction.

"See," Aodhan said. "It's like they're robots."

Before I could reply—or rip a chunk out of this giant's back with my teeth—we reached a cave. The warriors threw Aodhan and me into the cave and closed the entrance with an iron grate. Aodhan was up in an instant, his hands clutching the grate as he surveyed our surroundings.

"What's out there?" I asked.

"A bunch of nothing," he replied. I sat up, whimpering at all the new bruises I'd acquired when I hit the floor. "Are you okay?"

"Yeah," I replied. My shoulder and hip were sore where I'd landed on them, and the back of my neck where the warrior had gripped me ached, but I didn't think anything was broken. I spied Aodhan's duffle bag. It was still slung across his body, further proof that our captors were all muscle and little else. "Have you your phone?"

He grabbed his phone from his jacket as I withdrew mine from my back pocket. "No service. You?"

"Same." I squinted in the dim light, and as my vision acclimated, I noted the details of the cave, or perhaps I should call it a cell. The floor was relatively flat, but it was bitter cold and had a thin layer of damp grit upon it. The walls and ceiling were rough stone. Five paces took you the length of the cell—reduce that to three if you were Aodhan—and it was as many deep. The grate covering the entrance was the only way out.

Yes. This was definitely a cell, and we were prisoners.

I drew up my knees and hugged them to my chest. "What are we going to do?"

"I'm not sure." Aodhan sat beside me and wrapped his arm around my shoulders. "We'll get out of this, Mer."

"If you say we'll see this through together, I might hurl," I warned.

A familiar voice asked, "What if I say you'll be punished together?"

Aodhan and I looked toward the grate as one. Seamus MacCreehy—who was absolutely not a real school headmaster—stood in front of the grate, flanked by three warriors on either side of him. Part of me noticed how he looked like the odd duck in his jumper and trousers compared to the warriors' battle gear. The rest of me wondered why he'd brought six warriors to deal with the two of us.

"Why are we in a cell?" I demanded.

"You're criminals, is what you are, and criminals belong in cells," he replied. "You're traitors, just like your mother. A crime against the crown is treason."

"We're in Ireland, not Kilstiffen," Aodhan said. "There aren't any crimes against the crown here! What you're doing is assault, and kidnapping, and intimidation. You're the criminal!"

"Am I?" MacCreehy gestured to the man on his left. "Take the girl out and bind her hands and mouth, and be sure to make the gag tight. We don't want this one singing her way out of here."

MacCreehy stepped aside as two big men—bigger than the ones who'd hauled Aodhan and me into the cell in the first place—opened the grate and moved toward us. One had a length of cloth in his hands, and the other bore a set of manacles. I scuttled back from them on my hands and heels, pressing myself against the cave wall.

"Stay away from her," Aodhan yelled as he leapt up in front of me. "Don't you dare touch her!"

Another man entered the cave and grabbed Aodhan's arms and dragged him away from me, while the first man caught my forearm. All these people in the tiny cell made it difficult to move, or breathe. I opened my mouth to sing, but nothing came out, not even a squeak. Then Aodhan punched his captor on the side of his head, and all attention was on him.

In the commotion that followed, I squirmed away from the man holding me. I scanned the cave wall, desperate for a rock to throw or maybe hide behind, when MacCreehy started yelling. The warriors looked back, and I heard feet shuffling, and then a thunk. And another thunk, and then another.

The yelling stopped.

I covered my face with my hands, convinced Aodhan was dead, and I was next.

Fingers touched my arm.

I screamed.

"Meri." A gentle shake. "Meri, look at me."

I raised my head. My vision was blurred by tears and sweat and abject terror. "Aodhan?"

"I'm here." I'd never been so happy to see his blurry dark head. "Quick, come on."

I let Aodhan help me up. We crept out of the cave, stepping over the warriors' bodies as we did so. I wondered what had happened to them, then I saw MacCreehy splayed out on the ground.

"What happened?" I asked. "Are they dead?"

"No," said a voice from ahead of us. "They're just out for a bit."

My head snapped up, and I saw yet another warrior leading Aodhan and me out of the cave. I gripped his forearm and pulled him closer.

"Who is that?" I whispered. "Can we trust him?"

"Not him," Aodhan said. "Her."

I looked again, saw that this warrior was smaller than MacCreehy's goons, and that she had a blonde plait that reached almost to her waist. She extended her arm back and Aodhan grasped her hand, then the three of us plunged into a pitch black tunnel. We crept along, tripping over rocks and bumping into the damp cave walls, and eventually emerged near the ledge where Aodhan and I were first captured. Since we were at the far end of the ledge from MacCreehy and the rest, I hoped that meant we'd be safe for a moment or two.

The person leading us was outlined in the grey light, complete with the curve of a shield above her shoulder, and for a terrible moment I thought we'd been duped by one of Seamus's people.

I yanked Aodhan close. "How do you know she's not one of Mac-Creehy's?"

Aodhan smiled. "She's not, Mer." Aodhan moved aside, and I saw our rescuer's gold mail glinting in the shadows... mail with a triangle-shaped patch missing near her hip. I stepped out from behind Aodhan as my mother faced me.

"Mama," I said, as I threw myself into her arms. I'd imagined seeing her again so many times, what I'd say, what I'd do. None of those fantasies had me bawling against her leather breastplate.

"Meri, my Meri girl," she said as she stroked my hair. "I should wish you'd never seen this wretched place, but I can't. I've missed you so, my lamb."

"I missed you, too. We all missed you. I needed you so much." I buried my face against her shoulder. "When you sent us away at the Shannon Pot, I thought—"

Mama drew back and held my face with her hands. "I sent you away because it wasn't safe for you to be there, not with the others who were hunting me. It's not safe here, either." She stared into my eyes until I nodded, then she stepped back and looked at Aodhan. "He was with you before."

"Mama, this is Aodhan Sullivan. Aodhan, this is my mother." I paused, and wiped my cheeks. "Shall I tell him your name is Calliope Murphy, or have you got a new one?"

"I married your father, so we do share a surname," she snapped. "As for my given name, it is Aoife. Calliope is naught but a pet name."

"Why did you make Da forget your real name?" I asked.

Mama sighed. "I had to. The more he remembered, the more danger he was in. The more danger you all were in."

"Pleasure to meet you, Mrs Murphy." Aodhan stepped between us and shook Mama's hand. "Thanks for the rescue. Second rescue, now."

Mama cocked her head. "You're Bridgette's boy?"

"Yes, I am."

"I remember Bridgette," Mama said. "So kind, yet so lost within herself."

Aodhan stepped back; Mama had rattled him, which was no easy feat. "Ah, well, like I said. Pleasure to meet you. Meri talks about you all the time."

Mama gave me a look. "Does she?"

"And we have something of yours." He unzipped his duffle bag and withdrew Mama's sword, then laid the open bag at his feet. "We've no idea how you lost it, but it got scooped up from a river bed and taken to a museum. Meri nicked it from a few shady blokes dressed like those lot," he said, jerking his thumb toward the warriors in the lower chamber.

"Thank you, both of you," Mama said, beaming as she buckled her sword belt about her hips. "I always knew you'd be a warrior, Meri. Such a feisty babe you were, and when you first sang..." Mama saw something inside Aodhan's bag and jerked her chin toward it. "What's that?"

"It's a key. We found it on Slieve Callan." Aodhan withdrew the key we'd found at the ancient holy well and handed it to Mama. "It's fairly corroded. Don't know if it's really good for much now."

Mama rubbed the key and some of the green corrosion sloughed away. "It's not corroded. The key's been painted over." There was a shout from down below. Mama handed the key back to Aodhan and approached the ledge. "Keep that close. Meri girl, come see this."

I dutifully went to Mama's side. Fourteen years gone, and she still had that parental edge to her voice. "What is it?"

"Something's happening."

"Perhaps MacCreehy woke up and is calling for our heads," I suggested.

"That lot will be out for another hour, maybe longer." Mama scanned the gathering, then she indicated a corridor at the far end of the cavern. "They're readying themselves to march."

"These soldiers, they're the ones who have jumped off the cliffs and into the sea, aren't they?" Aodhan asked. "The ones who went missing and were never found."

"Yes," Mama replied. "That's how MacCreehy built his army, by telling lies and preying on the weak. Ever since I trapped him above, he's been compelling good people to leave their lives behind and join a cause that holds no purpose for them."

"You trapped him?" I repeated. "He's not a merrow like you?"

"He is, and he's not," Mama replied. "His mother was a merrow, and on his father's side he's descended from a fellow that once roamed the countryside, killing monsters in exchange for tribute from the common folk. When Seamus came of age, he joined the king's army. He did well, but a high rank wasn't enough for him. He wanted power, and decided that the best way to get it was to permanently open the portal."

"That can't be a good idea," I said, remembering Tourmaline's warnings about those from above and below needing to be kept apart for their mutual safety. "Why didn't the king try to stop him?"

"He tricked the king," Mama replied. "Seamus whispered lies into his ear until the king thought permanently opening the way below was for the good of all."

"I wouldn't think a king would fall for such tactics," Aodhan said.

"Normally I would agree, but Seamus appealed to the one thing the king loves most—his people." Mama shook her head. "For all that our king can be as naïve as a day old cat, he is the most wonderful old soul."

It was plain that Mama admired this king, who seemed too soft-headed to rule. "How did you trap MacCreehy above?"

"I stole the golden key that causes the city to rise." Mama smiled, a hint of pride in her voice.

"I imagine the king wasn't pleased," I said.

"No, he was not," Mama said. "I led them all on a merry chase above and below and above again. When no one could find me nor the key, Seamus swore a blood oath that he would personally retrieve the both of us, and that he'd remain above until he'd done so."

"Wait, so you tricked him into swearing he couldn't return to Kilstiffen until he had the key?" Aodhan asked, and Mama nodded. "You really are a badass warrior queen."

"Since Seamus was above, and didn't have access to Kilstiffen's army, he needed to raise another," Mama said, nodding toward the formation of warriors. "It's taken him nearly twenty years to do it, but there they are."

I studied the army. "He compelled people to jump into the sea, then he kidnapped them."

"Aye, that's just what he did."

"Are they just from the Cliffs of Moher, or are there faked suicides all across the world?" I asked.

"This group is only from where the sea meets the western edge of Ireland," Mama replied. "There are other portals such as this one scattered across the world. My sister guards the one off the coast of Scotland."

"I have an aunt?" I asked. "On your side?"

Mama smiled. "That you do, and she's a fair sight more interesting that Brian's sister, Donna."

I frowned at Mama's assessment of Aunt Donna. I'd always found her quite delightful. We turned toward the army below and observed them. Luckily, none of them glanced upward.

"They're dressed like Roman centurions," I said.

"Aye, the style is derivative," Mama said. "Everything Seamus does is a copy of what went before."

Aodhan grabbed my arm. "Do you see that man, second company, third row back?"

I scanned the company and found the man in question. He was dressed much as the rest, and carried the same spear and shield. The only thing differentiating him was that his skin was darker than the rest. "What about him?"

"That's my father."

THE MOST LAW ABIDING GANG IN IRELAND

"**I** thought your father was dead," I said, more loudly that I ought to have. Mama grabbed my arm and Aodhan's shoulder and hauled us back from the edge.

"Quiet, both of you," she hissed. "No attracting attention or carrying on, not unless you want the lot of them pointing their spears at us."

"Wow, you're strong," I grumbled, rubbing my elbow.

Mama ignored me, and asked, "Aodhan, you think you saw your father down there?"

He nodded. "It's him. I'd know him anywhere."

"Are you sure?" I asked. "He's been gone a long time. Maybe it's just someone who looks like him."

Aodhan shook his head. "You know how sometimes you're certain, like when you saw the sword in the museum and knew it was your mother's, and when we jumped into the Shannon Pot?"

Both of those times, I would have bet my life on what I was feeling in my gut. "Yeah. I do."

"I'm that certain." He leaned forward and peeked over the edge. "They never found his body, only the wreck of the boat. Everyone assumed he'd been swept out to sea." Aodhan spun around and grabbed my shoulders. "Meri, that's Lucas Sullivan down there."

"I believe you." I placed my right hand over his. He released my shoulders, took my hands. "I really do. Mama, how can we save him?"

"Right now, we cannot," Mama replied. When Aodhan began protesting, she continued, "Hear me out. Even if your father's in his right mind and wants to be rescued, how are the three of us going to manage that against an entire army? I can handle a few of them with the element of surprise, but not the whole lot at once."

"She's right," I said. "It would be suicide."

Aodhan looked toward the warriors. "Are they all jumpers down there?"

"Jumpers, castaways, and the like," Mama replied. "Those are the sort who hear the call."

"The call?"

"Aye. Places like this have their own song. A resonance, if you will. Those who are unsatisfied with their own lives are rather attuned to it."

Aodhan's fingers tightened against mine. We'd both heard the call many times. I wondered how much longer we would have held out before we went down to the portal, along with the rest of the jumpers.

"Do they remember who they are?" I asked. "Or did they leave it all behind?"

"I don't think they can remember," Mama replied. "MacCreehy has them under thrall. They live to carry out his orders, nothing more."

"That's terrible," Aodhan said. "They're like zombies."

The warrior that had picked me up and threw me in the cell had acted like a zombie, bereft of free will or opinions about the orders he carried out. I looked toward the army and felt my throat tighten. "Aodhan, if you hadn't caught me that day on the Cliffs, I'd be down there, mindless like the rest."

"No, you wouldn't," Mama said. "I wouldn't allow it."

"We have to save them," I said, my need to save the jumpers as strong as my need for fresh air and sunlight. Ostensibly, my quest was over; I'd found my mother, knew she was alive and well, and that remembered me. But I couldn't leave Aodhan's father to live out his days as a brainwashed follower of MacCreehy. I couldn't leave any of them behind, not if I could do something about it. "All of them. We have to get them back to their families, and their lives."

"We will save them," Mama said. "And we'll do that by stopping MacCreehy."

"If you don't mind my asking, who is Seamus MacCreehy?" Aodhan asked.

Mama cast an appraising glance toward Aodhan. The three of us had retreated from where the jumpers were located, and were following a winding path through the cave. This one inclined upward, and

I hoped we'd be on the surface soon. I'd never been underground for such a long time, and I desperately wanted to feel the sun on my skin.

"Who do you think he is?" Mama countered.

"I know a fair bit about him," Aodhan replied. "He's the headmaster of our school—"

"What?" Mama demanded.

"MacCreehy runs The Saints Academy, which is where Aodhan and I go to school," I said. "He came on right before Kevin enrolled."

"You must be joking," Mama said. "Brian allows you to attend a school overseen by my greatest enemy?"

I shrugged. "Don't blame Da. We didn't know MacCreehy was the enemy until last week."

Mama muttered a curse, then she gestured for Aodhan to continue.

"MacCreehy may run the place, but he's no academic," Aodhan said. "He takes over random classes and talks about weapons. He hates it when Meri and I are near each other."

Mama stopped walking. "Are you two together often, then?"

"We eat lunch together," I replied. "And we have all the same classes." I thought for a moment. "Actually, we used to have every class together, but this year it's only literature."

She nodded, and resumed leading us through the cavern. "That's Seamus's hand at work. He wants to isolate you, Meri, and probably Aodhan, too. A lonely soul is easier to sway. Fewer ties to the real world."

"Is that why you left?" I blurted out. "Because we were tying you to the surface?"

"No. I was forced to leave my family before Seamus hurt or captured you. Gods below, that one would have murdered you and Kevin in your cradles if he'd known about you, and I can hardly imagine what he'd have done to Brian."

"Well, he knows now," I snapped. "He's been after us all this time, and you weren't here to help us!"

"Meri," Mama began, but I held up my hand and turned away. I shouldn't have snapped at her, especially not now after I'd just got her back, but I had more emotions bubbling to the surface than I could handle.

"Is that what MacCreehy did to you?" Aodhan asked.

"What makes you think he did anything to me?" Mama countered.

Her hurt tone made me turn around. I saw Mama standing with her hands clenched at her sides, glaring at Aodhan.

"It is, isn't it?" I asked. "It all makes sense. He needed someone in high standing with a voice like yours. He got you on his side and used your voice against you, didn't he?"

"He did," Mama said. "For a time, I believed in Seamus's cause. When I realised how foolish I'd been and told him I'd have nothing more to do with him, he railed at me. Said I was ruining his plans, said he'd force me to help him, use any means necessary…"

"What happened next?" I asked, when she paused.

"That was when I stole the key to the city," she replied. "Without it, it doesn't matter who he sways to his cause. He needs the key to open the portal and raise the city, and he needs a merrow—not just any merrow, but a strong one—to gain the people's favour."

"That's why he wants Meri now, for her lineage," Aodhan deduced. "But her voice must be why he passed over Kevin."

I snorted. "Kevin couldn't carry a tune in a bucket."

Mama laughed. "Aye, he's just like his father, tone deaf as the day is long." Mama eyed Aodhan. "You're like Brian, too. He can see straight through years upon years of lies, see right down to the truth."

"I can?" Aodhan asked. "I mean, thank you."

"Is that why you loved Da?" I asked. "Because he saw the truth of you?"

"I love him for a thousand different reasons," she replied. "Gods willing, we can handle this mess quickly now, and I'll be able to tell him all those reasons myself."

We trudged on through the cavern and back toward the surface. I had no idea which direction we were heading in, since by then I'd seen so many rock walls that they all blurred together. I also hadn't said much of anything since my earlier outburst, which I felt just awful about. Despite that, every time I opened my mouth, I wanted to snipe at my mother.

That was unfair of me, and I knew it was... But wasn't it also unfair that I'd had to grow up without her? Wasn't it unfair that my mother had never taken me shopping for dresses, or shown me how to apply lipstick, or taught me how to bake a cake?

I glanced at Mama. She was the picture of strength in her leather armour and chain mail overskirt, the image enhanced by the shield on her back and the sword buckled at her hip. I didn't think she paid much attention to fashion or even owned a dress, and I doubted a warrior would wear lipstick very often. What's more, Da had taught me how to bake ages ago.

Maybe I hadn't been stuck with the short straw, after all.

Mama saw me watching her, and smiled. I wished I had her composure, and that I could just put aside my more inconvenient emotions and appreciate that my mother was alive and well and with me again. All of my fears—that I'd never see her again, that she was dead, that she'd never loved me and Kevin and Da and that was the real reason why she'd left us—had been proved false. I needed to get my head on straight and let her know that I was happy for her return, if for no other reason so she wouldn't ever leave us again.

But first, I had questions.

I cleared my throat. "Can I ask you something?"

"Of course," she replied. "Ask me anything."

"Why did you leave? I mean, I know it was because of MacCreehy, but what made you actually go?"

"Och." Mama stared at the ground for a moment. "Before I tell you—and I will—I need you to understand two things. One, I did not want to go. Two, I wasn't supposed to be gone this long."

I nodded. "I believe you."

"We—Brian and I—were well aware that MacCreehy and his followers were still searching for me, long after I'd married your father and changed my name," she began. "He went so far as to go to the guards and tell them I was his missing daughter. I should have left then, but I was carrying your brother." She smiled ruefully, and added, "It's a bit hard to go on the lam when you're carting a person around in your belly."

I returned her smile. "I imagine so."

"When the guards came to the house and questioned us, Brian and I told them we had no idea who this MacCreehy character was, and things were calm for a while. For a good, long while. Those were my happiest days, just the three of us, and then you were born and I was happier yet. Did your father ever tell you about the day you started singing from your cradle?"

I swallowed the sudden lump in my throat. "He doesn't talk much about singing. Whenever he does, he gets all weepy."

She frowned a bit, and continued, "Soon after your second birthday, things started to change. The tides came in wrong, birds and fish forgot to migrate, and people began throwing themselves into the sea in droves. Eventually, we figured out that MacCreehy had hatched a new plan. Brian and I made plans of our own…"

"What sort of plans?" I prompted, when she fell silent.

"We thought we could stop MacCreehy on our own, whilst I remained above with him, and you," she replied. "And would you know that every single one of those plans failed? Failure after failure, until the only thing left for me to do was leave the three of you in safety and face MacCreehy alone."

"That must have been heartbreaking," Aodhan said.

"It was," Mama and I replied in concert. "What happened next?" I asked.

Mama blew out a breath. "What didn't happen? I was captured, and spent time in chains. I escaped, and they pursued me. When it became plain that I could not defeat MacCreehy on my own, I rallied the merrows to my cause. Those who could joined with me, and we've kept the key hidden, and the portal from opening, for over twenty years."

"But it should open soon, yeah?" Aodhan said.

"Yes, which is why there's been so much activity above. The city cannot rise without the key, and they've not found it yet."

"Where is the golden key now?" I asked.

"It's close," Mama replied. "Close, and safe."

"What if we need it?" I pressed. "What if MacCreehy finds some other way to raise the city?"

"There is no other way." My face must have betrayed that I didn't quite believe her. "Meri, this isn't the sort of key where if it's been lost you can ring the locksmith for a replacement. It's enchanted."

"Oh." I thought on that for a moment. Of course, the key was a magic key, if it could raise and lower a city. On some level, I'd known Aodhan and I would encounter fantastical people and objects on this quest, just like in one of those table top games we'd played as kids. I just hadn't expected these fantastical objects to be as mundane as a key. For that matter, I hadn't expected a talking statue or legions of enthralled warriors, either.

I glanced at Mama. I wondered how strong she really was, what her voice could do beyond allowing us to breathe whilst underwater and spirit us across an entire island in the blink of an eye... I wondered what she was. She was a merrow, that much was true, but was she also a human?

Was I human? Or only half?

"I sang at MacCreehy and made him do what I wanted," I blurted out.

"Did you, now?" Mama said. "What did you have him do?"

"He was trying to stop Aodhan and me from leaving school, and I made him let us go," I replied.

"It was amazing," Aodhan said. "Like something out of a science fiction movie."

I frowned at Aodhan's assessment of what I'd done, and said to my mother, "You seem unsurprised."

"You're a merrow," she replied. "It's in your blood to change the world with your songs."

"Huh." I recalled one of the many taunts I'd endured, that if people heard me sing I'd lure them to their doom as my mother used to. "All those legends about merrows and sirens are true, aren't they?"

Mama caressed my cheek. "Most legends have a grain of truth to them. We merrows keep to the seas and yes, our songs have power. However, we are not fish or seals."

"So, selkies aren't real then?" Aodhan asked.

"I didn't say that," Mama replied.

"Did you ever change anything at the house, or in town?" I asked.

"Oh, yes," she replied, smiling at the memories. "I coaxed flowers to bloom out of season, snow to fall in summer, things like that. You and your brother would laugh and laugh when it snowed on warm summer days, and try to catch the flakes as they melted away on your hands."

"They why didn't you just sing at MacCreehy until he obeyed you?"

"Believe me, if I could have done that I would have," she replied. "We can only compel a body while we're singing. Once we stop singing, free will returns."

Aodhan looked back the way we came, toward his father and the rest of the warriors. "What about them? Do they wake up when the song ends?"

"MacCreehy has enough merrows in his employ to ensure the song never ends," Mama replied. "You understand now why it was vital for me to hide the key, being that he's brought so many over to his side."

"What if MacCreehy made a new key?" Aodhan asked. "Surely the people of Kilstiffen don't want to be trapped under the sea. Why not enchant a new one?"

"That could come to pass," Mama said. "However, there are precious few powerful enough to create such a key."

"MacCreehy hasn't tried to win any of them over?" I asked.

"He's tried," Mama said. "Tried and failed, but who's to say he won't encounter a wizard willing to help him?"

"Has he tried going below Kilstiffen, to Tír na nÓg?" I asked. It seemed to me that a land filled with gods and tricksters would be ripe with powerful beings of dubious moral character.

"That would be a last resort," Mama replied. "Even MacCreehy knows to avoid those below. The bargains they strike only benefit themselves."

Aodhan snorted. "Sounds like MacCreehy has some kindred spirits down there."

We reached the end of the tunnel and reentered Tourmaline's chamber, only the stone merrow was nowhere to be found. "Where's Tourmaline?" I asked.

"Why? Miss her?" Aodhan asked.

"You are jealous," I said.

"Who is Tourmaline?" Mama demanded.

"She's a stone merrow who helped us earlier," I explained. "She said she knows you."

Mama's brow pinched, then she burst out laughing. "Odds are you encountered Tallulah, a distant cousin of ours on my mother's side. She's always loved a good joke."

"Is she on our side?" I felt the wooden whistle, snug in my jeans pocket.

"Of course she is. A merrow never turns their back on one of their own."

"What about MacCreehy?"

Mama's expression soured. "That's the thing of it. According to MacCreehy, he hasn't turned his back on anyone. He believes that he is the righteous one."

"My dad always said that the worst villains were the ones who thought they were the heroes of the story," Aodhan said. "We can still save him, right?"

Mama patted his arm. "If he's alive, there is hope. In fact, now that I have you two to help me, there is a great deal more hope to be had."

"I don't know how much help we'll be," I said. "We don't know anything about warriors and portals."

"Then it's time you learned," Mama said. "I can recite the history of Kilstiffen, and teach you everything you need to know about merrows." She grimaced, and continued, "I do regret not being there to help you come into your voice."

"But, the warriors," I said, rather desperately. "I don't know anything about fighting!"

"You'll learn that, too," she replied. "I was a blooded warrior younger than you are now."

"Blooded?" I pressed my hand to my stomach, certain I was going to be sick. "I don't think I want anything more to do with blood. When Fitzsimmons fell on her sword I nearly had a panic attack."

Mama paused. "Fitzsimmons fell on her sword?"

"You know her?" I asked. I recalled how Fitzsimmons had taunted me with lies about Mama, but I hadn't realised they were actual acquaintances.

"Och, yes. That one's been a pain in my arse for too long." Mama continued, a gleam in her eye, "Her sword. She really fell onto it?"

"She did, right after I rolled an office chair into her. See that? I can't be a warrior. Who uses office supplies as weaponry?"

"It's all right, Meri," Aodhan said. "I imagine being a soldier's much like being an athlete. We can handle it."

"Maybe you can." I walked toward the stairway, and said, "If we're climbing out of the cave, we'd best get moving. I'm not sure when this place opens for visitors, and I'd rather not be caught inside by the authorities."

"What authorities?" Aodhan asked. "The cave guards?"

I glared at Aodhan. "By anyone who wants us to explain what we're doing here, especially since we broke in and did not pay the entrance fee."

"Right, then." Aodhan headed for the steps we'd descended earlier. "We're Murphy's Maniacs, the most law-abiding gang in Ireland."

"You're in a gang?" Mama asked.

"Sort of," I replied. "At the moment, the only members are me, Aodhan, and Kevin." I paused. "You can join, if you like."

"I would like that. Very much."

I smiled. I liked being in a gang with Mama.

We ascended the stone-cut stairs, and I was pleased that the way up was not nearly as treacherous as our descent had been. Or maybe the sight of dozens of armed and zombiefied warriors had made me reevaluate my definition of treacherous.

Soon enough, we were out of the cave system. I inhaled the fresh, sweet air, ridding myself of the stale and musty caves as best I could. The sun had risen while we were underground, and the car park was bathed in rosy light. I closed my eyes and tilted my head toward the sun, appreciating it like I never had before.

"Come on, we weren't underground that long," Aodhan said.

"It was long enough," I muttered.

"My people haven't seen the sun in over twenty years," Mama said. She, too, had her face turned toward the sun.

"They don't see that sun at all?" I asked.

"They can't, not without the key," Mama replied. "And it's all my fault."

"But you took it for a good reason," I said. "You took it to save everyone."

Mama smiled at me, but it didn't reach her eyes. "I hope my people see it that way, too."

"I'm sure they understand, Mrs Murphy," Aodhan said. "And even if they don't, once we stop MacCreehy and free my dad and the rest, we'll get the key and raise the city again! How could anyone stay mad once they experience a glorious sunny day like today?"

Mama's gaze slid toward Aodhan, then back to me. "Is he always this cheery?"

"He is. It's nice, most of the time."

Aodhan smirked at me, then he headed toward the car. The glorious sunlight we were enjoying did nothing to enhance Da's old banger. When Mama saw the car, she made a sound somewhere between a laugh and a wail.

"Brian still drives that old beast?" she asked. "I can't believe it starts up." Mama paused, her gaze darting about. "Is he here?"

"He's on his boat with Kevin," I replied.

Mama nodded. "Good, then. Our boys are safe." She glanced at Aodhan. "Most of them, at least."

My face went hot. "What do we do now?"

"We lure MacCreehy out of his nest, and then we trap him."

The Holy Island

The three of us enjoyed the sunlight for another moment, then we piled into Da's car. As soon as I shut my door, I realised I should have offered the front seat to Mama, but she slid into the back with nary a word nor glance toward the front. The back seat did offer more room for her sword and shield, so there was that.

"Where to now?" I asked.

"The petrol station, for starters," Aodhan replied. "I want to be prepared in case we end up going a fair distance again, like all the way to County Cavan."

I shuddered. "That was a long drive." I twisted around and asked Mama, "When you sang us away from the Shannon Pot, why did you send us all the way to Inis Mór, instead of just to the water's surface?"

"I was trying to send you home," she replied. "I suppose I overshot by a few kilometres."

I faced forward, and muttered, "More than a few."

Aodhan drove to the closest petrol station and filled the tank. While he took care of that, I popped inside to get us something for breakfast and three coffees. Mama stayed inside the car for obvious reasons.

After the petrol had been pumped and the food consumed, I asked, "How are we going to get MacCreehy to follow us? He must know we'll be setting a trap for him."

"He has an ego as vast as the sea, and he's quite sentimental, so it won't be too much of a bother," Mama replied. "We just need to poke him where he'll really feel it."

"But poke him where?" I wondered. "It would have to be somewhere significant to draw him out now, when he's so close to his goal."

"He is not close to his goal," Mama said. "He still does not have the key."

"He does have a rather large army," I retorted.

"What about Kilmacreehy?" Aodhan interjected. "Meri and I did a bit of genealogy research, and it led us to Saint MacCreehy. That's Seamus's ancestor, right?"

Mama stared from me to Aodhan and back to me. "Is there anything the lad doesn't know?"

"I call him Aodhan of the agile mind," I replied. "Well? Is Kilmacreehy a good spot?"

Mama shook her head. "A few years ago it may have been, but I've drawn him to that place more than once. Those wounds are a bit scabbed over. We need someplace that remains a bit tender."

"Have you ever led him to Inis Cealtra?" Aodhan asked.

Mama blinked. "Agile mind, indeed."

"What's Inis Cealtra?" I asked.

"It's an island in Lough Derg," Aodhan replied. "MacCreehy—the original one—set up there, but an angel made him leave. Right?"

"Almost one hundred per cent correct," Mama confirmed. "It's the Seamus we're acquainted with who was forced to leave the holy island." She tapped her chin. "If we lured him there, we could confront him away from most bystanders. We may even be able to trap him, and then haul him down to Kilstiffen."

"What will happen to him in Kilstiffen?" I asked.

"He'll be tried before the king, and punished," Mama replied.

Aodhan faced forward and started the car. "All right, then. Inis Cealtra it is."

It took us a little more than an hour to reach Lough Derg. The lough was larger than I'd expected, and the deep blue water was dotted with several islands. The three of us stood on the shore and gazed at the calm surface. After all that had happened that morning, and before we endured whatever was to come next, I needed a bit of calm.

"It's so peaceful," I said.

"Aye," Mama said. "This has always been one of my favourite spots."

"They say Saint Patrick killed a serpent here," Aodhan offered.

I shuddered. "I hope there aren't any more of those lurking about."

"Agreed," Aodhan said. "Here's hoping this watery adventure turns out better than our time at Shannon Pot."

"And that we don't get in trouble with the garda again," I added.

"I don't remember seeing any garda at the Shannon Pot," Mama said.

"We got on their radar after we stole your sword from the museum, and later at the Cliffs of Moher," I explained. "We ended up there after you sang us away to Inis Mór."

"I told you I was trying to save you!"

"I know. Thank you for that."

"You're welcome. What happened at the museum?"

"That's where your sword was, after it was hauled out of the river. Aodhan and I created a diversion, and I took it back." I took a deep breath. "Fitzsimmons killed an archaeologist at the museum. I saw the body."

Mama's face darkened. "No surprise there. She's always been little more than a mercenary. After MacCreehy gets his due I'll see she does, as well."

The thought of Dr MacElroy's killer being brought to justice gave me hope. "Which island is Inis Cealtra? And we need to see about renting a boat."

"I can get us across the water." Mama widened her stance, letting her hands hang loose at her sides. "Both of you, lay hands on me. No funny business, Aodhan," she added.

"Christ, you two are like sisters," he said as he set his hand on Mama's left shoulder. I placed my hand on Mama's other shoulder, then she sang a single clear note. One heartbeat later found us halfway across Lough Derg, and standing on the shore of Inis Cealtra.

"Whoa," Aodhan said. "Can Meri do that too?"

"Of course she can," Mama replied.

"I can?" I repeated. "How?"

"It's in your blood. All you need to do is learn which notes will lead to the outcome you desire, just like you did when you compelled MacCreehy."

I recalled how I'd felt when I'd forced him to let Aodhan and I leave school grounds. I'd been scared, and desperate, and almost sick to my stomach. "How will I ever control it?"

"With a great deal of practice, and even more patience," Mama replied. "Follow me. I know just how to irritate the old codger."

Mama led us inland, and I took a moment to examine our surroundings. We were walking toward a ruined church and a graveyard, and the whole of it was surrounded by a timbre fence. Next to the church was a round tower, and its walls were dotted with tiny windows and a single doorway that was at least three metres above ground. I assumed that there were once steps leading to the doorway; either that, or some exceptionally tall people once lived here. I could see the remains of other buildings nearby, some of which were so dilapidated they were little more than tumbled stone piles.

We walked straight through the graveyard and headed toward a small wooded area near the shore opposite from the one we'd arrived on. Mama walked with purpose, as if she'd been here many times before and knew exactly what she was after.

"Meri." Aodhan placed his hand on my elbow. "See those carvings around the church's door?"

I glanced at the doorway. The church was made up of grey stone, and the entrance was one of those wide arched doorways that peaked in the centre, typical architecture for one of these ancient sites. The top half of the arch was surrounded by carved heads, which probably represented local saints. "What about them?"

"They're watching us."

Nervous laughter bubbled out of me. "That's your imagination."

"Meri, the heads turned!"

Even as I opened my mouth to deny that possibility, one of the heads craned his neck toward me and grinned. I grabbed Aodhan's arm and pulled him away from the church. "Let's catch up to Mama."

We didn't quite run from the church and its nosy heads, but we did walk rather quickly across the churchyard, all the while navigating around gravestones and the occasional rutted ground. I wondered what sort of wildlife was digging holes on this island, perhaps the descendants of Saint Patrick's serpent. If there were a few offspring slithering about, hopefully they weren't still angry.

We found Mama clear across the area, standing on top of the low stone wall that bordered the graveyard. She was gazing up at a particular tree as if it was a long-lost friend.

"What's so special about this tree?" I asked.

"This tree is the entire reason why Seamus came here, and why he was sent away."

"Really. Looks like a regular tree to me." Even as the words left my mouth, I could sense that there was more to this tree than met the eye. The trunk itself was smooth and pale, the silvery bark offset by rougher patches of brown. The massive trunk split into three smaller branches, and the offshoots of those limbs climbed toward the sky. The topmost twigs resembled fingers trying to grab the clouds. There wasn't a single leaf on the tree, nor any moss or vines. Nevertheless, the tree teemed with life.

"It looks dead, yet it's alive?" I asked.

"It doesn't even have leaves," Aodhan added.

Mama turned toward us, and realised we had no idea what she was talking about. "Of course, you can't see it. Meri, sing with me."

She reached out to me. I took her hand, then she jumped down beside me. "Sing what?"

"Follow my voice," she replied, then she sang a clear, cold note. I matched her tone, her cadence. Mama nodded, and I sang louder, stronger. We sang together just as we'd done when I was a wee babe; those memories of us sharing rhymes and verses had been so perfect I'd worried I'd imagined them, but here we were, singing in concert once again. When we paused, she placed her hand on my cheek.

"That was beautiful, Meri girl," she said. "Look at what we've revealed."

"Revealed?" I repeated. Mama gestured toward the tree, and it was no longer an ordinary tree. The bark had changed from rough and mottled with brown to a uniform silvered grey. This new version had strong branches laden with leaves that glittered like so many dangling emeralds. Strange symbols wrought in coppery rainbow hues swirled across the bark and coursed around the trunk, sliding like ice across a pond.

"Those symbols," I said. "Are they a form of ogham?"

"They're runes," Mama replied. "It's an ancient language, one I can't hope to decipher. At least, not without a book to guide me. But I know exactly what the runes on this tree mean."

"What *what* runes mean?" Aodhan asked.

"What? Oh, of course." Mama touched the centre of Aodhan's forehead and sang. When his eyes widened and he gasped, I knew he could see the runes as well.

"This tree is sacred," Mama explained. "The sap is as sweet as honey, and a single drop will enhance a mortal's form."

"Enhance it how?" I asked.

"The sap will augment one's endurance, strength, things of that nature. Some say that if you ingest enough of the sap you'll extend your life by several years, maybe even decades. However, these gifts are only bestowed if and when the sap is carefully taken without doing harm to the tree. If you obtain the sap through violence—such as breaking off a branch or cutting into the trunk—you shall be rebuked and suffer a torment specially crafted just for you."

"Did MacCreehy have to leave the island because he wounded the tree?" I asked, and Mama nodded.

"Aye, that he did. He came here when he was young, long before he had notions of opening the portal to all and sundry. Some think this was his first stab at claiming power that wasn't his."

I thought for a moment. "What was his punishment? Is it why he's so ugly?"

Mama giggled. "He was born with that face. MacCreehy's torment is a mystery to all but himself, but I can guarantee it was something he'd rather not have endured."

I regarded the tree, wondering what sort of punishment it had extracted from Seamus MacCreehy. Based on the fact that he was a bitter, vindictive man, it must have been something especially terrible.

"Are we related to him?" I asked suddenly.

"Gods below, of course we're not," Mama replied. "Whatever gave you that notion?"

"When he went to the garda looking for you, he said his daughter was missing," I replied. "Ever since I read that report, I've been terrified he's my grandpa, or a weird uncle."

Mama shuddered. "Thank the gods you're wrong about that. After all of this is done, I will take you and Kevin down to the city and introduce you to your grandfather. He is the kindest man you'll ever meet, save perhaps for your father."

"I have a grandpa," I said. "How delightful."

"Is he a merrow too?" Aodhan asked.

"Yes, but he no longer moves between realms. He's much too busy."

"Too busy doing what?" I asked.

"He's the king of Kilstiffen," Mama replied. "Now let's set a burr in MacCreehy's bonnet, so he knows we're here."

Merrows And Stones

"What do you mean, your father's the king?" I demanded.

"I mean just that," Mama said with a shrug.

"Just like the story," Aodhan said. "The king's daughter stole the key."

"Exactly," Mama said, then she turned back to me. "Your grandfather is Steinar the Immoveable, Sixty-Seventh Lord of Kilstiffen and Guardian of the Portal."

"So he wears a crown, people do what he says, all of it?" I asked.

"Yes, of course," Mama replied.

"Will you stop saying of course!"

"Mer, you're a princess," Aodhan said. "Maybe when you meet your grandpa, he'll give you a tiara."

I tossed a glare at Aodhan, then I asked Mama, "Why didn't Da ever tell me about this? Is your royal status something else you made him forget?"

"No. Perhaps." Her head drooped. "When I sang the spell, we weren't sure exactly what he'd forget."

"He seems to remember an awful lot," Aodhan said. "He told us all about how he rescued you, where you're from, about that mad huge dowry—"

"What?" Mama demanded. "The whole point was for him to forget anything that could link him to me!"

"Maybe his head forgot, but his heart remembered," Aodhan suggested.

I threw my hands up in the air. "Wonderful. Da has a bad memory and a good heart. Exactly what else haven't you told me about our family?"

"I couldn't very well tell you about them if I wasn't here to do it," she replied. I crossed my arms over my chest and tapped my foot.

"Put it aside for the time being," she said. "We've more pressing matters at the moment." Mama turned away from me and toward the symbol tree. Since she was right, and damn it all, I did want to be more level-headed like she was, I stood beside her and regarded the tree. I squinted at the bark for a moment, and turned away. The coppery runes sliding across its bark made my stomach a bit queasy.

"How are we going to tell MacCreehy we're here?" I asked.

"If you and I sing together—not just any song, but a song that matches the symbols—we can project our voices toward him. That way, he'll know we're here, and it won't be long before he joins us."

"All right," I said. "How long will that take?"

"It won't be an instant, that's for certain. This will take half a day, at best."

"We could call him, instead," Aodhan offered. "That will get his attention within a few seconds rather than a few hours."

"How did you get MacCreehy's phone number?" I asked.

"I took over my dad's old phone plan, which is the number the school has," he explained. "Whenever they need to call my parents, I get the messages, and MacCreehy tends to make those calls from his personal cell. I saved his number, just in case."

I nodded. "So that's how you were able to miss all those days last week. The school was reporting your absences to you."

"On the nose, Meri." Aodhan withdrew his phone, then he grinned. "Instead of calling him, I've a better idea. Mrs Murphy, if you wouldn't mind, please stand a bit closer to Meri."

Mama positioned herself as he asked, then Aodhan put his arm around my shoulder, angled his phone and snapped a picture. He did a bit of typing, then he showed us the screen. It was a selfie of the three of us—Mama and I looking bewildered while Aodhan was grinning like a fool—with the symbol tree looming behind us. The caption read, "Wish you were here with us on Inis Cealtra."

Mama laughed softly. "That will certainly get his attention."

After Aodhan sent the picture of the three of us off to MacCreehy's phone, we retreated to the higher ground above the church. From that vantage point, we could see the ruined church and graveyard, and beyond that to the shore. Despite the frigid pre-dawn hours we'd endured earlier, the day had turned out to be quite lovely, with the sunlight reflecting off the lough's surface and the winds remaining calm. Too bad we were passing time waiting on a madman's arrival.

Aodhan declared he'd jog up and down the beach, and keep a lookout for MacCreehy's arrival. That left Mama and me standing together, staring at the lough. I opened my mouth to speak, but this was the first time we'd been alone with each other in fourteen years. I wracked my brain for something important to say, and came up with nothing. After seeing MacCreehy's army and being tossed inside a prison cell, everything else felt trivial in comparison.

"What is it?" Mama asked.

"What's what?"

"I can feel the words welling up inside you." When I remained silent, she faced me. "You can tell me anything, good or bad. I'll always listen."

"Okay. Um." I cleared my throat, swallowing down the emotions that threatened to overwhelm me. Why was it so easy for me to snap at her, and yet so difficult to talk? All I wanted was to talk to her, and have easy conversations like Da and me did all the time.

Mama touched my hand. "Meri girl."

"In the water, when you saw me wearing the pearl necklace," I began. "Your necklace. You were pretty mad."

"I was not mad," she said.

"You called me a thief." I scuffed my toe against the grass. "You didn't even recognise me."

"You can hardly blame me for that," she said. "The last person I expected to see while I was evading that lot was my daughter, who for all I knew was far removed from this mess." She smiled, and tucked a bit of hair behind my ear. "Nor did I expect to see you so grown. Even though many years have passed, I've always pictured you as my sweet Meri girl, singing in her cradle and catching sunbeams in her hands. Yet here you are, a babe no more."

I felt my throat tighten, then Mama pulled me into her arms. "So yes, Meri girl, when I first saw my pearl at your throat I did not recognise you, and I did assume my necklace had been stolen. I was wrong, and I am so very happy I was."

"I found it in the old cottage," I said, my words muffled by her shoulder. "Da must have hidden it there. I'll give it back to you, when we're home."

"Keep it," Mama said. "Your grandfather meant for it to go to you."

"He did?" Before Mama could reply, Aodhan returned from his patrol and saw us embracing.

"Aww, you two." Aodhan wrapped his long arms around Mama and me. "I love reunions. Soon, this'll be me and my dad."

Mama's arms tensed, then she caught my gaze and shook her head slightly. I took that as her sharing my fear that reuniting Aodhan with his father wouldn't be as easy as he hoped. Being that Mr Sullivan was one of MacCreehy's enthralled warriors, maybe it wouldn't even be possible.

"Did you see anything out of the ordinary during your patrol?" Mama asked Aodhan as she drew back.

"Not a thing," he replied, frowning. Since I didn't want to discuss the possibility of not rescuing Mr Sullivan any more than Mama did, I kept on distracting him.

"Shouldn't we be watching the docks, rather than the beach?" I asked. "I imagine that's where MacCreehy's boats will be landing."

Mama shook her head. "He has no need of a fleet. He and his will follow the river to where it meets the lough, and they'll do it all on foot."

"But how will they get across the water?"

"Not across. Under."

Realisation settled across my shoulders like a heavy coat. "How is that even possible?" I squeaked.

"His merrows will sing the army's way as they march along the riverbed."

I shook my head. "That is unreal."

Mama shrugged, as if warriors marching under water and across river bottoms happened all the time. Where she came from, I suppose it did. I shivered; what else could merrows accomplish with their voices?

"Won't that take an awfully long time?" Aodhan asked. "And how many warriors will he bring with him?"

Mama jerked her chin toward the water. "There's your answer."

As if they'd been privy to Aodhan's question, Seamus MacCreehy and his army marched up and out of the waters of Lough Derg and onto the island. MacCreehy himself was wearing armour across his chest and arms, though he wore metal plate rather than chain mail. The unmarred bronze plates reflected the sunlight like so many mirrors, making me wonder if he had ever fought in a battle. I bet he was one to let others do the fighting, and dying, for him.

The soldiers followed MacCreehy out of the water and onto the island, all the while keeping their tight formation. They weren't wearing any kind of breathing apparatuses, and they didn't have gills—at least, none that I could see—and I could hardly believe they'd walked right along the river bed and under the lough to reach us. MacCreehy and his merrows must be strong enough in their abilities to sing the air into dozens, maybe hundreds of sets of lungs, much as Mama had done for Aodhan and me at the Shannon Pot. That, or those soldiers really were zombies. For Aodhan's father's sake, I hoped that wasn't so.

Mama surveyed the warriors emerging out of the water and frowned. "Gods below, he's brought his entire army."

"Too bad we left the hard hats behind in the cave," I muttered. "Do you see Fitzsimmons anywhere?" I asked, imagining my mother telling that false archaeologist where she could stick her sword.

"Why would she be with MacCreehy?" Mama asked.

"I thought she worked for him," I said. "Isn't that why she was after your sword?"

"Fitzsimmons is an agent of Kilstiffen's council of lords," Mama replied. "The council has tasked her with recovering anything I brought above, including myself, should she get her hands on me."

"But your father's the king," I said. "Wouldn't this council work for him?"

Mama stared straight ahead. "Aye, Meri. That they do."

"Oh." I grasped Mama's hand. "Then we really do need to beat MacCreehy."

"Yes. A sound beating is what is needed."

I squeezed Mama's hand, then I glanced at Aodhan. He stood tense, with his hands fisted at his sides. "Can you see your father?" I asked.

He shook his head. "No. What with him wearing the same kit as the rest, they're all blending in together. It's like MacCreehy stripped them down to nothing, then made them all the same."

"Like those manky school uniforms we wear," I teased.

"Meri, this is no time for jokes," Mama admonished. Aodhan's mouth quirked, then something caught his attention.

"What are those blokes for?" Aodhan asked. "The odd ones on the corners of the companies. Are those horns they're carrying?"

I followed his gaze, and saw that regularly spaced among the warriors were other people clad not in armour but in long, loose garments that almost reached the ground. Chains were wound around their torsos, keeping their arms tight against their bodies. Large metal harnesses were balanced on their shoulders, and were held in place with heavy leather straps and rusted buckles that clasped over their abdomens. Attached to the harnesses were curving gold horns that wouldn't have looked out of place on Da's antique Victrola. The mouthpieces of the horns were perched directly in front of the marchers' mouths. And while the sound was faint, I could hear their songs wafting up from the water.

"Those people, the ones in the grey robes? They're his merrows," Mama said. "The horns are used to amplify their songs." I returned my gaze to MacCreehy standing at the head of the company. He had his mouth shut tight, and he was glaring at the rune tree as if it was his mortal enemy.

"MacCreehy isn't singing," I said. "He's relying on the others for the brunt of it."

"He also hates that tree," Aodhan added.

"Odd," Mama said, then she glanced at the rune tree. "That's it! When Seamus hurt the tree, it must have cost him his songs."

"If the tree hobbled him like that, he must have done more than hurt it," Aodhan said.

"If he can't sing, then why are those merrows helping him?" I asked.

"Look at them, Mer," Aodhan said. "The merrows aren't his helpers. They're his slaves."

I noted the heavy chains wrapped around the merrows' arms, and how they all gazed dejectedly at the back of the person in front of them. "Oh, Aodhan, they look miserable."

"Kilstiffen does not practice slavery, not on merrows or any other living creature." Mama drew her sword. "This ends today."

"What do we do?" Aodhan demanded.

"We engage the enemy, stand our ground, and hold for reinforcements," Mama said.

"Just the three of us against so many?" I scanned the approaching warriors. "There must be a hundred of them. Maybe two hundred."

"The rest of the merrows—the ones that stand with me against MacCreehy—will have felt a force of this size moving through the water," Mama replied. "They'll be here soon."

"We need help now," I said.

"We are all the help we have right now," Mama snapped, but she was wrong. I withdrew the whistle Tourmaline had given me and blew.

"You're trumpeting our location straight to our enemies' ears," Mama said.

"Tourmaline told me to use the whistle if I needed help!"

"*Tallulah* is a trickster," Mama snapped, then Aodhan grabbed my arm.

"Look there," he said, pointing at the church. "At the door!"

The carved heads that outlined the church's entrance were pulling themselves loose from the stone and mortar structure, all the while making the horrible scraping noises of rock on rock. Once the carvings were free, anthropomorphic forms oozed down from their necks until each head had a torso and four rudely crafted limbs. The stones dropped to the ground with a flourish, like so many carved acrobats, then they loped across the field and stationed themselves between the three of us and MacCreehy's army.

"Gods below," Mama said, her gaze moved across the stone army. "Tallulah did something right."

I caught movement in the corner of my eye. "There's more coming from the churchyard."

"More of these... these stones?" Mama turned around, and clapped her hand over her mouth.

It wasn't just the stone heads that had rallied to the whistle's call. Statues and carvings were pulling themselves free from the other ruined buildings and even the tombstones, and they quickly grew to human size. Added to our army were ancient monks, lanky skeletons and winged skulls, and several sets of enormous praying hands. We Irish are a morbid lot.

"I did not think this was the sort of help we'd be getting," I said.

"Neither did I," Mama said. "These stone beasties are on our side?"

"I think so," I replied.

"Let's hope you're right. With them we have the numbers to match MacCreehy's army." Mama rolled her shoulders and raised her sword. "Seamus!"

MacCreehy moved to the front of his army. The sunlight reflecting off his well-polished armour was blinding. "Aoife, first lady of traitors," he yelled. "I accept your surrender."

"Let the merrows go," Mama said, ignoring his insult. "Enslaving our own kind is low, even for you."

MacCreehy clenched his fist. "Give me the key, and I will set every last one free."

"I give you nothing," Mama ground out. "No quarter, no mercy."

"It is for the king to grant mercy," MacCreehy said. "Have you forgotten our ways so completely? Is that why you betrayed everything you knew and dirtied yourself with a surface man?"

I stepped in front of my mother, and yelled, "My father's a better man than you'll ever be!"

A slow smile spread across MacCreehy's face. "I knew you were her daughter. I will keep you alive, Meredith, and present you to the king in a cage. He likes his pets."

I spun around and faced Mama. "He's stalling," I said. "That, or he's crazy."

"A bit of both, I'm afraid." Mama glanced at the stone army and pointed her sword at MacCreehy. "We will leave off this banter. All of you, forward!"

The stones didn't move. Panic skated over Mama's face, then she glanced at the whistle in my hand.

"Right. They're your soldiers, Meri," she said.

"They are?"

"You called them to life. You're the only one they'll follow."

I clutched the whistle, feeling the edge of it bite into my skin. "Is that some kind of supernatural whistle rule?"

"If I say yes, will you order them to advance?" Mama demanded.

"All right." I held the whistle aloft, and shouted, "Stones! We are fighting those warriors!"

The stones organised themselves into a rudimentary company and faced the shoreline. MacCreehy's warriors continued their march up from the water and toward the interior of the island, and halted when their front line was about five metres away from the stones. The two companies stared at one another for a moment, the island so quiet you could hear the wind rustling in the grass.

"Stones," I yelled. "Advance!"

Both sides uttered bone-chilling war cries and charged toward each other. The stones had the advantage of running—or rather, tumbling—downhill, not that Seamus's warriors were about to let a pesky little thing like gravity deter them. The warriors fought tooth and nail against the stones, unfazed as their swords glanced off hard, rocky forms, and as their spears cracked and splintered to pieces. They didn't even scream when the stones struck back, knocking them off their feet and into the dirt. Some of the warriors didn't get back up.

My mother, Aodhan, and I hung back from the fighting, and watched from the sidelines in case some of MacCreehy's men tried to circle around behind us. I was caught up in the thrill of battle, egging on the stones as if they were a sports team. Then one of the warriors lost his helmet, and I saw his face. He was a white-haired old man, someone who should be sitting outside a pub and talking with friends, not caught up in a madman's battle. He had probably never heard of a merrow or Kilstiffen, and now he'd die for both.

Frantic, I looked at some of the other fallen warriors. Some lay at odd angles, and some were bleeding.

"The stones are hurting MacCreehy's warriors!" My hand flew to my mouth, a futile attempt to quell my fears. I'd never seen a battle before, and I was unprepared for the reality of it. "The warriors don't even know what they're fighting for!"

Aodhan grabbed my arm and pointed. "Meri, look!"

One of the enormous praying hands swept through the human warriors, knocking the breath out of them and leaving them flat on the ground. A woman's helmet fell off as she rolled onto her back, and I saw her face. She was my literature teacher, Sister Mary Katherine. So that was why MacCreehy had taken over her class that day. He had kidnapped not only innocents, but also our teachers to fight for his mad cause.

This had to stop.

I leapt in front of Mama and flailed my arms. "MacCreehy's warriors aren't the problem here! We need to help them, not beat them senseless!"

"Agreed, but as long as they're under MacCreehy's thrall, they want to beat us senseless," Mama said. "If we don't fight back, we're done for."

I grabbed her shoulders and forced her to look at me. "We have to do something! This isn't right!" Mama looked past me to the injured yet still fighting warriors, and bit her lip.

"You're right. It's not." Mama surveyed the battle, then she sheathed her sword. "I'm going in for a closer look. Stay with Aodhan."

Mama melted into the battle, evading both stone and human fighters. Aodhan stayed right beside me, alternately craning his neck as he searched for a glimpse of his father and pulling me out of harm's way. With the stones guarding us, we remained in the thick of it, until one of MacCreehy's men tripped and sent a spray of gravel and sand toward me. I shielded myself, but not before the gravel chips struck my face and eyes, temporarily blinding me.

I pressed my hands over my eyes and dropped to my knees. Not a smart move in the midst of an all-out battle, but I couldn't think past the pain. Then Aodhan was there, his hands on my shoulders as he tried rallying me.

"What's wrong?" he demanded.

"I can't open my eyes," I replied. "Sand or something got in them."

"We're in the middle of everything." Aodhan pulled me upright and looped my arm around his elbow. "Hold on to me. When we get to the edge, we'll see what we can do about your eyes."

I nodded, then he was weaving through the warriors and stones. I was in total blackness, my eyes burning as I held on to Aodhan for dear life.

He stopped moving and said something I couldn't make out, then his arm went loose. I assumed we were out of the fighting, so I withdrew my hand and tried forcing my eyes open. After a moment, they did open; I went down on my knees and blinked slowly, tears coursing down my cheeks as the bits of sand washed away.

Finally able to see again, I stood. It wasn't long before I had my bearings, but as I took in my surroundings my stomach dropped. I was at least five metres removed from the battle, and I was alone.

Aodhan was gone.

RELIABLE

"**A**odhan?"

I scanned the crowd, only seeing grey stone bodies and kitted out warriors, and the occasional captive merrow warbling their dull notes. I couldn't find Aodhan anywhere.

"Aodhan!"

He wouldn't have left me of his own accord, of that I was certain. Aodhan was the most reliable man on earth, and he would have stood guard over my pathetic blind self until sundown if necessary. For him to have left my side without even telling me where he was going meant that something had happened to him.

"Aodhan!"

I recalled the sight of Sister Mary Katherine falling under a stone's blow, and clenched my fist. MacCreehy was the reason my mother had been gone for so long, why my father was a drunk, and—with his lack of punishments to Kelsey and Sarah—the source of my incessant bullying at school. He'd kidnapped my favourite teacher. And now, something had happened to Aodhan.

I'd had enough of MacCreehy ruining my life. Today, I will stop him.

"Stones," I called, and the six closest stones stopped what they were doing and formed a circle around me. "I've lost Aodhan. I need you to help me move into the battle so I can find him."

Four of the stones wasted no time in reshaping themselves into a many-legged platform like so much modelling clay, while the other two stood guard on either side. Once the platform was complete, the guards set me on top of it, and eight stone legs picked their way down the hillside and into the fight.

As the platform bobbed and jostled me into the fray, I cupped my hands at my mouth and yelled Aodhan's name. I searched the faces of those near me, but I couldn't find Aodhan's dark head anywhere. What I did see were innocent people of Clare, elders and school-age children mixed in with adults, fighting and falling before my stone army.

"Don't hurt them," I called out. "Subdue the warriors, but don't hurt them."

The fight raged on. It might have been my imagination, but the stones appeared to be pulling their punches.

One of the stone guards pounded on the platform I was on, getting my attention. My gaze followed where it pointed, and I saw MacCreehy scaling the round tower, impossibly thrusting his fingers into the mortar between the stonework in order to make hand holds, with a man's body flung over his shoulder. The man had a sack over his head, but I recognised that godawful blue track suit.

"Aodhan," I screamed. I jumped off the stones' platform and landed on my knees in the dirt. I got up and ran toward the tower, trying to climb up after him. I couldn't make my own handholds, and Mac-Creehy's were too far apart for me to reach. I fell against the tower, scraping my hands and elbows against the stone blocks. Then Mama was there, helping me to my feet.

"MacCreehy has Aodhan," I said, flailing my arms toward the tower.

"I know." She held me back when I would have attempted to scale the tower again. "No, Meri. We need to out-think him, not fall into his trap alongside Aodhan."

I stilled myself. "The tower is a trap?"

"With MacCreehy, everything is a trap."

"What's he going to do with him?" I backed away from the tower and watched as MacCreehy stood atop the wall's curved edge. His arm was around Aodhan's waist as he held his body upright, then he snatched the sack off of Aodhan's head, and it fluttered to the ground. Aodhan glanced around, then he kicked back at MacCreehy. MacCreehy made a movement I couldn't track and Aodhan jerked, then he went limp.

"He plans to use Aodhan as a bargaining chip, most likely. Gods, is he even still alive?" Mama asked. Aodhan's head lolled to the side, and his body was lax against MacCreehy.

"Don't say that," I said. "He has to be. Aodhan's only mixed up in this because of me. He can't get hurt."

"Aoife," MacCreehy bellowed. "The key for the boy."

"I accept your terms," Mama said, her voice ringing clear and true across the din of battle. "Small problem, I don't have the key."

"What?" MacCreehy's face purpled. "You've lost it?"

"No. I hid it." Mama spread her arms wide. "Give me a bit of time and I'll retrieve it for you. As a gesture of good faith, why don't you let the boy down."

MacCreehy clasped his hand around the back of Aodhan's neck and dangled him off the side of the tower. "As my own gesture of good faith, I'll give you until my arm gives out and the boy drops."

"That boy dies and you'll never go below again," Mama shouted.

"God, why is this happening?" I wailed. At my wit's end, I scanned the battle. My gaze landed on a merrow, glassy-eyed as she sang into her burnished horn.

"Stop singing," I shouted. Remembering what I'd done in the car park, I sang, *"You're all helping him do this. All of you, stop it! Stop it now!"*

Every single merrow fell silent.

The warriors stopped fighting, as did the stones. Every last set of eyes on the field turned to me.

"W-what just happened?" I asked.

"You commanded the merrows to stop singing, and they obeyed," Mama said. "MacCreehy's warriors and the stones obeyed you, too."

"I did all of that?" I asked. I'd only wanted the merrows to be silent.

"Your voice is strong," Mama said. "You lack training, but you have an innate understanding of your power. Meri girl, your grandfather will be so proud of you. I am proud."

"Pride won't help Aodhan," I said, pausing when there was a commotion behind us. One of Seamus's warriors had broken free of his regiment and sped toward the tower, barrelling into it like a raging bull. His armoured shoulder connected with the tower... And nothing happened. The tower had withstood centuries, after all.

MacCreehy didn't loosen his grip on Aodhan. Realising this, the warrior backed up a few paces, then he took off his helmet and threw it at Seamus. His aim was true, and the helmet struck MacCreehy's shoulder, knocking him off balance.

MacCreehy dropped Aodhan.

I screamed.

The warrior sprinted forward and caught Aodhan, breaking his fall. He went into a crouch, cradling Aodhan against his chest. I was there in an instant, feeling Aodhan's hands and wrists and searching for the pulse points in his neck.

"Aodhan, are you all right?" I asked. "Aodhan, wake up!"

The warrior held Aodhan tighter. "It's all right," he murmured. "I've got you now."

"Why did you save him?" I asked. The warrior raised his head, his expression betraying that he thought I'd asked the most ludicrous question. He had dark skin, even darker than Aodhan's, wide brown eyes, and close cropped black hair. What's more, he had an American accent...

"You're Lucas Sullivan!"

"I am," he said. "Thank you, for breaking me free from whatever MacCreehy did to me." He reached over Aodhan's torso and squeezed my shoulder. "If you hadn't, I might not have caught him in time."

"I'm just glad it worked," I said, since I didn't fully understand how I'd broken MacCreehy's magic.

"Who are you?" Mr Sullivan asked.

"I'm Meri," I replied. "I go to school with Aodhan."

Mr Sullivan nodded, then he jerked his chin toward the stone tower. "And who is that?"

I followed his gaze and saw Mama pacing at the base of the tower. Her sword was out, glinting in the sunlight. "That is my mother."

"Is she going to stop MacCreehy?"

"Yes," I said with confidence. "She is."

"You're beaten, Seamus," Mama yelled. "Surrender!"

MacCreehy ignored her command, and screamed for his merrows to resume singing. They inhaled as one, ready to comply with their master, but I had other plans.

"No," I sang, and they hesitated. *"Stay silent!"*

As MacCreehy stood dumbfounded, my mother sang a lifting note and leapt to the top of the tower, alighting opposite him. He drew his sword, but he was still off-balance, and he faltered. Mama brought her shield down on his sword, and he tumbled into the centre of the tower.

"Stones," I yelled as Mama jumped down to the ground. "Seal him in!"

The living stones swarmed the tower like a colony of ants. Once at the top, they reshaped themselves into blocks and sealed the tower's roof, then they worked their way down to the narrow windows, and finally the arched doorway. At long last, Seamus MacCreehy was trapped.

"Will he be able to breathe in there?" I wondered.

"Would it be so bad if he couldn't?" Mama countered. "But I'm sure he'll be fine. Men like him tend to survive whatever scrape they've got into, and live to a ripe old age."

"What do we do with him now? Should we leave him in there?"

"If only we could," Mama replied. "I'll send a message to Kilstiffen's guard. They'll collect his sorry arse and return him below for punishment. While that goes on, we can work on setting many of his wrongs to right."

"Which one should we start with?" I asked, since MacCreehy had committed his fair share of sins.

"We've already started." Mama gestured toward the now un-en-thralled warriors. They were looking around as if they'd just woken up, and were still wound up in their dreams. I saw Sister Mary Katherine sit up, look down at her strange attire, shake her head and laugh. Thank God, they were going to be all right.

"It's like they finally remembered who they are," I said.

"We always knew," Aodhan's father said. "We were trapped within ourselves but had no free will. It was like a waking nightmare. It only ended when you ordered us to stop following him."

Aodhan opened his eyes, squinting up at the sun and his father. "Dad?"

"Yeah, kid," he replied. "I'm here."

Aodhan blinked, then he threw his arms around his father's neck.

Mama watched Aodhan and his father's reunion and smiled. "We did a good thing today, Meri."

I leaned against my mother, shaking and unsure if I was about to laugh or cry. In one day's time, I'd found her, and Aodhan had found his father, and we'd stopped a madman and rescued hundreds of captives. "That is an understatement," I said. "Possibly the most egregiously under-stated statement of all time."

Mama looped her arm around my shoulders and kissed my hair. "I could sing a song about it, if you'd like."

I smiled as happy tears flowed down my cheeks. "I'd like that, very much."

Happy Endings All Around...

"Dad, I can't believe it," Aodhan said. "I never thought I'd see you again, yet here we are." Aodhan and his father had got to their feet and were grinning at each other. "When we saw you this morning, and you were brainwashed with the rest, I was gutted."

"You saw me this morning?" Mr Sullivan asked.

"In the caves, when you were with the other warriors," Aodhan replied. "We were looking for clues to stop MacCreehy."

"Well, you did great," Mr Sullivan said, gesturing to encompass the entire island, including the freed merrows and warriors.

"How are you free?" Aodhan asked, and I remembered that he'd been unconscious when I'd commanded the merrows and warriors to stop following MacCreehy.

"It's all because of Meri," Mr Sullivan replied. "And..." He looked at my mother, and cocked his head to the side. "Are you Aoife Murphy?"

It was Mama's turn to look shocked. "You remember me?"

"Sure do. My wife grew up alongside your husband."

Aodhan stilled at the mention of his mother; someone, probably Aodhan, was going to have to break the news to Mr Sullivan that she'd remarried. Before Aodhan or I could say anything, Mama surveyed the field.

"We'll catch up later," she said. "Right now, we need to assess if anyone is injured and get them whatever medical attention they need. Meri and I will see to the merrows, if you and Aodhan will check in with the warriors."

"Will do, ma'am," Mr Sullivan said. I turned to follow Mama, but Aodhan caught my hand in his.

"I'm so sorry I left you alone on the field," Aodhan said. "One of the warriors grabbed me from behind and stuck a bag on my head. When MacCreehy took it off and I saw you so far below me..."

"You were awake for that?" I asked, and he nodded.

"At first. Then he choked me, and I passed out."

"I was so scared he'd hurt you, or worse."

"Hey." Aodhan moved closer and smiled down at me. "You really think I'd let a creep like MacCreehy take me out before we had our talk?"

"I know you wouldn't. You're far too stubborn for that." I squeezed his fingers. "I'm so glad you're okay."

Aodhan smoothed the stray hairs back from my forehead. "I'm glad you're okay, too," he said, his lips against my forehead.

"Don't ever leave me like that again," I blurted out. "Please. I-I was so worried about you."

I felt his mouth stretch into a smile. "I won't. Promise."

We broke apart, and each followed our respective parent, our hands remaining in contact until we were out of reach. I glanced over my shoulder, and caught him looking back at me. Perhaps our upcoming talk wouldn't be so bad.

"How long have you and Aodhan been together?" Mama asked.

"Together?" I squeaked. "We're just friends!"

Mama raised a single brow. "Is that so? Perhaps you should tell that to the lovesick boy."

"What?" I turned back to Aodhan, but he was following his father. I glanced at Mama, saw her smirking at me. I squared my shoulders, and said, "We should check the tower, make sure it's secure."

"As you say, Meri girl."

Mama and I walked around the base of the tower, and were pleased to learn it was as solid as the day it was built. Even so, we could hear MacCreehy wailing and cursing from within. I posted the remaining stone warriors as guards, just in case. That done, Mama and I set about freeing the merrows from their harnesses.

I don't know which lot had been worse off. The warriors had been enthralled to do Seamus's bidding, but he'd put the merrows in actual chains. The harnesses that held the brass horns before their mouths had worn deep, red indentations into their shoulders and arms. Two of the merrows that had been Seamus's prisoners for the longest had stooped backs from the weight of it all, and their spines were twisted into unnatural angles. I wondered if either of them would ever stand upright again.

"What's your name?" I asked the oldest merrow. His arms were emaciated from lack of use, and I was massaging his hands in the hopes of getting the blood flowing to his fingers again.

"I am called Daveth," he replied.

"Good to meet you, Daveth, though I wish we'd done so under better circumstances. I'm Meri."

"I know who you are," Daveth said. "We all know who you are."

My hands stilled. Before I could ask Daveth exactly who everyone was and how they all knew about me, Aodhan plopped down beside me.

"I thought you were seeing to the warriors," I said. "With your dad."

"He's still with them. They're figuring out their next move. They all seemed like they needed a bit of space to do it, so I gave it to them." He turned toward Daveth and grinned. "Hello, Daveth. I'm Mer's friend, Aodhan."

Daveth's eyes narrowed. "You're no merrow."

"No, I'm not, but I am an excellent swimmer. What's this about everyone knowing Meri?"

The old merrow looked at me and smiled, his brown skin crinkling around his eyes. "You're Aoife's girl, and King Steinar has always said that if his daughter couldn't save Kilstiffen, then his granddaughter would. As it turned out, you did it together."

"Wait. The king knows about me, too?" I demanded.

"Of course he does. He knows of your brother, as well. He has eyes and ears everywhere."

"What do you mean, everywhere?" I asked.

"So Meri really is a princess," Aodhan said over me. "Tell me, Daveth, does her position involve a tiara?"

"Ignore him," I said to Daveth. "If it's not too much for you to speak of, would you tell us how MacCreehy captured you?"

"It is not too much, and in the beginning we worked alongside him," Daveth replied. "Seamus came to each of us individually, and beseeched us our help. He had been wounded, you see, the worst sort of wound a merrow can suffer and survive from, and I daresay he touched our hearts. We all went to him willingly, at first."

"He must have been hurt rather badly," I said. "He lost his singing ability, didn't he?"

"He did indeed," Daveth said. "For a merrow to lose his songs, it's as if the world has ended." Daveth's face darkened. "And we helped him, sang what he needed sung. When his true plan became known and we spoke against him, that was when he chained us."

"Oh." My hands trembled on Daveth's forearm.

"Now, Meri, don't be sad for us," Daveth said. "Be proud that you ended our suffering."

I smiled at Daveth. "I can do that."

After the warriors had sorted themselves out, and we'd done all we could for the merrows with our limited resources, it was time for us to get back across the water to the mainland. Mama wasn't sure if the merrows could sing all of the warriors across the water in their weakened state; I'd asked why she couldn't do it herself, and she explained that one voice can only carry two, maybe three passengers at a time, so for her to take on the job alone—or even with my help—would take days. In the end, we conscripted a few of the tourist boats, and while it wasn't a quick journey, it was much faster than if Mama and I had handled it ourselves.

As for the merrows, they had dispersed on their own, slipping into the water in twos and threes and quickly disappearing from view. Mama and I stood on the beach as we watched the last of them depart.

"Do you wish you were going with them?" I asked.

"No. I don't." Mama turned to me and smiled. "I do miss Kilstiffen, but it's not time for me to return. Not yet."

"When will it be time?"

"When I next return to the city, it will be to present you and Kevin to the king," she replied. "It's time you two learned about the other side of your heritage."

So I'd be going below, at least halfway. I made a mental note to ask Da if he'd ever met this King Steinar, Guardian of the Portal blah blah blah, and what he'd thought of him.

After the last boatload of warriors arrived on the mainland, Aodhan, myself, his father, and my mother all piled into Da's car. Since Aodhan was the only one qualified to drive—Mama and I didn't know how, and Mr Sullivan hadn't driven so long, he didn't think it was a good idea for him to make the attempt—he took the wheel. His hands were shaking, and instead of his usual breakneck pace, he crawled down the road. That was just as well, since the remaining warriors marched along behind us in an ordered column. That column included none other than Sister Mary Katherine. I'd tried to get her into the car with us, but she'd refused to leave her regiment. She was a loyal soldier, if a bit frustrating.

"Is this really a good idea?" Mama asked.

"Is what a good idea?" I countered. "Going home?"

"Having all these people descend on the town at once. There's just so many. The garda will have fits." She worried her lower lip. "Perhaps I should bring them somewhere else first, somewhere they can rest."

"Where can they rest better than with their families?" I asked. Mama didn't reply. Instead, she kept looking all around the countryside, and leaning forward to see what was waiting for us up ahead.

"You don't have to be nervous," I said, and she stilled. "Da wants to see you. He's not angry."

She laughed through her nose. "Brian is never angry. He's so understanding it's enough to drive you mad." She watched her hands, clasping and unclasping in her lap. "We had an agreement, your father and I. I was to return no later than seven years after I left, because if I couldn't halt Seamus by then the portal would have opened regardless of my efforts. I was to return home, and the four of us were to flee."

"Why didn't that happen?" I asked, remembering Da's days-long bender that had happened around that time.

"When the seventh year came, I was in chains in the bottom of a cave," Mama replied. "And since the key was elsewhere, and hidden, the city did not rise and the portal remained closed. I fear that's when Seamus lost whatever was left of his sanity."

"But you escaped," I said.

"That I did, but I'd missed our meeting. I'd failed, both my family and my city."

"You didn't fail us. It just took you a bit longer to succeed that you'd anticipated. Da will be overjoyed to see you again."

Mama smiled, but it didn't reach her eyes. "Gods below, I hope you're right."

Soon enough, Aodhan parked near the docks where my father moored his boat. The sun was descending toward the water; we'd been at this all day, and neither Aodhan nor I had updated Da or Kevin as to what was happening. I hoped they weren't too worried, or mad about our lack of communication.

We left the car and walked the rest of the way toward the water, Mama and me and Aodhan and his father leading the rest of the jumpers out of the darkness and back to their lives. I wondered how they would fare, how they would get on with the families and jobs they'd left behind. No matter what happened, I knew they'd be better off. Anything would be better than being slave in Seamus MacCreehy's army.

I heard Mama gasp. I followed her gaze and saw Da and Kevin standing at the edge of the docks, the sea at their backs. Da had his arms crossed over his chest, his stance wide and powerful. As he stood there, lit from behind by the setting sun, I understood why my mother had chosen him. He was strong enough to bear both her secrets, and his own.

Da saw us, then his gaze fixed on Mama. "Calliope?"

Mama stopped moving. "Brian, I—"

She raised a hand to her face, and I saw her tremble.

"What's wrong?" I asked.

"Brian looks just the same," she whispered. "And... And is that my Kevin?"

"Calliope," Da called, again. Next to him, Kevin frowned.

"Go on." I nudged her forward. "They missed you."

I didn't have to tell her twice. Mama ran down the road and onto the docks, and straight into Da's arms. They were crying and holding each other, and a moment later Kevin was mashed between them.

Da looked over Mama's shoulder and saw me. "Meri!"

And then I was mashed right along with my parents and brother. I don't think I've ever been happier.

After a few minutes, Kevin and I stepped back. Da held Mama's face in his hands and kissed her brow.

"Calliope," he murmured. "My Calliope. I searched for you every day."

"I know you did. And call me Aoife." She bit her lip. "I'm sorry I made you forget. I'm sorry it took so long for me to return. Brian, I'm so sorry about the way things went."

Da brushed his thumbs across her cheeks. "You promised you'd return to me, and here you are. The way I see it, there's nothing to apologise for."

They kissed, and I turned away. Aodhan came up behind me and draped his arm across my shoulders. "I love a happy ending," he said.

I leaned into him. "Me, too."

"Too bad we never found the key."

Mama peeked around Da's shoulder at Aodhan. "You already have the key."

Aodhan blinked. "I do?"

Mama untangled herself from Da and held out a hand. "Let me have that bag of yours."

Aodhan's duffle had remained in Da's car while we'd dealt with MacCreehy. He jogged back to the car and retrieved it, then he handed the bag to Mama. She rooted around inside it for a moment and withdrew the key we'd found at the well on Slieve Callan.

"But that's just someone's old offering," I said. "It's not even gold."

"Isn't it?" Mama worried the edge of the key, and the green paint sloughed away, revealing shining gold underneath. "After I stole the key from the king's chambers, I painted it. No one above or below was looking for a green key."

"Meri knew the key was important the instant she saw it," Aodhan said. "I wanted to leave it behind, but she took it anyway."

I stared at the key in Mama's hand. "You mean the key everyone's been searching for has been in Aodhan's bag all this time?"

Mama's smile widened. "Aye, that it was. Now we can return it to Kilstiffen, and the city will once again rise as it is meant to."

Aodhan's arm snaked around my waist, and he pulled me against him. "When MacCreehy had me, by default he had the key, too. Good thing he never had a merrow demand I produce it."

"Good thing," I murmured, then I leaned up and kissed him. Aodhan hesitated, then he drew me closer and kissed me longer than I'd intended, tightening one of his arms around me as his other hand cupped the back of my head. When we parted, he grinned.

"We've got happy endings all around, huh, Mer?"

"Finally, we all get one."

But It's Not Yet The End

As it worked out, the ending wasn't happy for everyone.

The least happy of all had to be Seamus MacCreehy himself, and he'd earned every last drop of his misery. We had left him in the tower on Inis Cealtra with the sentient stones watching over him, and the day after Mama's return, she darted off just after dawn and sent a message below. Later that day, a merrow appeared at our door and handed Mama a scroll. She accepted it, then the merrow gave a quick nod and was gone.

"Is that Kilstiffen's version of the post?" I asked.

"I suppose it is." She unrolled the scroll onto the kitchen table and held it flat with her hands.

I picked up one of the gold end caps that had kept the scroll intact. "Must be pricey."

"Not so much." She glanced at the weighty piece of gold in my hand. "Well, not pricey in Kilstiffen's terms. The city has a great deal of gold in its treasury."

"Really?" I remembered Da's story about the gold bars. "Where does it all come from?"

"Oh, many places. Underwater mines, tributes from other lands, taxes…" Her voice trailed off as she read the scroll, then she smiled. "This is a message from the king himself. Your grandfather. MacCreehy has been taken to the gaol and will be punished accordingly. The exact punishment isn't mentioned, but I'm sure it will be long and unpleasant."

I flopped back in my chair and breathed a sigh of relief. "We're safe from him, then? At least for a little while?"

"We're safe from him forever." Mama leaned across the table and grasped my hand. "We can live in peace now, as a family."

And live in peace we did, though it was the noisiest peace you'd ever experienced. The four of us quickly established a routine: we woke at dawn, even Kevin, and began our day with a huge breakfast cooked by myself and Da. Once the food was consumed and the dishes washed, we tumbled into the garden and set about putting all those overgrown hedgerows to rights. Now that Mama was back, Da wanted to revisit his dream of overseeing a working farm supplying produce for his very own restaurant. We didn't know how long it would take to renovate our neglected lands, or where this restaurant would be located, but that was all right. We were together again, and we had all the time we needed.

While the Murphy household was the happiest it had been in years, all of the affected families weren't experiencing blissful reunions. The re-introduction of so many people who'd been assumed missing or dead caused a great deal of confusion for the town folk, and many headaches for the garda. One woman had been gone almost twenty years, and returned home to find her family had moved out of Clare over a decade ago. Most stories were similar, with people having moved on, literally and figuratively, in the wake of their loved ones' disappearances, and the question became what to do with those who had returned. The garda ended up establishing an office near the docks tasked with tracking down relations and reuniting families, and finding housing for those who were now alone in the world. Their success rate was, shall we say, uneven.

Aodhan's father had been away just over seven years. He was gobsmacked to learn that his wife had married his business partner, and had gone on to have a few more children without him. As for Mrs Dumhach, it seemed that she couldn't decide if her first husband's return was a joyous occasion or more of an annoyance.

"It's a good thing we have that little apartment behind the shop," Aodhan said. We were sitting in my kitchen, having tea and eating the leftover cinnamon rolls Da had made for breakfast. A few weeks had passed since MacCreehy's defeat, and the town was finally settling down. "Looks like Dad and I will be roommates for a while."

"I bet you two will have a grand time of it," I said in a rush. Aodhan hadn't yet moved his things out of my house, and he'd been sleeping here almost every night while helping with the yardwork during the day. His initial reasoning for staying had been that when his sisters came home to spend time with their father, there hadn't been enough room for him, but Anne and Mary had both since returned to university. Maybe Aodhan preferred the Murphy house over the surf shop's back room. I know I'd got used to having him close.

We hadn't yet had our talk, the one we'd promised to each other in the dark and damp cave far below ground. Much had changed since we made that promise, and part of me wanted to pretend it had never happened. The rest of me wanted Mr Sullivan to get a place of his own, so Aodhan and I could have the shop's apartment all to ourselves again.

We also hadn't kissed again since that day at the docks, what with our families always hovering around us. Perhaps if Aodhan's father move out of the apartment, we could have ourselves a bit of privacy, and not just for kissing. Although, having time for kissing would be nice.

"I'm sure we will," he replied. "That apartment's just a bit cramped for two."

"You can always stay here," I said. "For that matter, your father can, too. We've got more than enough room, and, ah, Kevin likes having you around."

"Kevin, eh?" Aodhan grinned, and I laughed.

"Well, he does." I slid my hand across the table and squeezed Aodhan's fingers. "I'm sorry your dad isn't getting a happy ending out of all this."

"That's because it's not the end, Meri," Aodhan said. "I reckon we're not even at the middle yet. There's a lot that still needs to get done."

"There certainly is. Want to work on it together?"

He grinned. "Thought you'd never ask."

I hope you enjoyed Meri and Aodhan's first adventure! If you did, please consider leaving a review. If you can't wait for their next adventure keep scrolling for a sneak peek from the sequel, Death's Door.

Remember: they're Meri and Aodhan, and together they can do any-thing.

Happy reading!

DEATH'S DOOR: CHAPTER ONE

"Stop. Fidgeting."

I glared at Kevin even as I stilled myself. We—me, my brother, and our parents—had been waiting for the golden gates of Kilstiffen to open up for us for what seemed like forever. We were down here because Mama was taking Kevin and me to meet her father the king, just as she'd promised. She was also due to return the golden key that controlled when the city rose and fell, which meant this was a momentous occasion for one and all. It had taken weeks of sending messages back and forth to arrange this meeting, and now the day had finally arrived and here we were, waiting to experience all that Kilstiffen had to offer.

If the gates ever opened, that is.

And what magnificent gates they were. They were three times my height and almost as wide as they were tall, and the whole of them was covered in finely-wrought designs featuring undersea scenes and creatures. I wondered if the doors were made of solid gold. If so they must weigh a literal tonne, maybe more.

"It's not my fault I'm nervous," I whispered to Kevin. "I've never been here before."

"You have," Mama said. "When you were three weeks old I presented you to your grandfather, as I did Kevin before you."

"Events I cannot remember don't count," I grumbled.

"Don't fret, Meri girl," Da said. "Your grandfather was quite taken with you then, as he was with Kevin. He'll be glad to see both of you."

I looked up at Da, but before I could speak I heard gears turning. Finally, the gates opened. Four armed warriors stepped forward, and arranged themselves around us. Mama took one look at them, tucked her hand into Da's elbow, and strode past the warriors through the gates and into Kilstiffen. Not knowing what else to do, Kevin and I followed.

"Shouldn't the men with the spears be going first?" I asked. Our escort was dressed almost identically as Seamus MacCreehy's enthralled warriors had once been, and their look was not inspiring confidence in me.

"You forget, Ma outranks them all," Kevin replied. "She can probably outfight them, as well." I opened my mouth, but Kevin held up a hand. "Save your questions. Look around, Meri!"

I did, and noted that we were walking along a wide, flat causeway, not unlike the cobblestone paths of County Clare I'd been walking on my entire life. Then we crested a small rise, and I saw the city of Kilstiffen for the first time.

"Oh," I breathed.

"Quite a sight, eh," Kevin said, as he nudged me with his elbow.

Stretched below us were dozens, maybe even hundreds of white walled houses roofed in gold. I could see verdant gardens woven between the bright white buildings like a string of emeralds. An impossibly bright blue river meandered through the city and encircled a many-spired castle clad in gold and shimmering white tiles reminiscent of mother of pearl. Having grown up in a poor fishing village, I was awed by the casual display of wealth. I was also glad I'd listened to Mama when she insisted we wear our best clothes. Even though my dress and shoes were brand new, I still felt a bit raggedy compared to my surroundings.

I was also amazed by the amount of light in the city. I'd expected Kilstiffen to be dark as a cave, what with its current location under the sea, but it was as bright as noon was above ground. The sky—or whatever was above us—was even a pale blue. I wondered if it rained down here, too.

Missing from the scene were Kilstiffen's residents. Save for our escort the city streets were empty, as were the windows and doorways. I found that odd; wouldn't the opening of the gates and the return of the king's daughter be a good reason to turn out?

We crossed a gold and ivory bridge and entered the castle proper. The interior was all polished white and gray stone, with colorful tapestries adorning the walls and deep blue carpets on the floors. We walked through several outer rooms, each larger than the one that came before, then up a small flight of stairs into a chamber so large it seemed the whole city could fit inside. The floor was highly polished white marble, and the ceiling was painted deep blue like the night sky, with lines and bobs of silver making up the zodiac and other constellations. In the very center of the room was a throne, and upon the throne sat the king.

Mama had said many, many times that her father was one of the kindest men she'd ever met. The man on the throne did not appear kind. He wore a crown of golden shards, his hair and beard were white as sea foam, and thanks to his scowl his brows were so low I had no idea what color his eyes were. He was swathed in deep green silks and velvets edged in dark fur, and a pair of golden shoes peeked out from under his robes.

"He's like an angry Neptune," Kevin whispered. I bit the inside of my cheek, and tried to keep a straight face.

"Approach," the king ordered. We did, and I saw people assembled in the rear of the room behind the throne's dais. So there were others here, at least in the castle. I was beginning to wonder if the king lived all alone.

We halted a few meters in front of the throne. Mama and Da stood in front of the king and bowed. Behind them, Kevin and I exchanged a quick glance and did the same.

"Aoife," the king boomed. "My youngest, fiercest child."

"My lord," Mama said. "Thank you for receiving us."

"When did I become a lord to you, instead of your father?" he asked.

"About the same time I was accused of treason," Mama replied.

The king's head drooped. "You know well that I never accused you. What's more, all now understand that you were the one in the right." He glanced up, and Mama smiled at him. "I'm told you have something for me?"

"Yes, my lord. Father." Mama stepped forward and withdrew the object she'd stolen from him over twenty years ago, which was the golden key to Kilstiffen. All of the green paint she'd covered it with had been carefully removed, and it had been polished until it gleamed. The king gazed at her for a moment, then he descended the dais and claimed the key.

"My people, we are saved," he declared, holding the key aloft. "My daughter has delivered us from darkness. We will see the sun again!"

After the king had admired the key for a suitable amount of time, a few of the servants stepped out of the shadows and ushered us into an intimate dining room that was every bit as opulent as the throne room. All of the dinnerware was made of cut crystal and heavy gold, and pearls the size of my palm and silvered coral were heaped in the middle of the table in lieu of a floral arrangement. The ceiling was painted like a noonday sky, and the surrounding walls were rolling green meadows. If I squinted just so I could pretend I was standing on Ireland's soil, rather than far below it.

The king took his place at the head of the table, with Da and Kevin seated on his left across from Mama and me. At first I was relieved I didn't have to sit next to my grandfather, then I noticed Mama's straight spine and squared-off shoulders, and how Da's mouth was a slash across his face. I wondered if the king had purposefully separated them.

The king set the key next to his goblet and smiled. "I knew you'd do it, Aoife," he said. "Others were skeptical, but not me. I was certain you would stop MacCreehy and return the key to its rightful home. As ever, Aoife, you remain our champion, and our guardian."

"As I always will be," Mama said. "My only regret is the length of time it took me to complete my mission."

"That is my regret, as well." The king's gaze slid toward Da. "I assume it was a great shock and surprise when my daughter returned to you."

"It was one of the happiest moments of my life, my lord," Da said.

"I'm certain it was. Kevin, how is your singing coming along?"

"Good, my lord," Kevin replied, which was a complete untruth. Kevin couldn't carry a tune to save his life. Realizing he had just lied to the king, he added, "I'm still working on a few aspects."

The king grunted, and signaled a servant. Moments later bowls of clam-scented broth were set before us. We watched as the king sampled a spoonful; when he nodded in approval the rest of us picked up our spoons and began eating.

"Meri," the king said. I fumbled my spoon. "I'm told you've come into your voice."

I gaped at him. "Have I?" I asked, with a desperate glance at Mama.

"She surely has," Mama said, rescuing me from certain doom. "She commanded an army of enchanted stones to victory, and single hand-edly broke the merrows free from Seamus's thrall."

"That is quite impressive," the king acknowledged, but I wasn't interested in praise.

"How are the merrows?" I asked. "Did they all manage to return home?"

"They did, and they are recovering," he replied.

"Daveth is well, then? Can I see him?" I asked, before remembering one didn't make demands of a king. If my rudeness bothered him he hid it well.

"He is doing very well," the king replied. "You learned some of their names?"

"I learned all of their names," I said. "And most of the soldier's names, as well. Many were from my village."

The king nodded. "That is good, Meri. That is very good. Perhaps later, you will sing for me."

A servant whispered in the king's ear, thus saving me from an acapella performance over our soup bowls. The king stood, and the four of us followed suit.

"Come, all of you," he said. "The room is ready."

We rose and followed the king out of the dining room and into a smaller chamber. In this latest chamber the ceiling and walls were painted in layers of rose and gold, with a floor of deep blue tiles.

"This room is like a sunset, the last was noonday, and the throne room was night," I said. "Why is everything painted like the sky?"

"To remind those who cannot go above on their own what the sky looks like," the king replied, his voice heavy with sadness. "To ensure that no one forgets the sun." I pursed my lips, and resolved to keep my wonderings to myself.

The king approached a golden wall—honestly, Kilstiffen was packed with so much gold this latest installation may as well have been painted wallpaper—and opened a small hinged door in the centre. Beyond the door was a mechanism made of several copper gears, and into that mechanism the king placed the key. We stood with bated breath for a heartbeat, two... Then the king frowned and removed the key, and shut the door.

"The window has passed," he said. "It will be another seven years before Kilstiffen may rise again."

Mama lowered her head. "Then I did fail."

The king placed his hand on her shoulder. "You did everything you could, with the little you had available," he said. "We've held out under the waves this long. A few more years will not matter overmuch. Now, let us return to our lunch."

Get your copy of Death's Door here: https://books2read.com/Merrowkin-DeathsDoor

Glossary Of (mostly) Irish Terms

Céilí – a gathering where those in attendance dance and play traditional Irish music. These gatherings may be held in a home or a public location.

Cliffs of Moher – sea cliffs located at the southwestern edge of the Burren region in County Clare, Ireland. They run for about fourteen kilometres. At their southern end, they rise one hundred twenty metres above the Atlantic Ocean at Hag's Head, and, eight kilometres to the north, they reach their maximum height of two hundred fourteen metres just north of O'Brien's Tower, then continue at lower heights. The closest settlements are the villages of Liscannor six kilometres to the south, and Doolin seven kilometres to the north.

Gaol – prison.

Great Famine – also called the Great Hunger, was a period of mass starvation and disease in Ireland from 1845 to 1849.

Kilstiffen – a lost city beneath the Cliffs of Moher which sprawls grandly over the Atlantic Ocean on the western coast of Ireland. The city once rose every seventh year, but now it remains submerged until the golden key to the gates is found.

Merrow – a mermaid or merman in Irish folklore.

Milesians – the Milesians (sons of Míl) are Gaels who sail to Ireland from Iberia. When they landed in Ireland they fought with the Tuatha Dé Danann. The two groups agree to divide Ireland between them: the Milesians take the world above, while the Tuatha Dé Danann take the world below.

Ogham – an Early Medieval alphabet used primarily to write the early Irish language, and later the Old Irish language.

Oisín – regarded in legend as the greatest poet of Ireland. He spent three years in the Otherworld with the sea god's daughter, but it was three hundred years in mortal time. When he returned to Ireland the centuries caught up to him, and as soon as his foot touched Irish soil he withered and died.

Press – Irish term for a cabinet or cupboard.

Time Team – long-running British archaeology programme.

Tuatha Dé Danann – literally, "the folk of the goddess Danu". They comprise the Irish pantheon of gods who dwell in the Otherworld.

ACKNOWLEDGEMENTS

Fun fact: writing acknowledgements stresses me out more than writing the actual novel! As is the case with all of my stories, I've gotten a great deal of help from some pretty amazing people, and I'm always afraid I'll forget someone. Well, here goes!

First of all, have you seen the amazing cover? That was created by the brilliant and talented Lisa Amowitz. Many people helped the story along the way: Lisa Gail Greene, Rose Santoriello, Suzanne Reynolds Alpert, and my entire former MFA class beta read this story at various stages and offered notes. My sister Suzanne helped me understand what it was like to attend Catholic school; for better or worse, my education was decidedly secular. Without all of their help, Merrowkin would not be the story it is today.

Finally, a big thank you to my Patrons: Jessica Worthy, Aurora Slinkman, Amanda Raymond, and Keri Maniquet. Your support means more to me than you know.

ALSO BY JENNIFER ALLIS PROVOST

The Chronicles of Parthalan, a six volume epic fantasy (and one short story collection)

Heir to the Sun

The Virgin Queen

Rise of the Deva'shi

Pieces of Parthalan: Six All-New Stories From The Land Of Parthalan

Golem

Elfsong

Sunfall

The Copper Legacy, a four book urban fantasy:

Copper Girl

Copper Ravens

Copper Veins

Copper Princess

A duology based in the Copper world:

Redemption

Salvation

Poison Garden, an urban fantasy filled with seers, witches, and one seriously hot detective:

Belladonna

Oleander

Bleeding Hearts

Thornapple

Wolfsbane

Mistletoe

Mandrake

Gallowglass, an urban fantasy set in Scotland and New York:

Gallowglass

Walker

Homecoming

Winter's Queen, an urban fantasy set in Scotland and Elphame:

Touch of Frost

Giant's Daughter

Elphame's Queen

Merrowkin, an urban fantasy set in Ireland above and below

Merrowkin

Death's Door

Manannán's Pearl

Changes, a contemporary romance:

Changing Teams

Changing Scenes

Changing Fate

Changing Dates

About the Author

Jennifer Allis Provost is a native New Englander who lives in a sprawling colonial along with her beautiful and precocious twins, a dog that thinks she's a kangaroo, a parrot, a junkyard cat, and a wonderful husband who never forgets to buy ice cream. As a child, she read anything and everything she could get her hands on, including a set of encyclopedias, but fantasy was always her favorite. She spends her days drinking vast amounts of coffee, arguing with her computer, and avoiding any and all domestic behavior.

Find Jenn on the web here: http://authorjenniferallisprovost.com/

For up to the minute sale notifications, follow her on Bookbub here: https://www.bookbub.com/profile/jennifer-allis-provost

For exclusive content, follow her on Patreon: https://www.patreon.com/jenniferallisprovost/

Friend her on Facebook: http://www.facebook.com/jennallis

Follow her on Instagram: @jenniferaprovost

Happy reading!